G000161021

HEAT IN THE DESERT

A DESERT LOVE NOVEL

ANGELINA KALAHARI

FlameProjects
London
www.flameprojects.com

Publisher's Note: This is a work of fiction. Names, characters, places, and incidents are a product of the author's imagination. Locales and public names are sometimes used for atmospheric purposes. Any resemblance to actual people, living or dead, or to businesses, companies, events, institutions, or locales is completely coincidental.

Heat In The Desert
ISBN 978-0-9954877-6-5

To the people and animals of Namibia

THANK YOU

For buying *Heat In The Desert.*

I hope you enjoy reading the novel as much as I've enjoyed writing it.

To receive occasional email notifications about freebies, new stories and novels, YouTube videos, podcasts, short stories and much more, you can subscribe to my Newsletter here – https:// angelinakalahari.com/contact/.

The first thing you'll receive upon subscribing, is an exclusive novella called Diary of Naomi, a Desert Elephant – it's the story of what happens to ellie Naomi.

Elephants in Namibia are the toughest in Africa. But orphaned elephants are the toughest still. And they need to be.

All elephants must travel great distances to find food to live on and they're renowned for their magnificent memories and deep emotions.

We first come across ellie Naomi in Under A Namibian Sky.

In this novella, discover what happens when she finds the people responsible for making her an orphan?

If you prefer, you can email me at angelina@agelinakalahar-i.com or please go to the end of this novel for more details.

ONE

The second Saira stepped off the plane, the heat lashed at her. It was a quick reminder of the other sweltering situation she'd left behind in London. However, she couldn't blame that on the climate there.

The frigid London winter weather hadn't prepared her for the instant struggle to breathe in the oppressive Namibian heat. Saira tilted her head back to see if it would help her breathe easier. But it only made the air feel thicker, too thick, like breathing fire. She swallowed down the panic rising inside her.

Even vacations in the humid heat of India on their family farm was nothing compared to this. How to live and work in this place for the next month? Please let it be less than a month.

Come on, girl.

She shook her hair away from her face and pushed her shoulders back; the actions restoring a semblance of confidence. Getting it done as fast as possible was the best option.

Fanning herself with her passport, Saira followed her fellow passengers along the hazy sun-softened tarmac to the airport's entrance. She couldn't help noticing the heat waves forming in the air ahead of her when she'd have expected to see those in the far distance. She twirled her hair around her hand and threaded it through a loop of its own. Getting the strands of sticky, damp hair away from her neck, didn't help much as the sun's rays found her soft skin and burned her like the passion from a fiery lover.

She cursed under her breath and admonished herself for being so unprepared for the weather here.

She noticed most of her fellow passengers now wore hats. It would have been an excellent idea to stick one in her bag. To add to the discomfort of her lengthy flight, a trickle of sweat ran down her back, causing her white silk shirt to stick to her body.

What had possessed her to wear silk?

She hoped sweat marks weren't visible beneath her armpits.

Her well-cut black trousers had felt comfortable and smart in London. Now, it clung to her perspiring legs. Every step felt as though she was suffocating from the bottom up and drowning in sweat. But after the lengthy flight, she was too exhausted to care about her appearance.

Her case, even though small enough for the overhead cabin, was heavy. She fought with the wheels that kept catching in the cracks on the tarmac, cursed under her breath. Her second since landing, and before she'd even entered the country. But her patience was wearing thinner. Memories of the lecherous older guy who couldn't keep his hands and his lust to himself on the plane still tasted bitter. She hadn't quite shaken the energy of the experience, and the heat and her stupid case just added to her darkening mood.

As she walked through the airport's doors, the blast from the air conditioning was almost too cold. Goosebumps formed all over her body. Still, she welcomed the respite. The heat had pressed down on her, making even her smallest movements a battle against lethargy.

It wasn't the first time she'd wondered if it was all worth it?

Would any of her efforts even register with Max Galbraith? He'd made it clear he wanted something special for MaxPix to sell to a large terrestrial television channel, and he didn't care which one. With his reputation, he'd most likely have the pick of the bunch.

Saira followed the line of passengers. But now her thoughts had turned in that direction, she couldn't prevent the anxiety rising into her chest.

Thoughts of her boss linked to those of Jonathan. Would she have severed the relationship by now if Jonathan wasn't Max's son?

She tossed her hair back as though to fling all thoughts of Jonathan from her mind. Instead, she focused on the reason she was here.

Wasn't this just the opportunity she'd needed to prove herself to Max once and for all? The reason for her reluctance to take this assignment, still alluded her, or did it? Oh, who was she kidding? Hadn't she thought this might be what she needed to prove to herself she could do it, do her own thing?

As she continued moving along the queue, she heard the voices of the naysayers in her mind. The words came from her frenzied thoughts and besties, Manda and Peter. Their fears pummeled her mind, the loudest her own.

"You're too young to start your own company."

"You owe Max a few more years after all he's done for you."

"What if you fail?"

Even though her parents didn't know of her plans yet, their sincere faces flitted past her mind's eye. Hadn't they always taught her through their example? But their plans for her had never included working in the television industry. The path they'd wanted for her corresponded with theirs, a lawyer or something in investment banking. Their worried eyes carried the questions they'd never asked since she'd passed the three-year mark at MaxPix. Perhaps they hoped she'd come to her senses sooner, but now, they had to accept it was her chosen career path.

She sighed away the images in her head and continued to follow her fellow passengers down the long corridor. At least the rigmarole of going through passport control and then collecting her suitcase from the luggage carousel brought extended relief from the heat outside.

Saira had expected someone with a plaque bearing her name waiting for her in arrivals. Instead, she heard her name being called over the airport's PA system.

She swore under her breath.

The lengthy flight and the unbearable heat immediately on landing had taken its toll.

Saira was hungry and thirsty and didn't feel like having to deal with a problem now. Better to get it over and done.

Her sigh revealed her frustration.

She shifted her bag to her right shoulder to give the left one time to recover from where the straps had dug into her. Pulling her suitcase behind her, kept her handbag in place on her shoulder. She experienced a twinge of gratitude for minor mercies when she found a trolley. It made moving around the airport smoother.

Apart from the information agent, only one other person stood next to the counter. Saira assumed he was there for her as he looked as though he might be local. His sun-darkened skin, sun-streaked blonde hair and safari uniform gave the impression of a life spent mostly outdoors. His skin color almost matched hers, though she didn't acquire hers through a suntan, but through her Asian heritage.

As she walked closer to the man, the small badge on his shirt confirmed he was a safari guide from Desert Lodge. But he had the body of a god-not that she could imagine him working out in a gym. His physique had to be because of his lifestyle. He was tall and perfectly proportioned, and his biceps strained against rolled-up sleeves. Broad shoulders and a muscular torso looked as though it belonged on a model and not a desert guide.

What work could he do at Desert Lodge to produce such muscles?

Her thoughts of Desert Lodge were a reminder she'd hoped it wasn't too far away. Every pore in her body screamed for a shower and a bed. She'd think about work tomorrow.

As she extended her hand toward the man, she almost stumbled back in surprise when his blue eyes, like the deepest ocean, locked onto hers. She hadn't foreseen he'd be so striking. A little flutter in her stomach caught her off guard.

His eyes ran over her body with unexpected boldness, and her mouth was suddenly dry.

But she determined to remain polite and professional even though her voice sounded tight to her ears.

"Hi, I'm Saira. From MaxPix."

Her conscious effort to lower her voice at the end of the phrases presented a sense of confidence. It was a trick she'd learned to use when she was tired, so she'd be taken seriously. Though, why she'd want to impress a desert guide, she couldn't fathom. What she hadn't expected was the connection she felt when the man's hand enveloped hers. Unlike her sweaty palm, his hand was huge and felt firm and dry. She pulled her hand from his to hide her embarrassment.

His voice sounded relaxed and musical to her ears and far friendlier than he appeared because his greeting contained no smile or warmth.

"Gerhard. Desert Lodge. Follow me."

Gerhard turned and walked toward the exit.

Saira settled her handbag on her shoulder and pushing the

trolley, followed him. She was too surprised and too tired to comment. The man was a rude buffoon.

He hadn't even offered to help her with her luggage. She hoiked her handbag closer to her body and pushed the trolley with more zeal than she thought possible in her exhausted state. Even though she was bristling at his behavior, Saira had to admit he was interesting-looking, but she didn't appreciate his brusqueness.

Was his behavior the norm in Namibia?

But she dismissed the thought as soon as it popped into her head. She'd been in contact with the owner, Naomi and her manager, Kerri, at Desert Lodge over the past few months, and although very different from each other, both seemed friendly. She could work with them.

Saira had to walk faster than she'd liked to keep up with Gerhard. But the exercise woke her up, and she felt a spurt of energy flood through her body.

Her work at Desert Lodge shouldn't involve Gerhard. God knows, she had enough on her plate right now and could do without the usual stress of dealing with demanding clients. Not that Desert Lodge was a client. Not yet. But she hoped to persuade Naomi and her team to allow her carte blanche while shooting an exciting TV series there. All she had to do first, was get their signatures on the agreement she carried in her bag, and then shoot a spectacular pilot that would impress Max. But only after she'd impressed herself.

From her conversations with Naomi and Kerri, Saira had to admit the place sounded interesting. But she could think of a thousand better things to do with her time when Max Galbraith had talked her into this trip. Traipsing around in the desert hadn't featured in her plans. However, after her initial resistance to the project, she'd surprised herself. She realized she was looking forward to it.

The lengthy flight here had given her ample time to consider once more the repercussions of her decision to accept Max's offer. But she wasn't stupid. She was aware Max had given her the assignment because she was the only young female producer at MaxPix, and this show was about weddings. It could have offended her. It should have offended her. But wasn't it typical of the industry, this sexism? How often had she wanted to scream at them all to sod right off?

Her competitive side, however, renewed her resolve to go after her dream. It meant ignoring her friends' advice because it wasn't their dream, was it? It was also the perfect opportunity to get away from Jonathan. The flight had given her time to think about Jonathan and her future with or without him. T

he thoughts in her head still tormented Saira when she noticed they'd reached the exit. She steeled herself for the intense heat that awaited them outside.

But as Gerhard opened the door, the sun seemed to want to show off how brutal it could be. He surprised her when he took her suitcases from the trolley and walked ahead toward a small Cessna plane sitting to the left of the airport. Saira followed him out of the air-conditioned building and found the heat even more overpowering. Once again, she fought for every breath as she made her way to the plane.

But as she got closer to it, Saira stopped for a moment. The aircraft was much smaller than she'd imagined. A slight panic shivered in her chest.

Gerhard must have sensed her trepidation. Against her better judgment, she liked his light, reassuring hand on her back and allowed him to lead her toward the plane. He surprised her further by not only opening the door for her but also helping her up into her seat and closing it once she was seated. Then, he stowed her luggage in a compartment behind the wing.

The cabin was sweltering even though the plane stood in

the building's shadow. Each breath felt as though it burned down Saira's throat into her lungs, and the overwhelming smell of heated plastic and leather almost made her gag.

To distract herself, she watched Gerhard instead.

As he walked around the plane, it looked as though he didn't even feel the heat. But when he opened the door and slid into the seat beside her, it followed him and blasted into the small cabin.

Would it be like this the whole time she'd be here? How would she endure it?

If there was a hell, this must be it.

Gerhard fiddled with the knobs. The plane's sudden roar and shaking made Saira sink into her seat and grip the armrests.

Together, in the close quarters of the cockpit, Saira noticed Gerhard's imposing physique and immense presence. When his leg touched hers, concern stirred through her mind. She could feel how muscular his leg was as it rested against hers. How would she manage the journey with him sitting so close? She moved her leg away and tried to think of something else.

She was just about to ask Gerhard how long the flight to Desert Lodge was. But he'd already donned his headset and was talking to the control tower about taking off. The knot in Saira's stomach became tighter as they taxied down the airstrip. Her hands were getting sweatier, but she couldn't let go of the grip she had on the armrests. The plane felt too small, too exposed, too much like a tin can.

When Gerhard opened the throttle, and the small craft raced down the airstrip, Saira shut her eyes as tight as she could and felt her lips mimic the action.

They wobbled and vibrated as they took to the air and the engines screamed their protest at having to lift away from the ground, echoing Saira's feelings. She didn't believe in prayer but prayed anyway, even though she wasn't aware of actual words.

How did she ever believe getting into such a flimsy-looking thing was a good idea?

Please don't let this be her last day on earth.

But as the wobbling died down, and she felt the plane leveling out, becoming steadier, she opened her eyes.

Saira could have sworn she saw an amused smile flit across Gerhard's face. But she must have imagined it, or he was a master at hiding his emotions because there was no trace of it when he nodded at her and handed her a headset.

Once she'd put it on, she could hear his voice in her ears.

"Are you okay? Do you need anything? There's water behind your seat."

Wow, the silent one could speak.

Saira nodded and found a bottle of water in a small refrigerated cabinet behind her seat. She unscrewed the top and took a long welcoming slug of the cold liquid. The bottle against her forehead felt wonderful as she held it there for several seconds. Its icy coldness forced her to forget about the heat for a moment. But when she removed it to take another sip, there was the heat, a sweltering thing she couldn't escape.

She took care to tip the bottle over her wrists, keeping the top of the container in touch with her skin so the water could reach her pulse without pouring out everywhere. Then, she poured a tiny amount into her hand and ran it over her neck, cheeks and forehead. It seemed to work. She felt revived, and no longer parched. The breeze, cooled by the forward motion of the plane through the windows Gerhard had left open a little, also helped somewhat.

Saira could feel Gerhard's eyes on her, but when she looked at him, he was staring ahead into the distance.

Feeling better, gave her the courage to peek through the window at her side. They were on the outskirts of Windhoek. As she watched, the houses and greenery of the trees and lawns and blue swimming pools made way for the unending desert sands that stretched to the horizon.

Saira had seen many pictures and documentaries on Namibia and knew it was a beautiful country. But the scene that met her was breath-taking. Red dunes, sprinkled with dried yellow grasses and the odd tree, reached into the distance to meet a cloudless, milky blue sky. The only other moving thing, as far as she could see, was the shadow of the plane that followed them as it undulated over the dunes below.

Again, she wondered how long it was before they'd reach Desert Lodge.

But before she could ask, Gerhard surprised her.

"We'll arrive at Desert Lodge in about an hour. Relax, and enjoy the view. We'll be flying over some interesting terrain."

His blue-blue eyes rested on her for a moment before he looked ahead again, his face a mask once more.

Saira stared at the handsome man beside her.

She never found herself without words. But now, not only had her mind drawn an unexpected blank, her questions had evaporated under Gerhard's brief gaze. The unfathomable expression she'd seen in his unusual eyes had somehow reached out and touched her heart in a way she'd never experienced before.

She shook her head.

Oh, for goodness' sake, she wasn't even at Desert Lodge yet, and already potential trouble had found her. She didn't need any complications-certainly not this kind. Hadn't she just left something similar behind in London with Jonathan?

A sudden, loud bang brought Saira back to the present. The plane shook at once. A thin, pale plume of smoke blew past them.

When she turned to look at Gerhard, she saw that his

knuckles were white on the yoke and his eyes narrowed in concentration.

His voice sounded deliberate and calm when he spoke.

"We need to make an emergency landing. Make sure you fasten your seatbelt."

TWO

The small plane banked violently. Saira squeezed her eyes closed. Once again, she felt her fingers dig into her seat's armrests.

Rivulets of sweat felt sticky and ticklish as they ran down her back and squelched against her body where it met the seat. Her hands were dripping, but she didn't know whether it was from the heat or from being panicked. The muscles in her stomach and calves were aching as she tensed and willed her body to stop the plane.

She wasn't paying attention to Gerhard sitting next to her, but she could feel the force of his exertion as he tried to land the small craft.

They were getting close to the earth. Saira thought she was prepared for the impact, but the jar as the plane hit the ground rattled her bones and her teeth. They bumped along the sand for moments that felt like forever before they came to a shuddering stop.

When she opened her eyes, all she could see around her was the red dust storm the plane had kicked up. As it settled, she realized they were in the middle of nowhere. There was nothing: no trees, no dunes, no bushes. Stretching out in all directions were miles and miles of flat sand.

Saira felt more panic rising inside her body. Her fear was irrational, she knew, but she felt as though the sand would smother her. There was no escape.

She noticed her fingers were still digging into her seat's armrests and unclamped her hands. As she stretched out her fingers and tried to relax, her muscles screamed with the pain she'd inflicted on them when she'd tensed every single one in her body.

Next to her, Gerhard sat still, his hands on the plane's yoke.

As his body relaxed, he turned toward her.

"Are you okay?"

"What do you think? You've landed us in the middle of nowhere. How long will we be here? Can you fix the plane?"

Gerhard shrugged, and Saira wondered how he could be so relaxed about it all?

She'd seen television shows and read about people being stranded in the desert and dying of thirst. Would it happen to her? She didn't relish the idea.

Gerhard's voice was far too controlled for Saira's liking when he spoke.

"I'll see what I can do. But we may need help."

"Help? Where do you see help around here?"

"Well, it won't be easy, but I'm sure we can summon some."

Saira was sure the temperature rising inside her had nothing to do with the heat in the desert. She was getting mad as hell. What was the man playing at?

Gerhard opened the door on his side, and scorching air blasted into the already boiling cabin.

Saira put a hand on her chest as she struggled to draw the heated air into her lungs. She opened her door, but even more hot air streamed into the cabin.

Gerhard placed a firm, dry hand on her forearm.

"I wouldn't go outside if I were you."

"You don't seriously expect me to stay in this oven while you go outside?"

Gerhard removed his hand and nodded.

"Trust me. It's safer here than out there."

Safer? What was he talking about? Would she have to deal with wild animals as well on top of this disaster?

"What do you mean, safer?"

Those blue eyes locked on hers, and she understood he wasn't used to being challenged.

"I mean, it's hotter out there than in here. Out there, you risk sunstroke."

Saira shifted in her seat.

She didn't want to sound petulant, but she was feeling more than annoyed. The perpetual clamminess her entirely inappropriate clothing for such weather had produced, didn't help things.

"I still think it would be better if I sat in the wing's shade."

Gerhard got out.

He spoke through the open door, his back toward her.

"Suit yourself."

This time, Gerhard didn't help her. As a result, when she jumped down from the plane, she sank into the sand. She tried to muffle the loud yelp that came with the unpleasant surprise. The difference between the surfaces underfoot almost made her lose her balance. More importantly, the heat from the sand penetrated her shoes at once. She couldn't get her feet away from the burning sand fast enough. The muscles in her face contorted, but she refused to give Gerhard the satisfaction of seeing her distress. She pulled herself together, reached back, grabbed her water from the cabin, and rooted through her bag for her jacket to sit on. Even though the wing of the plane had given the illusion of shade, the sand underneath was scorching.

Saira had forgotten they'd only just landed here. The sun had been baking the sand into what felt to her like grains of fire beneath her. She jumped up as the heat penetrated through her jacket and burned her backside.

Though Gerhard was apparently ignoring her, she was sure she'd seen him smirk when she'd jumped down onto the blistering sand. And she thought he did it again when she'd leaped up as the heat had penetrated her behind.

Meanwhile, Gerhard had opened the bonnet on the side of the plane. He was tinkering away, a frown deepening between his eyebrows.

Saira watched him and didn't care for the frown.

She walked closer to him.

"Well?"

"Well, what?"

"Can you fix it or not?"

"I'm not a mechanic."

Saira had to walk away before she lost her temper. She placed her hands on her hips. Staring off into the distance might help her get a grip on her emotions. But it didn't help.

Oh, God, they would die here. She knew it.

When she had her breathing a little more under control again, she turned to face Gerhard.

"But if you're not a mechanic, how the hell are you going to fix this thing?"

Saira could have sworn she heard Gerhard mumble "give me strength," or something like it.

Not only was she stranded in the desert, but she had to deal with a jerk like him. Being hunky didn't make up for it. Life could be so unfair.

Damn, she should never have come. What a stupid idea.

Bloody Max. He'll have a lot to answer for when she gets back to London.

All of a sudden, she didn't want to be anywhere near Gerhard. She eyed the area under the wing furthest away from him and walked there as fast as the sand would allow her without tripping and falling. But the clanging and banging of his tinkering grew in volume, and she couldn't help wondering what he was doing. Another small prayer went up that he didn't damage the engine even more. Unable to contain her curiosity, she peeped around the plane.

Gerhard was fumbling inside the cabin and ignoring her. When she saw him unpacking a bundle of wood from underneath his seat, and reaching for a lighter in his pocket, she couldn't believe it.

Was he going to make a fire? In this heat?

She walked closer.

"Fire? I thought we only need it at night to prevent predators from eating us alive."

"I'm not building a fire for the wildlife."

The man was impossible.

Saira felt the urge to stamp her foot but wouldn't give him the satisfaction of seeing he'd got under her skin.

Why couldn't he be civil? Men with manners were in such short supply these days. Why were they all like Jonathan, instead of like her father?

Saira watched in silent fascination as Gerhard built a fire. He'd collected some straw-like plant matter she hadn't noticed before. The way it blended in with the color of the surrounding sand, was perfect. Gerhard placed it over the pieces of wood, like kindling, started the fire and blew on it until it took hold.

God, he was a real Neanderthal.

But when he took off his shirt, Saira almost gasped at the

sight of his beautiful torso and had to cough to hide her faux pas.

Gerhard's body wasn't only beautiful, toned with perfect muscles, but he looked far more like a model than a Neanderthal. Just the right smattering of hair on his chest made him appear even more manly. His all-over tan made her wonder why he spent so much time without his top? Perhaps he had a lot of leisure time. That he was pure male and nothing like Jonathan, just made him seem more mysterious. He moved with ease and elegance, felt as though she was watching a dancer instead of a Neanderthal. Only now he had his back to her, could she admire his toned bum and thighs.

But the beauty of his body couldn't disguise the fact that the fire was now roaring and smoke was everywhere. It made Saira's eyes water. The sudden uncontrollable coughing fit that gripped her wouldn't let go and didn't help the situation. The heat from the fire added to the already unbearable conditions.

Just as she was about to say something, Gerhard grabbed the sleeves of his shirt. He held the shirt over the fire for a few moments, then removed it and repeated the action over and over.

Saira could see the effect. The smoke curled into the air above them into an upright column since there was no wind to disperse it.

Okay, he was cute. But what the hell? Are we in a cowboy movie now?

Saira took a few steps toward Gerhard because she didn't want to shout and come across like a banshee. Besides, she didn't trust her voice to carry after the coughing fit.

"I don't understand. Why make a fire? Why don't you just call someone?"

Gerhard spoke without stopping what he was doing.

"Have you tried using your phone in the desert? It doesn't work here."

Saira hadn't considered that. A sizeable stone fell into her gut. Would she really be stranded here?

"But what about the plane's radio?"

"I'm not an electronics engineer."

Saira narrowed her eyes.

What the hell did he mean by that?

Gerhard spoke as though he'd read her mind.

"The radio is dead. Something must have gone wrong with the radio's wiring when the engine blew."

Saira felt tears of panic sting her eyes.

She wouldn't cry. She wouldn't cry.

"I saw you had a walkie-talkie?"

"The battery is flat."

Shit. She knew it. She would die here for sure. Who could ever see these puny smoke signals?

Saira looked up into the vast sky. Only someone with binoculars glued to their eyes and looking in the right direction would see such small puffs of smoke.

She wasn't in the mood for one of his stupid answers she didn't understand but somehow couldn't stop the question leaving her mouth.

"But who would see this?"

The sun was glistening off the sweat on Gerhard's back, and droplets were dripping down his temples. But he didn't seem to be suffering in the slightest. Saira envied him.

Again, he didn't look up as he spoke.

"You'd be surprised."

What does that mean? Why does he have to be so weird? For goodness sake, why couldn't he just spell it out? He must know she knows nothing about this lifestyle. Wasn't he a guide? The guides must meet people from lots of different backgrounds. She reckoned most of their guests didn't understand about conditions in the desert or this kind of lifestyle, either.

Was it her imagination, or was he actually smiling?

Just as she turned around to walk away, Gerhard's voice sounded behind her.

"You'll just have to trust me."

Saira almost snorted with indignation.

We'll see about that.

She didn't respond.

Instead, she went back to the plane to get more water. Her stomach grumbled with hunger, and an inordinate thirst wanted her to drink all the water they had-another symptom of the panic she didn't want to acknowledge? Not only that, but she experienced an increasing and much-needed urge to pee. But what to do? There were nowhere to go, no trees or bushes as far as she could see, and she would not do anything in front of Gerhard.

Saira checked her watch. Four o'clock. No wonder she was so hungry. She'd eaten little on the plane. Airplane food played havoc with her digestion, and she never ate it if she could help it. But the water only somewhat relieved her hunger pangs. As she focussed on everything that felt uncomfortable, the other need became overwhelming. She'd have to make a plan.

She was still trying to figure out if the wheel would protect her, when Gerhard spoke without looking at her.

"If you need to pee, I suggest going behind the wheel. I won't be able to see you from here."

What? Was he psychic? So, why didn't he also know she needed his assurance they'd be okay?

Saira turned to look at him. But making smoke signals still focused his attention. She couldn't help noticing the fire was dying down now. Perhaps they had no more wood. Otherwise, he would have used it, wouldn't he? She didn't want to think about it too much in case she panicked more. Instead, she delved through her purse and found some tissues.

As she walked to the back of the plane, she replayed scenes from films and documentaries she'd seen of people stranded in the wilderness. When their water ran out, they'd had to drink their urine. She shuddered. Drinking her own would be bad enough, but God forbid she'd have to drink Gerhard's.

She took up a stance behind the wheel, turning this way and that to make sure Gerhard couldn't see her. Then, she quickly pulled down her pants and relieved herself. Relief was the right word for it. At least one need was now satisfied.

Saira couldn't wait to have something to eat and a shower. But she didn't want to fantasize about a shower too much and stress herself out because she didn't know how long they'd stay stranded in the desert.

As she came walking around the plane, she could see Gerhard wafting the final bits of smoke from the fire. Only smoldering pieces of wood and ash remained now.

Gerhard had his shirt on again but had left it unbuttoned, allowing his gorgeous chest to peep out. For a moment, Saira wondered if he'd done it on purpose, but he seemed oblivious to the effect he'd created. How did such a handsome man not know he was beautiful? But he behaved as though it was just a normal thing for him to walk around like that and most likely, Saira reckoned, it was.

Gerhard walked back to the plane. He rooted around in the small fridge behind his seat and took out several packets of food.

He looked up at her.

"I hope you're not a vegetarian?"

"Well, if I were, I wouldn't care now. I'm far too hungry."

Again, Saira wondered if she'd seen a smirk on his face. But she must have imagined it because it wasn't there when she focused on him, and he said nothing more. Instead, he opened the luggage compartment and took out a bag containing a hand-held grill, plates, mugs and cutlery. Everything was made of thick, sturdy plastic, Saira guessed because of its durability in the desert.

Gerhard placed the sausages on the grill and soon, Saira cursed her stomach for rumbling as loud as it did. Why she was shy about Gerhard hearing it, she didn't know. But the delicious aroma of barbequed sausages made it difficult to ignore her gnawing hunger pangs.

When the sausages were done, Gerhard produced a thermal blanket which he opened onto the sand underneath one wing. From the small fridge, he took out a Tupperware bowl with salad. He set everything out on the blanket and indicated for Saira to sit down.

"I know it's not much, but I hope you enjoy your first meal in Namibia."

Saira eyed the food on the blanket. It wasn't what she was used to, but it looked and smelled divine. She couldn't wait to tuck in. Gerhard sat down beside her and dished sausages and salad onto a plate for her.

She sniffed at the sausages, which made her mouth salivate.

"What kind of meat is it?"

"Kudu. Chef at Desert Lodge makes it himself. You'll get used to his amazing cooking."

Saira took a small bite of the sausage. She didn't fancy burning her mouth on the hot meat.

"Hmm... It's delicious. Why do you call him Chef? Doesn't he have a name?"

"He prefers Chef. I think it's because he's had to work so hard to become one. The owners of Desert Lodge paid for him to study in France."

"Then it's a shame he's hidden away working at Desert Lodge, isn't it?"

Saira had been speaking in between mouthfuls of food and felt much more civil now she had something in her stomach.

It seemed Gerhard felt the same way.

"Yes, I suppose he could work in France. But all his family live in Namibia, and it's a source of pride for them he's achieved this status. Also, we get a lot of high-profile clients visiting Desert Lodge. They can be demanding, and it helps that we can offer them first-class food."

"Well, our meal was absolutely delicious. Chef hasn't wasted his talents."

They stayed sitting on the blanket, drinking the cold Namibian beer Gerhard had poured for them. After Saira's initial concern about drinking anything alcoholic, she discovered that not only did she like the taste of the beer, but it was also surprisingly refreshing.

Though Gerhard wasn't the world's most eager conversationalist, he told her exciting things about the desert. His voice was soothing, and she loved the excuse to stare into his intense, mesmerizing blue eyes. It was almost enjoyable. But every time she looked around her, she remembered they were stranded in the desert, and her breathing became a little shallower.

The temperature was still as high as it was when they'd landed. But when Gerhard got up and took a storm lamp from the plane's luggage compartment, switched it on and packed away their dinner things, Saira saw the night was upon them.

The changing sky over their heads was awe-inspiring. In the West, the sun was setting with brilliant red and orange hues across the blue sky, while in the East, darkness was descending. With it, thousands of stars appeared on the black velvet of the night sky.

In the distance, Saira could hear the sounds of animals beginning to echo through the night. She didn't recognize what kinds of animals they were and prayed they weren't coming to eat her. But Gerhard seemed calm, so she decided they had to be safe. Otherwise, he'd say something, right?

Still, she had to check.

"I don't suppose there's any more wood, is there?"

Gerhard glanced at her, his eyes narrowing as he considered her question.

"There's no need. We can't make smoke signals at night."

"No, I didn't mean we needed a fire for smoke signals. I meant; don't we need a fire for protection against predators?"

Gerhard laughed. The sound bubbled up from his stomach.

If Saira wasn't so annoyed, she might have found his laughter more than pleasing.

What the hell? He was laughing at her, now?

The laughter was still present in his voice when he responded.

"No, we'll be safe here from predators. We have the storm lamp. But we need to get back into the cabin."

So, it wasn't as safe out here as he'd like to make it sound?

But as Saira slid into the cabin, she realized she'd be sitting very close to Gerhard again. He smelled of wood smoke and sweat and barbeque. She wasn't sure she could handle being that close to him again. Not now, she'd seen how beautiful his body was underneath his clothes. At least, he'd buttoned up his shirt. So, perhaps he was a gentleman.

Gerhard had left the storm lamp outside on the sand. Its beam shined away from them into the deep blackness of the desert.

Saira checked her watch. Seven-thirty. She ached for a shower and bed. The traveling and the time difference between here and London were to blame for her sudden exhaustion.

She blew her breath through pursed lips.

"So, when are you expecting our rescuers to arrive?"

Gerhard sat back in his seat, pressed a button and lowered

it, so he was lying down. The extra space helped him to extend his long legs in front of him.

He closed his eyes before responding.

"Oh, they'll get here when they get here."

Saira couldn't relax. She sat upright and looked through the window at the darkness beyond the storm lamp.

"What does that mean?"

"What I said. They'll get here when they get here."

Saira crossed her arms and sighed. It might be a long night. She was prepared to believe that every situation allowed her to learn something. But what she had to learn from this, she had no idea. Perhaps it was a test of her patience? Yes, that, on every level.

Saira reconciled herself with the idea that she had no alternative but to wait. She sat back and closed her eyes. It might be better to think about what she'd like to achieve with the filming at Desert Lodge, instead.

From Gerhard's regular breathing, she could tell he'd fallen asleep. She wished sleep would claim her, but she was too wound up. It always happened when she traveled somewhere new. Instead, her discussions with Max about the project played in her mind's eye. It went round and round in her head.

Just as she felt herself drifting off against all expectations, there was a light tap on Gerhard's window.

At once, Saira sat up and looked to see what it was. All she could see was a hand against the window. It was amber, small like a child's, but ancient and looked like a claw that belonged on a mummy.

An involuntary scream escaped her lips.

Gerhard, who had also awoken at the tap on his window, sat bolt upright at Saira's scream.

He grabbed her hand.

"What? Are you all right?"

Saira realized her hand was shaking as she pointed to his window.

"There's a hand..."

She could hear the panic in her voice and hated herself for it.

Gerhard let go of her as though she'd burned him.

"Yes, it's our rescuers. They're here."

She didn't mean to, but she almost cried from the relief. Her voice sounded weak and anxious to her ears.

"Oh, thank God."

THREE

Saira couldn't help staring at Khwai when Gerhard introduced her to the older man. Khwai was the kind of age Saira couldn't even conceive of. In the dim light of the night, she marveled at the many lines that crossed his face and neck. But though he was small and skinny and ancient, his bearing was youthful with an energetic, upright posture. His eyes captured her attention at once. They were bright and curious and displayed none of the age the rest of his body suggested. His powerful spirit shined from them. But she'd never come across his type of energy before. He was as alien to her as was the country of his origin.

Saira thought it a miracle he'd found them in the middle of the night. But her admiration for him increased as he drove the truck through the black night. The road went on forever and revealed itself in the truck's headlights only a few feet at a time. She relaxed as the journey continued, happier in a vehicle rather than in a plane. Gerhard's presence beside her brought more comfort, and she dozed off, her head resting against his muscled shoulder.

SHE'D EXPECTED Desert Lodge to be in darkness and everyone asleep by the time they arrived. But as they drove through the gates, to her surprise, the big old house was lit up in the lights attached all around it. It blazed like a beacon in the black night.

Both Naomi and Kerri were waiting for her, their smiles welcoming.

Naomi held Saira's hand in hers as she spoke.

"Well, of course, we'd wait for you. Khwai told us about Gerhard's smoke signals and said he'd taken the truck to collect you. It must have been a scary experience, but we were confident you'd be safe with Gerhard while you waited for your rescuers."

Saira liked Naomi. She imagined it was usual for the owner of Desert Lodge to carry such an authoritative air even though Naomi was still young. But despite being the owner of such a prestigious lodge, Naomi had remained down to earth.

Saira nodded.

She didn't want to acknowledge just how terrified she'd been but was grateful for Naomi's comforting words. It made her feel as though she was safe all along. Over the past few weeks, she'd been in touch with Naomi and Kerri daily. Kerri's managerial skills had impressed her. Now, seeing them together, Saira realized they made a formidable team. She could feel their energy and enthusiasm and was looking forward to working with them.

But Gerhard seemed eager to get away. He bid her a stern good night before taking long strides through the door.

Saira frowned.

How rude. He didn't have to make getting away from her as fast as possible so obvious.

Kerri must have noticed Saira's small reaction because she laid a sympathetic hand on Saira's forearm.

"He has a very early morning safari group to take into the desert. We're lucky to have him. He's not usually so curt."

Saira wondered if Kerri was just being kind about a colleague. She'd had a much different experience of Gerhard. His rudeness shouldn't have surprised her.

After confirming Saira wasn't hungry, Naomi and Kerri both accompanied Saira to her suite, and Khwai brought her luggage.

Saira didn't know what she'd expected. But the suite was stunning. Much larger than she'd imagined. Beautiful African decorations were everywhere. The room felt bright and airy even though low lighting cast a warm, welcoming glow. After her new Desert Lodge friends made sure Saira felt comfortable and had everything she wanted, they left.

For moments, Saira stood still. She'd never experienced such silence, except earlier today in the desert. The slight breeze and distant sounds from birds and animals had pervaded the daylight. But here, the quiet was part of the darkness that enveloped her. It surprised her to realize it felt comforting.

Even though it was already late, Saira unpacked. She'd be at Desert Lodge for the next month, at least, and didn't fancy living out of a suitcase all that time. She hung the clothes she wanted to wear the following day in the bathroom so the steam from her shower could get the creases out of it. It didn't take long to unpack everything and stow her suitcases away in the beautiful wardrobe. A furniture maker had fashioned it from some local wood she'd never seen before. When she'd finished, she undressed and went to have the shower her body had craved all day.

Feeling refreshed and clean, Saira stepped from the shower. She rubbed her hair with a towel so it could dry naturally and went over to the tiny kitchenette to make herself a cup of tea. As she sat down at the table, she noticed her room keys and the message Kerri had given her. The piece of pink paper looked important, and someone had written the words in neat handwriting.

Your father called. Could you call him back as soon as you get this message?

Saira checked the time. It was two o'clock in the morning. So, it would be four o'clock in London. Her parents would both be asleep, and it would be unfair to wake them up, knowing how hard they both still worked. But on the off-chance their worry about her kept them awake, Saira sent a text message.

It was her first time to Africa and her first big solo assignment. Though each in their own way, her parents had eventually supported her decision to come to Namibia. But they couldn't disguise their anxiety from her. She wondered who worried more about who.

Even though Saira had been exhausted earlier, now she felt wide awake. Might as well check her other messages.

Her father had left his message with reception.

Her mother had sent a text to say, I'm thinking of you. Take care. Love you lots.

It was easy to see the message was a disguised plea for connection and confirmation that Saira was okay.

Three other messages were all from Jonathan. The first said he was sorry about the argument they'd had, and she must please forgive him. It smacked of the assumption that she would. This time, he had another think coming. He should count himself lucky she hadn't come to this point sooner in their relationship. Perhaps she should thank that bimbo who posed as a secretary to Max.

The second was to inform her the mechanic had returned her car after he'd repaired it. She'd have to trust Jonathan with her vehicle even though she knew his penchant for driving the sports car far too fast along the narrow streets of London.

Despite his protestations otherwise, it was Jonathan who had broken something by driving that way and had landed the car at the mechanic. But as usual, Jonathan insisted he was innocent. He could be so annoying.

Saira couldn't believe the third message. It seemed to imply Jonathan was coming to Desert Lodge to join her. He had to be joking. Jonathan was the last thing she needed right now. Wouldn't Max have told her if Jonathan were going to join them?

Saira shook her hair from her face as though to shake away all thoughts of Jonathan.

Instead, she dug out the schedules for the next day and the sheets that contained information on each of the crew members she'd be working with. Might as well familiarize herself with the names and faces of her new crew in their photos. According to Kerri, several of the crew members were already at Desert Lodge. The rest would arrive in the morning. Saira went through the notes, making sure she was secure in everything she wanted to say to the team.

Her heart beat a little faster as she thought about the project. It would be an excellent thing if she could decrease its importance, but wasn't this her big chance to show Max what she could do? If she did an outstanding job, Max might ask her to do more of these. Max would be successful selling the programs to the highest bidder, she had no doubt and then, her name would be in the credits. Saira didn't want her imagination to run away with her. Still, she could already imagine the awards nights, the beautiful clothes, lots of people and an Oscar in her hands.

She smiled to herself.

Okay, maybe not an Oscar, but a prestigious award. Awards were good for only one thing-to help take her career to the next level or on to her own business.

But Saira couldn't shake the idea that this opportunity was it. This project was her dream. It was the secret she'd kept from everyone, including her parents. Only Peter and Manda knew, and they were obliged as best friends to support her ideas no matter what she suggested. But when she'd told them about this yearning to have her own company and to use this opportunity to make it happen, both were less than enthusiastic about it. She knew they were scared for her. Perhaps this idea was so far out of Manda's comfort zone, she couldn't imagine it for Saira either. Though Peter was the best stylist and designer Saira had ever met, he was chaotic in his creativeness. Saira couldn't imagine him ever having his own company. He couldn't either, and perhaps he couldn't imagine Saira having hers.

But it was more than that. Saira loved how quickly the three of them had become brilliant friends because they were newbies having started work at MaxPix around the same time, and they had bonded in their newness. Now, three years on they'd seen how those who left never came back despite their promises to do so. However, the three of them had sworn they'd stay in touch forever. It was that promise that allowed Saira to share her dream with them. She'd even imagined they'd work in her company. But she hadn't told them about that idea yet, and she couldn't let the fears of her friends stop her.

Satisfied she had everything for the next morning's meeting, she went to bed, switched off the bedside lamp. The room tumbled into complete darkness. But sleep eluded her.

Instead of thinking about aspects of the filming or meeting her new crew in the morning, all she could think about was Gerhard. Why he of all people would dominate her thoughts, she couldn't fathom. But her eyes wouldn't unsee his gorgeous body and his stunning eyes. And her body wouldn't unfeel his powerful, pervasive presence, or the way he'd made her feel when he looked at her or when their hands touched.

OPENING her eyes the next morning and seeing sunlight streaming through the cracks in the curtains, Saira felt happy to know she'd slept. She stretched and yawned. Despite the late and shaky start to falling asleep, she'd had a good night's rest.

She was just about to get up when the phone next to her bed rang.

"Yes?"

Kerri's voice sounded perky on the other end.

"I have your father on the line for you. Can I put him through?"

"Of course. Thank you."

Hearing her father's voice almost brought tears to Saira's eyes. Even though she'd seen her parents only two days ago to say goodbye, knowing she was this far away from them made her feel homesick.

Her father's lovely deep baritone voice reassured her, as it always did.

"Thank you for your text message last night, Saira."

"I thought it was too late to return your call."

"The receptionist informed me there had been a problem with the plane to Desert Lodge?"

Saira could hear the fatigue and concern in her father's voice. She didn't want to worry him further.

"Yes, we had problems with the plane. We had to land in the desert. But I'm okay. The pilot, Gerhard, who is also a guide here at the lodge, looked after me. When he realized his walkie-talkie's battery was flat, he made a fire and sent smoke signals to their head tracker here who came to find us last night."

There was a lengthy pause.

Saira wondered if her father was still on the line. Then, he spoke again.

"It's unthinkable you had to go through such an ordeal, Saira. Your mother and I are very concerned. We couldn't bear anything happening to you. I'm happy to send the jet to collect you. It could be there by this evening. It would be wiser if you came back. We know you like your job with Max, but it's not worth your life. You can find another, much better job. I will help you find whatever you want to do. I'm not without influence."

Saira knew her father meant it. He would send the jet to collect her, and he would use his influence to get her whatever job she wanted. But she was not after a job, and she was no longer a little girl. She was a woman with a career. He had to learn that. She had to show him.

"Please don't send the jet, Daddy. I'm okay, I promise. Landing in the desert was a little scary, but everyone here is so friendly and helpful, I feel safe... felt safe. Please don't worry about me. I'm a grown woman, you know?"

"You may be a woman, but you're still our little girl, our only baby girl. Wait 'till you have a child of your own. Then you'll understand. We could never stop worrying about you."

Saira said nothing. Tears welled in her eyes at her father's love for her.

But another, firmer feeling sat in her body. She had no intention of remaining a little girl.

FOUR

The unbearable heat seeped through the open windows and multiplied inside the room. It was such a marked difference from the chilly desert evening last night.

Saira's body felt clammy as she ruffled through the clothes in the wardrobe she'd deposited there last night. The outfit she'd hung in the bathroom now seemed too hot for this weather. This being her first foray into working on her own, she wanted to make a wonderful impression. Thank goodness she'd had the foresight to bring along lighter clothes. The white linen trousers with the short-sleeved navy top looked smart but casual. She tied her hair back with an embellished clip and applied minimal but tasteful makeup. Satisfied with her image in the mirror, Saira gathered her notes and bag and left the room.

Breakfast appeared to be a noisy affair. Saira could hear the cacophony of eager voices the minute she left her suite. Crew members who'd arrived from South Africa had joined those who'd been at the lodge since yesterday, friends catching up.

Saira followed the unmistakable sounds of breakfast, infused with the excited voices. She realized it was coming from a structure beside the pool and remembered Kerri had called it the Lapa. The sounds coming from there echoed over the swimming pool's ripples left by the early morning swimmers. She'd have to be careful because she could so easily feel this was a holiday. The place was stunning. The morning sun invited her to investigate her surroundings instead of going to work.

As Saira walked into the Lapa, Kerri came to greet her.

"Good morning again, Saira. I hope the call from your father wasn't anything serious?"

Saira returned Kerri's warm smile and shrugged.

"You know, fathers. He just wanted reassurance I was safe and happy."

Saira glanced around the Lapa, making mental notes of the new members of her crew whose files she'd studied the previous night.

"So, where's our fabulous cameraman?"

A frown appeared between Kerri's eyes.

"It's grim news, I'm afraid. As you know, a few members of your crew arrived yesterday, and the cameraman was among them. We've met George before because he shot the videos for our promotions here several years ago. As he was already familiar with the lodge, he took some of the boys with him into the dunes on the fabulous Armati buggies we have here. You know they are prototypes, available only at Desert Lodge courtesy of Naomi's husband, Luca Armati?"

Saira nodded.

She'd read about Luca Armati and Naomi getting married. She even remembered seeing pictures of the stunning couple in glossy magazines. A brief flutter in her stomach showed she was looking forward to meeting Luca. He was an international celebrity, after all. She waited for Kerri to continue, and knew curiosity shined in her eyes.

Kerri's frown had deepened, meanwhile.

"I wouldn't say George is reckless, but something went wrong. He broke his arm."

Saira clasped her hand to her chest. It was not what she'd expected Kerri to say. An enormous fist clamped over her heart as the shock of the situation landed in her body. This project was too important to have a cameraman derail her plans.

"Oh, no. I'm guessing it means George is out of action?"

In response, Kerri bit her lip and nodded.

"I'm afraid he is. He's right-handed, and that's the arm he broke."

Saira was silent for a moment. She had to think fast. Time wasn't her friend and another cameraman from London would take too long to get here.

She looked up at Kerri before she spoke.

"There has to be more than one cameraman. Especially in such a beautiful country as Namibia?"

Kerri's nod was slow, comprehension bright in her eyes.

"You're right, Saira. There are many wildlife cameramen in Namibia. Maybe one of them can shoot the pilot episode. Good thinking. I'll make some calls. Excuse me."

Saira watched Kerri walk away toward the main building and to her office. Saira's palms felt clammy. She remained rooted to the spot. She didn't expect trouble of this kind to hit on her first day here. It could severely affect the pilot and be her first and last shot at delivering a completed project to MaxPix.

Shitshitshit.

Come on, girl. You've been in worse scenarios. You can handle this.

Her pep-talk to herself seemed to work, albeit only to still her beating heart and get her breathing under control.

She blew a breath through pursed lips, went to the bar, poured herself orange juice and found a seat at the table nearby. Members of her new crew sat around the table, and Saira plopped down in the only empty chair. She would just have to wait for Kerri to find someone and prayed it happened quickly.

Saira smiled to herself. For someone unused to praying, she'd been doing a lot of that since arriving in Namibia. She hoped it would help and looked up. The faces surrounding her were young. Their eyes were gleaming with enthusiasm.

Saira tried to remember the names of those around the table.

Shona, the girl with the lovely red hair and freckles, beamed as she spoke. Perhaps because she was young and excited, her voice was high, yet mellow and smooth to Saira's ears.

"I couldn't sleep last night. I was so excited. Just imagine. Maybe we'll all go to London. It's always been my dream."

The guy with black hair curling over his ears sat back in his chair and contemplated Shona.

Even though Saira knew he wasn't much older than Shona, his voice was deep, and he spoke with a slowness that came from natural confidence.

"I doubt it. Crew members like us don't get such opportunities. When we finish here, we'll all just go back to South Africa. So, I'd treat this as your journey abroad if I were you."

Saira recognized him from his picture on his file and identified him as Tony. She knew he was one of the grips.

The second guy at the table had mousy brown hair and wore thick glasses. A researcher, Saira remembered.

Eric looked up from his breakfast.

"I fear Tony is right, Shona. Such accolades are only given to the cameraman, the director, the editors and the producers. But it's not for the likes of you and me."

Saira couldn't help noticing that Eric spoke in short, clipped bites like beats of data. Something about him reminded her of Peter back in London. She wished Peter were here now. Both Peter and Manda would have been useful, but as they rarely worked with her, she couldn't request them. The team Kerri got together from a film agency in South Africa, seemed great on paper at least.

Saira was much too worked-up to concentrate on breakfast and had a quick coffee and a banana while she continued to work on her tablet. It was a relief none of the people at her table tried to pull her into their conversation.

But when she gauged her new crew had come to the end of their breakfasts, she got up and clinked her knife against her glass to get everyone's attention.

"Good morning, everyone. My name is Saira. I'll be producing and directing our pilot episode for this new series. I've received all your files and tried to familiarize myself with your names and faces. But please forgive me if I mispronounce your name or forget something as there are quite a few of you."

Saira looked from one face to the next as expectant gazes rested on her.

"I know several of you already know each other, but let's introduce ourselves to those who don't. Before we start, I have something to announce which may not surprise some of you.

"Twenty-five of us were supposed to meet here today, but we've had unpleasant news about our cameraman this morning. He won't be joining us. Those of you who were with him yesterday, already know he's broken his arm. Perhaps after surgery, he'd be able to join us on future episodes of the series, should our pilot be successful. Meanwhile, the manager here at Desert Lodge is helping to look for a replacement cameraman."

Saira paused and looked each crewmember in the eyes before she continued.

"Our success rests on us. I hope you're all up for a marvelous adventure and hard work."

She smiled at the wild applause and exuberant whoops, explicit confirmation of their commitment to the project.

Saira nodded.

"So, to begin, I am Saira Shah. I've worked in the London office of MaxPix for the past three years, but this is my first time shooting such a pilot. It's also my first time in Namibia, and I look forward to working with all of you. I believe we can produce a wonderful show here. We only need to get over the first hurdle of the pilot."

She'd meant it as a joke and was awarded for her effort when they met her comment with good-natured laughter.

Saira indicated for Shona to introduce herself next and sat down.

After everyone had made their introductions, Saira once again stood up, applauded her new crew and smiled when they joined her.

"Right, as we know who everyone is and who's doing what, let's get started. We have some serious prepping to do. They have allocated us workspace in the lounge in the main building. Grab something to drink and let's be on our way."

Saira didn't need to invite the crew twice. Each took a drink of orange juice or coffee. Saira knew they'd walk up the little pathway, through the French doors, up the corridor and into the lounge. She'd already seared the way there into her brain. But just as she collected her bag and printed materials, a shadow fell across the table. She looked up, expecting Kerri with news about another cameraman. Instead, she looked into Jonathan's pale blue eyes.

His voice was stern with annoyance and imitated the ice in his eyes.

"What do you think you're doing?"

Saira was aware her eyes had widened with shock and a boulder had fallen into her stomach.

Jonathan was the last person she'd expected, even though he'd made a few noises about coming to Namibia to "rescue her production attempt," as he'd put it.

Like she needed rescuing, and if she did, he'd be the last person she'd think to turn to. Hadn't he proved repeatedly that chivalry wasn't in his makeup? But she never imagined he'd follow through on his threats. He was such a city boy. She couldn't imagine him in a wild place like Namibia.

Saira hid her shock by tidying her papers, putting them in order and refusing to make eye contact with Jonathan as she spoke.

"What are you doing here?"

He remained standing close to her, to taunt her, Saira knew.

Then, he surprised her again by sitting down in the chair opposite hers.

"Need help with that?"

Saira knew it wasn't a genuine offer of help. She understood he was sarcastic as usual. Thanks a bunch, to the unfair gods. Jonathan was a complication she didn't need in her life right now. She thought she'd left him and all his nonsense behind in London.

She threw her hands up toward her shoulders and slapped them down on her thighs to show her annoyance at his unwelcome appearance.

"I don't know what to say to you, Jonathan. I have work to do. Enjoy your time here."

Before she could leave, Kerri came around the corner.

"Good, you're still here, Saira. I have excellent news for you."

But before Kerri could continue speaking, Jonathan jumped up and offered his hand.

"Hi, I'm Jonathan, Jonathan Galbraith from MaxPix."

Kerri's eyes told of her confusion as she looked from Jonathan to Saira. But she took Jonathan's proffered hand and allowed him to shake hers.

"Oh, I wasn't aware MaxPix had sent two producers instead of only Saira?"

Despite herself, Saira had to admire the ease with which Jonathan ingratiated himself with Kerri. He was tall and charismatic, and no one could guess at the temper and nastiness that belied his friendliness. Kerri couldn't know the truth behind Jonathan's sudden charm toward her.

Kerri smiled at him.

"It's lovely to meet you, Jonathan. Welcome to Desert Lodge. Have you just arrived? I'm afraid we haven't received a reservation for you, but I'm sure we could find you a suite."

Jonathan drew himself up even taller before he spoke.

"Thank you. No, I won't be staying at Desert Lodge. I have a suite booked at the Safari Sands Hotel in Windhoek. My pilot will fly me back and forth every day. It's not too far by plane."

Saira almost choked at the arrogance in Jonathan's voice. Still, Kerri didn't seem to notice, or if she did, she'd chosen to ignore it.

Instead, Kerri smiled and offered him refreshments.

As Jonathan was trying to impress Kerri, Saira felt safe to leave.

But as she walked away, she couldn't help wondering what the hell Jonathan was really doing here. He did nothing without an agenda. She'd call Peter and Manda as soon as she could. They'd find out what was going on. Her mind made up, she walked with a new resolve toward the lounge to prep her crew.

It shouldn't have come as a surprise when half an hour later, Jonathan appeared in the lounge. Saira knew him well, and understood she had to take charge of the situation at once. Otherwise, Jonathan would impose himself on the project.

Saira wouldn't allow it. This project was too important to her. She would fight tooth and nail to keep the leadership of it. Besides, what did Jonathan know about weddings? Or reality shows? She couldn't believe Max would have sent him. They'd never discussed Jonathan's participation in the production.

Before Jonathan could speak, Saira clapped her hands together to get everyone's attention.

"Everyone, this is Jonathan, also from MaxPix. He's Mr. Galbraith's son. Jonathan has come to Namibia on vacation and dropped by Desert Lodge to see what we're doing. Let's welcome him and make him feel at home."

Saira looked up at him, and clapped, but her smile didn't reach her eyes. The crew joined in and applauded Jonathan.

Jonathan smiled and bowed ever so gentlemanly.

Saira couldn't help noticing two of the young female crew members' eyes widening at the striking figure Jonathan posed.

What a waste. That someone physically so beautiful should be such a shit. Not for the first time the thought had crossed Saira's mind.

Jonathan's melodious voice carried through the lounge.

"Thank you for the warm welcome."

Jonathan looked at Saira, his smile still on his lips, but it took on a hardened edge now.

"Though I loved the introduction, Saira, I'm not sure why you think I'm on vacation. I'm here to oversee this little project, and it looks like I'm just in time. Your cameraman has a problem, doesn't he? But he's only one cameraman. I'm sure we can find someone even more suitable."

The crew applauded with enthusiasm. Whistles and whoops showed their acceptance of Jonathan on the team.

Jonathan looked around the room and gave the crew his most beautiful smile.

Saira watched in dismay as her crew fell under his spell. She understood it all too well. Hadn't she fallen like that many moons ago?

Jonathan continued to smile and looked around the room at the faces before him, at last turning to Saira.

"Well, carry on, Saira. You seem to have everything in hand. I'll liaise with the London office to send another cameraman."

With a wave at the crew and long strides of his athletic legs, Jonathan left the lounge.

Saira watched him go, and wondered how the hell she would pull off a successful pilot episode with him here.

Soon the sound of a Cessna plane told her he'd left Desert Lodge in favor of whatever entertainment he could find in Windhoek. She put him out of her mind as best as she could and instead, concentrated on her work and her new crew. There was a lot to go through, a lot to teach the new team, and not much time. She only had a month in which to complete the entire project.

MUCH LATER, after everyone had left the lounge pursuing their individual tasks, Saira slumped down in one of the big old leather chairs. She sank her head into her hands and rested her elbows on her thighs. Not only did she have to prove herself to Max and her parents, but now she had Jonathan to battle, too. The situation felt like the David and Goliath story from the Christian Bible. She was David with just a slingshot and her wits, and Jonathan was the giant Goliath, with his sword aloft and the MaxPix machine behind him.

Bloody Jonathan.

The door was open, and Saira looked up as she heard footsteps, thinking Jonathan had returned to continue to torment her.

But Gerhard walked past, saw her and waved. She'd forgotten how sexy his smile was.

FIVE

The next morning, just as Saira put the phone down, a sharp rap came at her door.

Please let it not be Jonathan.

Her voice sounded guarded and defensive to her ears.

"Come in."

The door opened, and Kerri's smiling face peeked around the door frame.

"Hi."

Saira's spirits rose at once as she got up.

"Looks like you have good news for me?"

Kerri walked into the room. Her presence exuded excitement and confidence.

"Yes, I have. I've found you the best wildlife cameraman in Namibia, Bill Furie."

Saira couldn't help laughing at the comical expression of glee on Kerri's face.

"Thank you so much, Kerri-"

Before Saira could say anything more, Kerri interrupted her.

"Come on. Bill is waiting for us in the Lapa."

Kerri's excitement was contagious, but Saira's body tensed at the thought of meeting Jonathan there.

Kerri must have noticed the look of trepidation on Saira's face because she hastened to add, "Don't worry. We have the Lapa to ourselves. Your crew was with Jonathan 'till late. I'm sure they're all still sleeping."

At the shock of hearing Kerri's words, Saira felt herself stepping back, her hand clutching at the back of the chair she'd just vacated. She couldn't believe it.

Bloody Jonathan. What was he playing at?

It was a stark reminder of her intention to call London to find out from Peter and Manda what Jonathan was doing here. She had to make that call soon.

Kerri watched Saira's face in earnest.

"I don't want to interfere, but am I right in thinking Jonathan's arrival came as a surprise?"

Saira didn't want to appear unprofessional in front of Kerri. She had to keep Kerri and Naomi on her side. They hadn't signed the agreement for the filming yet.

Saira knew she had to be careful.

"Well, Jonathan also works for MaxPix. He's Mr. Galbraith's, son."

"And your boyfriend?"

"Kind of."

Saira folded her arms across her chest.

"Jonathan had mentioned he was thinking of coming to the shoot. But I had no idea he would actually turn up. I can only hope his presence here disrupts nothing. He hasn't worked on a reality show before."

Saira thought it best not to mention neither had she.

"It surprised me when you said my crew had been with him till late last night. I didn't expect that."

Saira saw Kerri was no fool. Kerri understood the situation perfectly.

Kerri's eyes narrowed as she tilted her head to one side.

"In that case, I think it's even more important you meet with your new cameraman as soon as possible, Saira."

Saira collected her papers and bag and followed Kerri out of the room to the Lapa.

A tall, handsome, sunburnt, middle-aged man got to his feet as they approached.

"You must be Saira?"

He extended his hand toward her.

Saira nodded and shook his hand.

Kerri indicated toward the man.

"This is Bill, Saira."

When everyone had taken a seat, Bill asked about Saira's requirements for the shoot. As she explained things to him, Kerri went to order coffee for them.

Bill opened his laptop and clicked on his show reel.

Saira got lost in the stunning videos of Namibia's wildlife, only just aware that Naomi had also joined them. But it felt as though the three people at the table knew each other well, and Saira didn't get the sense they wanted her to hurry. She took her time to click through Bill's incredible work. Even though she appreciated what a find he was, she couldn't help thinking they were wildlife videos.

Bill must have sensed something from Saira's body language because he lent forward, a conspiratorial glint in his eye, and winked.

"If you have the patience to film wildlife, humans should be a doddle."

His small joke relaxed Saira.

She sat back in her chair and spread her hands on the table in front of her.

"Your work is amazing, Bill. I'd be delighted if you'd work with us. But I can't offer anything beyond the pilot, for now, at least."

"That's fine. I expected nothing else. It would make a pleasant change from being alone in the desert."

Saira liked Bill at once.

Naomi and Kerri excused themselves while Saira and Bill got down to the business side of their agreement. But it didn't escape Saira that both women seemed excited about the shoot and the part they'd played in introducing Bill to her. Saira hoped it meant there would be no problems when it came time to sign the agreement. Now, she had to cast a bridal party. Kerri had already placed several ads for the competition couples could enter to win the wedding of their dreams at Desert Lodge. The only caveats were they had to be available immediately and agree to appear on camera for the TV show.

After Bill left, Saira went through her emails. Several were from the members of the crew updating her on the status of their tasks. Everyone was doing a brilliant job and had already achieved more than she'd expected from them. It would be such a pity if Jonathan messed it all up.

As though thoughts of him could conjure him, he appeared before her. He scraped a chair away from the table and sat down, extending his long legs in front of him.

He folded his arms and contemplated her with a look of boredom on his face.

"So, what are you up to today? It seems you have delegated everything to your team."

He leaned forward, pretended to whisper and tapped against his nose.

"Well, except for the cameraman."

He sat back.

"But don't worry, I'm working on it."

A smug smile hovered around his lips. He looked pleased with the news he'd imparted.

Saira wished she could see his eyes, but his sunglasses prevented her from reading the truth she knew she'd find there. Instead, she felt like punching his face. Damn him. She wondered if Max even knew where Jonathan was?

She'd have to call London soon to find out, and she needed privacy to make the calls.

Saira was too mad at Jonathan to confront him now about what he was doing with her crew. That conversation would have to wait. Her anger sat like a bitter goblin in her belly. She wouldn't let him bait her, either.

"Well Jonathan, it might appear to you that I've delegated everything, but if you'll excuse me, I actually have work to do now."

He said nothing, but as she walked away, she could feel his eyes burning into her back.

As soon as she opened the door to her room, the air conditioning hit her. It reminded her how hot the day outside had already become despite the early hour. She closed the door at once to keep the lovely chilly air in the room. Staff had made the bed and vacuumed the floor. The room smelled like the fresh lilies that stood in the vase on the bedside table.

Saira stood for a moment with her back against the door, her eyes closed. Why couldn't things be straightforward for once?

Her sigh told of her frustration.

Turning around, she looked through the peephole. She was half expecting Jonathan to have followed her, but the view outside was clear. Pushing herself away from the door, she went to check that the windows were shut. They had to be because of the air conditioner, but she wanted to double-check.

As she closed the curtains, she smiled to herself. Paranoid much?

Manda's voice answered on the third ring.

"Hi there. Are you having fun yet?"

"Hi yourself. Did you know Jonathan would be here?"

"Oh. My. God. You. Are. Kidding?"

Saira sighed again.

"I wish I were."

"No wonder you sound so pissed off. God, I can't believe that man. Not only does he have to make your life hell when you're here, but now he's followed you half-way around the world to do the same there. Leave it with me, I'll find out what's going on."

"Thank you, Manda. You're a proper mate. I don't know what I'd do without you."

"Neither do I, but you're the one who's talking about..."

There was a pause before Manda whispered, "...leaving."

"Don't speak of it there. Wouldn't you rather work with me when I have my new company?"

A tiny squeal came over the phone.

"Do you mean it?"

Saira could hear the ill-concealed excitement in Manda's voice. She had to laugh. Manda's expressive face danced in her mind's eye.

"Silly mare. We'll discuss it in detail when I'm back."

Manda whispered again.

"So, you've decided then?"

"I'm thinking hard about it. We'll talk later. Is Peter nearby?"

"I'll transfer you to him. Hold on."

"Before you do, please find out everything you can about why Jonathan is here, what he's up to, and how I can get rid of him?"

"Sure, sure. Hold on."

There was a rather lengthy pause, and Saira knew Manda

was giving Peter the low-down on Jonathan's appearance in Namibia.

Then, Peter was on the line.

"Hi darling, how are you?"

Saira felt tearful at the sound of her sympathetic friend's voice. It was still so unexpected how she had developed a fast and deep bond with Peter in a way she'd never experienced with any other human being before. Peter seemed to understand her in a way no one else did, and he allowed her to see him in such a vulnerable way it awed her. She loved him like the older brother she'd always yearned for.

"I could be better, thanks, Peter. Jonathan's turned up."

"Yes, Manda just told me. I'm guessing you didn't expect him?"

"No. Well, Jonathan mentioned in passing he might want to join me, but I thought he was just talking nonsense, as usual. You know what he's like."

"Yes. A snake in the grass."

Saira smiled.

Peter had often chosen the most inappropriate moments to deliver a tirade about Jonathan's inadequacies as her boyfriend.

"I hope you meet some gorgeous desert prince while you're out there. It's time for an end to the Jonathan era."

When Saira didn't respond straight away, Peter jumped on it at once.

"Oh, there's a prince already?"

"Don't be silly."

"Come on, tell Uncle Peter. What's his name?"

"If you must know, he's not a prince. Gerhard landed us in the middle of the desert when the plane broke."

"Oh, my God, are you okay?"

Saira filled Peter in about what had happened. She told him how her father had wanted to send his jet to rescue her from the desert. Peter made it clear he wanted to know more, but Saira could hear Manda's raised voice behind him.

"Darling, Manda's here, and she's practically jumping out of her skin. So, I'm guessing it's fabulous news."

Saira could imagine Manda grabbing the phone from Peter's hand. Her excited voice came on the line, but her whisper was too soft.

"Manda, please honey, speak up. I can't hear what you're saying."

"Sorry. Is that better?"

But before Saira could respond, Manda continued talking.

"Did you know Max has a new secretary? No, you probably didn't. Well, I've just met her. She's stunning, tall, blonde... you know the type. I'm sure Jonathan had a hand in her being here and only because Max isn't in the UK at the moment. Can't imagine Max putting up with her for long because she seems entirely vacuous. Of course, I might be wrong."

Saira sighed.

"Manda, get to the point."

"Oh, right, yes. Well, Cindy is new, so I offered her a friendly tea and a chat. She told me Jonathan had called Max's private phone last night, but Max was already out of the country. Not sure why Jonathan didn't know his dad was traveling? Anyhoo, Cindy answered, and Jonathan asked that she send him details of the three best cameramen we use here at MaxPix."

In the background, Saira could hear Peter's voice as he escorted someone else out of his office so she and Manda could continue their private conversation.

"So, did Cindy find a cameraman?"

"No. She's still looking, poor love. I've kindly sent her a file of camera operators we normally use, but they're in the expired file."

Manda giggled at her plan, and Saira wanted to join in the amusement because she knew Manda was referring to the retired list. But she found nothing about it funny.

Saira glanced at the time. Almost nine o'clock. She had to rescue her crew from Jonathan.

"Okay, Manda. Thanks for being such an amazing friend. I have to go. Please keep up the outstanding work and let me know anything you can find out. Be careful."

"I will, honey."

Saira shook her head as she ended her conversation with Manda. She knew Manda's petty attempts at sabotaging Jonathan's efforts to get a cameraman out here would dissipate the moment Max came on board. It was the best thing he was away on a business trip.

Saira still had half an hour before meeting with the crew. Might as well respond to their emails before the meeting. She flipped open her laptop.

A knock came at her door just as she typed her name at the bottom of the last email.

"Come in."

Jonathan opened the door and walked into her room.

"Jonathan! What do you think you're doing? I said I was coming."

"I wanted to check whether you are, in fact, working or if you were taking a nap after our exhaustive chat earlier."

Saira folded her arms.

Dear God, she had to make Jonathan leave, or she might kill him, the infuriating egotist.

SIX

Saira stopped in the door and placed her fists on her hips as she regarded the room.

What the hell?

Someone had completely altered the lounge, their HQ, that she and Shona had taken such care to adapt for the duration of their stay here. The tables they'd arranged in groups, with laptops and PC monitors facing outward so everyone could see each other, had been shoved to one side of the room. Papers and dirty plates were scattered all over the tables, and half-full mugs of cold coffee had left marks on the dark wooden surfaces. The chairs stood in rows and faced two large flip boards with lots of writing in thick black marker pen.

Saira's sigh told of her frustration and of her renewed determination to wrestle back the project from Jonathan. She didn't have even a sliver of doubt that he was behind this chaos.

Closing the door, she walked down the corridor to Kerri's office. Kerri's door was open. She was sitting behind her desk, phone clutched to her ear. Saira raised her hand to knock on the frame. But Kerri noticed her at once.

Kerri smiled and indicated the chair in front of her desk.

Saira returned Kerri's smile and sat down. She wasn't listening to Kerri's conversation. But the tone of Kerri's voice carried the impression she was dealing with her own problems.

Instead, Saira's thoughts revolved around what had happened in the lounge and Jonathan's role in the chaos. She'd have to do something about it, and soon. It was clear he was trying to take over the project and may already have damaged it. The only good thing about Jonathan's presence was that now, she had to focus on him instead of thinking about Gerhard all the time. That way lay even more trouble.

Kerri finished her conversation and leaned forward, questions shining in her eyes.

"Anything wrong, Saira? How can I help?"

Saira spread her hands on the table.

"Looks like you have troubles of your own. I didn't mean to interrupt. But I didn't want to be rude and just leave before speaking with you."

Kerri slumped back in her chair, her eyes on her phone.

"No, you interrupted nothing. I was going to contact you, so I'm glad you're here."

As Saira watched Kerri, a feeling of doom fastened itself in her gut. Saira couldn't help noticing Kerri appeared to have difficulty meeting her eyes. It could only spell more trouble, and Saira prayed it wasn't more from Jonathan.

Kerri folded her arms across her chest as though she was preparing herself for Saira's adverse reaction and lifted her chin toward the phone.

"That was Bill."

Saira sat forward.

"You mean Bill Furie, the cameraman?"

"Yes. I'm sorry, Saira. The BBC has offered Bill a commission for another program. He called to apologize, to explain he'd be away in the desert for months and he won't be able to take part in your project."

Kerri looked up. Her brown eyes big and filled with remorse.

"I hope you'll accept my apology as well? If we'd known Bill would be so unreliable, we'd never have recommended him for your project."

Saira tried to make her voice sound upbeat, but to her ears, she sounded anything but.

"I see. Don't worry, Kerri. I wasn't able to offer him more than the pilot, anyway. So, if the BBC has offered him a better project, how can I blame him?"

But even as Saira said the words, she felt her stomach tighten in an anxious knot. This was an added complication she didn't need, not with Jonathan playing silly games.

Kerri looked up. Her expressive eyes showed concern.

"I'm truly sorry, Saira. We called several camera people when we were looking for one the first time around. It doesn't mean there aren't any others and we'll continue to try."

Kerri paused and nodded to herself as though she'd decided.

"I'll put out feelers to all our contacts at once. You never know, things might have changed, and someone who wasn't available before could be now."

Kerri started typing on the keyboard in front of her.

Saira was grateful for the small respite. She didn't want Kerri to see her level of apprehension, but it was mounting by the minute. In particular, after Jonathan had shown his cards. Until now, Saira had been in two minds about the project, but Jonathan's shenanigans had clarified everything. This project was far more important to her than a mere skirmish with Jonathan. Somewhere deep inside her, Saira knew it was exactly what she needed to start her own company, to begin her dream. She could already see the entire thing.

Why did only a crisis ever reveal how important something was?

Kerri startled Saira from her thoughts as she stopped typing, sat forward, elbows on the table, fingers interlinking under her chin.

"Am I right in thinking you're in a hurry to get the project finished?"

Saira nodded, glad someone understood.

"Yes. The longer we take to shoot the pilot, the more of the budget I'd have to use on things other than the production, and I'd rather not spend the budget on food and drink for the crew."

The instant glint in Kerri's eyes made Saira wonder what she was up to?

Kerri's excitement appeared to grow and showed in her voice when she spoke.

"I have an idea. I don't know how you'd feel about it, but it's something to consider. There is someone here we use for our marketing purposes. He takes the most beautiful pictures and videos for our website and marketing materials. But he's not a professional cameraman, though he could have been–he's won several prestigious photographic competitions and his work is often featured in local magazines and on Namibian TV. However, it might be worth looking at his work because he could be the answer to your prayers. He works fast, he won't charge you the earth and could be available at once."

Saira sat forward again. Hope flooded her body as she returned Kerri's smile.

"Who is this magician?"

"You've already met him... Gerhard."

Saira frowned.

It couldn't be. There was no way Kerri could mean the sexy, but the rude, silent guy who crash-landed them in the desert and didn't even have a working walkie-talkie on him? The gorgeous guy with eyes that made her melt when he looked at her? The guy who occupied nearly all her thoughts. That guy?

Kerri's next words revealed she thought Saira's furrowed brow meant she was trying to remember him.

"You know, the guide who came to collect you at the airport."

"Oh, I see."

Kerri laughed.

"I can see you're not a fan. Don't worry. I wasn't either when I first met him. But Gerhard isn't all he seems at first."

Saira couldn't imagine Gerhard doing anything creative or artistic. He gave the impression of a man of action. She felt a twinge of shame at having called him a Neanderthal, even if only in her head. But she had to acknowledge she'd based her feelings about him on him landing them in the desert. Then there was his annoying, curt manner. She wasn't basing her opinions on an in-depth conversation or knowledge of him.

Kerri continued to smile and talk as she watched Saira consider her suggestion.

"I'm sure you've seen our website. Gerhard was responsible for the images and videos on our site. You'd need to see his show reels properly to decide. But if I were you, I'd consider him. You may know several Hollywood A-listers have already been on vacation here with us, and we're expecting more to arrive later this year. We've also catered to several famous movers and shakers. So, our advertising must be of the highest quality. I'm sure you understand."

Kerri seemed so sincere but couldn't disguise her enthusiasm.

Saira had to laugh at the expression on Kerri's face.

"Okay, I'll look at his work. You've sold him to me, at least on paper. You're right, I've had a look at your website before coming here, and the videos and images impressed me. They showed how unique and beautiful Desert Lodge is, and also how stunning Namibia is. But I didn't dwell too much on them at the time because I was more focussed on reading about you and Naomi and what you offer. My boss had already decided for us to shoot the pilot here, so I didn't have to choose. But I feel he made a perfect choice."

Kerri smiled and dialed Gerhard's number as she spoke.

"Thank you, Saira. I'm glad you feel that way. Let me make a quick call to see if Gerhard is available to show us his work."

Saira waited until Kerri started speaking with Gerhard before pulling her phone from her bag.

She sent a quick text to Manda and Peter.

Please help! Jonathan has kidnapped the project! xxx

Within seconds, Manda's text response appeared.

Don't worry. On it. Got you covered this end. xxx

A few seconds later came Peter's response.

Fucktard! Don't worry, darling. We'll sort everything. It's war! xxx

Saira smiled as she texted back.

Thanks, guys. xxx

She put her phone away as Kerri's call to Gerhard ended.

Kerri got up.

"Right, Gerhard is ready for us. He's waiting outside in the truck to take us to his study where he'll show you his work."

Saira wondered if she'd heard Kerri correctly.

"Oh, I see. Doesn't he have his show reels in digital format on a website or something? I thought he'd email the link."

Kerri's laughter bubbled up from her stomach.

"No. He's not a professional photographer or cameraman. He doesn't have a website. But his work is amazing, and he takes it seriously. He has a wonderful studio in his study where he stores everything. No one else has access to it. It's why we now use him also for our marketing. Every image is unique. We no longer rely on anyone else from outside. And it works better for us because Gerhard knows both Namibia and Desert Lodge very well."

Saira glanced at the time.

"How long will it take? I have to re-schedule my meeting with my crew as they weren't in the lounge and I have no idea where they are."

Kerri collected her bag and phone as she spoke.

"I didn't imagine they'd be up this early. The night staff heard them leave the lounge around four o'clock this morning. I should think they're all still fast asleep. But viewing Gerhard's work won't take long..."

Kerri glanced at her wristwatch.

"... two hours tops?"

Saira felt the rage build inside her anew.

Bloody Jonathan. He had her crew working until four o'clock in the morning?!

She'd deal with him later. She shook her head as she followed Kerri out the door.

It felt strange to be that close to Gerhard again. An acute awareness of his presence felt overwhelming and disturbing in the confined space of the truck.

Saira had been unable to get him out of her head since their first meeting. Falling asleep each night had been difficult because that was when thoughts of him wouldn't leave her. Just as she was ready to drift off, there he'd be, larger than life, preventing her from falling asleep. It was quite irritating, and she blamed him one hundred percent, but couldn't make him disappear.

Apart from nodding in her direction, real-life Gerhard seemed unperturbed by her nearness. His focus was on driving and the occasional chat with Kerri.

Saira sighed and sat back against the seat, trying to get control over her wayward beating heart.

Even though Gerhard had the air conditioner on in the truck, the idea of the heat outside continued to concern Saira. She was grateful she'd opted to sit in the back. It gave her a brief space away from Gerhard's intensity. But it remained difficult to deal with her feelings around him. It also made sense to move out of his eye line in the rear-view mirror because every time she looked up, and their eyes met, to her annoyance, her heart would beat faster again.

The noise from the truck, and not being penetrated by those blue-blue eyes, made it easier for her to ignore the conversation between him and Kerri. Sitting in the back, also meant she had more room to move out of the sun as it burned through the windows onto her arms.

The road ahead was an endless straight line of sand with nothing growing beside it. Saira wanted to contemplate the mystery of how anybody or anything could live and thrive in this desolate country. But she couldn't stop her thoughts and the gloomy feelings around Jonathan and the problems he posed.

Who knew what he'd told the crew to get them to abandon the schedule she'd set for them?

The car's movement, and the pleasant drone of Kerri's and Gerhard's voices as they continued their conversation, lulled Saira. When she couldn't resist any longer, she gave in to the call of her heavy eyelids. Sleep would, at least for a few moments, ferry her away from the anxiety Jonathan and unreliable camera operators had caused her.

The sudden change in movement woke Saira as they drove over a grill through some gates.

Kerri glanced back at her and smiled when she saw Saira was awake.

"I didn't want to wake you. You seemed to need the nap.

But Johan called. He'd never forgive me for not bringing you to see the elephant orphanage, especially since it's on the way to Gerhard's place. Are you ready to overload on ellie cuteness?"

Saira pinched her thumb and forefinger over the bridge of her nose.

"That's a lovely surprise. I adore ellies but never imagined I'd see any on this trip."

Even though the detour would add an extra burden to her already stretched schedule, Saira could do with the distraction. It might help to put things into perspective again.

Johan, and several dogs of different sizes and levels of excitement, were waiting to greet them as they drove up to the huge old house.

The Victorian-German architecture Saira had encountered so far, seemed foreign yet fitting to the desert landscape around it. Johan's house, with its austere gables and wraparound veranda, was no exception.

His booming voice matched his imposing physique. He opened Saira's door and extended a hand to help her out.

"Welcome. Welcome to your first visit to the Namib Elephant Orphanage, Saira. I hope it's the first of many."

He glanced at Kerri and Gerhard.

"Great you guys could make it. We're just about to let the youngest ellies out to play."

Johan took Saira's elbow, steered her toward an enclosure and walked her through the gate, talking all the while.

"You'll love this, Saira. These are our youngest ellies. They can't join the herds yet, but as they've been with us for a few months now, they have acclimatized to us. It's important for their development and socialization that they play together every day. That way, they create a herd of their own, so when they're old enough, we can free them back into the wild together."

Saira forgot all about Jonathan and the mess he'd created as she watched the ellies. They were even cuter than Johan had promised, or than she'd expected, and much smaller. Their comical struggles to play with a ball almost as large as the smallest of them, had her smiling through tears and clutching a fist over her heart.

Johan appeared sensitive to the impact that seeing the orphaned baby elephants had on her.

"Most of these ellies are only a few days old, and sometimes, only a few hours when our anti-poacher units find them near their dead mothers. It's heart-breaking. But we do everything we can to help heal the trauma they experienced. We create a safe environment for them here and, in time, return them to the wild where they belong."

When Gerhard spoke, Saira's heart skipped a beat. Only now did she realize he'd followed them into the enclosure and was standing close behind her. The warmth from his body was far more immediate than the heat of the day.

"Luca has done a lot of work with Johan and several local anti-poacher units to end the poaching. It's slow going, but we've had some success so far with the drones."

Saira noticed Kerri wasn't with them, but before she could ask, Gerhard spoke as though he'd read her thoughts.

"Kerri had something to see to in the house. She'll join us soon."

It was both distracting and comforting to have Gerhard so close-by. But soon, the ellies captivated Saira's attention once again. They were so adorable. She almost forgot to take the video of them she'd wanted. Her father would love them, she knew, and she made several short videos to send him.

Kerri had re-joined them, meanwhile.

"Right, guys, I guess we'd better skedaddle as we need to get Gerhard back to Desert Lodge in time for his guests."

Saira followed the others with reluctance, unwilling to leave her experience with the ellies. Johan hugged everyone and surprised Saira when he slapped Kerri's bottom. But, Saira reckoned, they clearly knew each other well and were excellent friends.

Johan waved as he bent down to scratch behind the ears of one of his dogs.

"See you soon!"

As the car's air conditioning kicked in, Saira couldn't help being grateful to be out of the scorching sun. The red sandy road stretched ahead of them again in a never-ending straight line. Once again, Saira sat back, leaned her head against the headrest and closed her eyes. But this time, instead of sleeping, her mind's eye saw only the ellies playing with the ball in the desert dust. They were excellent medicine against anxiety.

It must have been half an hour later, she felt the car turn and opened her eyes, blinked a few times, and almost gasped aloud at the sight before them. On either side of a straight track, tall, dark green trees lined the path ahead to the house that looked more like a castle from a fairy-tale than anything that belonged in the desert.

As they drew closer to the house, Kerri turned around to face Saira, her grin spreading wider as she saw the wonder on Saira's face.

"Not what you expected, right?"

Saira could see Gerhard's face in the rear-view mirror. He appeared to be unfazed by Kerri's excitement and oblivious to the expression of amazement Saira knew must sit in her eyes. Yet, as he locked his eyes on hers for a few seconds, Saira felt herself flush and another flutter curled in her stomach.

What the hell?

Kerri's voice interrupted the weirdness as she continued to convey her enthusiasm.

"It feels like being transported into a fairy-tale, don't you think?"

Saira had to smile at Kerri's words because they echoed her thoughts.

"It's very unusual. Not something I'd expected to see in the desert."

Gerhard pulled the truck in front of the house and got out. As he walked away up the stairs, opened the front door and disappeared through it, Kerri spoke again.

"If you think the outside is amazing, wait till you get inside."

Saira smiled.

The day just got even better. Saira had to remind herself again she wasn't here on holiday. She opened the door and stepped out of the truck but stopped dead in her tracks as a cheetah appeared around the corner. It headed straight for her.

But Kerri came to Saira's rescue. She walked toward the cheetah, squatted down and stroked its head. She looked at Saira over her shoulder and smiled.

"Come, meet Rundu. Gerhard rescued him when hunters killed his mother. When he was a small cub, he lived at Desert Lodge for a while, so he's very tame. He won't attack you."

Saira's hands were clammy as she closed the door, but she took a deep breath and a few hesitant steps forward.

"You're sure he's safe?"

"Oh, yes. The only danger from Rundu is he might love you to death."

Saira said nothing. But she couldn't shake the thought she didn't like the death thing, no matter how it might happen. It was no joke, and she'd rather not be left alone with the cheetah, no matter how tame he was, thankyouverymuch.

SEVEN

Gerhard appeared in the doorway and clicked his fingers.

"Rundu! Here, boy."

The cheetah dashed up the stairs to Gerhard, who stroked the animal's head.

"I wondered what had happened to you guys, but I see Rundu has worked his charm on you. Come on. Safari guests are waiting for me at Desert Lodge."

The women followed Gerhard and the cheetah into the house.

Saira wanted to ask if she should close the front door, but no one else seemed bothered by it being left open. As they were in the middle of nowhere, she reckoned, there were no problems with safety and security.

But as Saira entered the house, she stopped in her tracks once again. Kerri had been right. Inside, it was even more magnificent.

Stunning, massive tapestries covered every wall. They lent an air of old Europe to the place. The entrance hall, lavished in polished wood, reflected the light from the windows high above. Saira's eyes traveled over the stunning floor to the ceiling high above the balcony that revealed the next level of the house. The place felt welcoming but austere at the same time.

Saira wanted to shiver. But the feeling passed almost as soon as it started. Instead, she walked closer to the nearest tapestry.

Perhaps the tapestries depicted something from Gerhard's European ancestry? The place carried an air and sense of old Europe. It reminded her of English castles and holidays in France and Germany.

Looking around the enormous hall, the massive sweeping staircase leading up to the upper floors captured Saira's attention. Its wooden banister had been polished to a dark luster.

She couldn't miss the gigantic chandelier dangling from the high ceiling. As the light caught its crystals, it projected tiny multi-colored slivers, like a shield of angels, against the top of the walls and the ceiling.

But before Saira could indulge her visual senses any further, Kerri's head popped around the doorway of a room to Saira's right.

"In here. This is where the magic is."

Kerri's smile said she understood Saira's reaction on first seeing the inside of the house.

As she neared the doorway, Kerri whispered, "not what you expected, right?"

Saira nodded.

She didn't know how to express her amazement at such beauty, and even more so since she hadn't expected it from someone like Gerhard. It seemed so at odds with him. But now she'd seen him here, she couldn't imagine him living anywhere else. Even his curt manner made sense in the otherness of his home.

But if the entrance hall had impressed her, the room she now entered took her breath away. On one side, floor-to-ceiling windows allowed the sharp desert light to fill the room. Bookcases and books covered two of the walls. And on the other wall, behind what was Gerhard's desk, a massive television flat-screen occupied the space.

Gerhard was standing by the desk.

Saira thought he looked the embodiment of an aristocrat, comfortable in his skin, king of his world. But there was something else about him, something sensual and earthy in the way he carried himself. She watched as he picked up a remote control and pressed the buttons. The massive screen came to life. It changed the way the room felt. The room receded in the images that appeared on the screen in 3D, and she marveled at the technology he could access in this desolate place. He had to have serious connections somewhere nearby, but she didn't see any towers or poles outside. Perhaps they were further away from the house?

Image after image of the desert, sunsets and sunrises, and the beauty of Namibia appeared on the screen. After several images, one replacing the other, stunning videos followed.

Saira was surprised to see Gerhard had also worked with people in his videos. It was a relief to know he had that experience, unlike Bill, who'd only shot footage of animals and landscapes. It shouldn't be too tricky for Gerhard to transfer those skills to the TV project, she reckoned.

She nodded to herself. Perhaps the saying was true, there was a reason for everything.

But why Jonathan was tormenting her, she couldn't guess. Other than he enjoyed doing so for its own sake. At least the reason for losing the other cameramen might have happened so Gerhard could film the pilot. He was more than capable of it, judging by the latest ad campaign he'd shot for the lodge, and that was now playing on the massive screen.

Kerri sat down on a chair and indicated for Saira to take the other.

Meanwhile, Gerhard left the room without a word, followed by Rundu.

One stunning video followed another, and mesmerized Saira. The quality of the work was superb. She could feel Kerri's eyes flicking toward her now and then and was aware of a gigantic smile that wouldn't leave her face.

"So, what do you think, Saira? Have you found your new cameraman?"

The expression in Kerri's eyes spoke of her sincere wish to help.

A sudden emotion washed through Saira's body. She had to blink to stop the tears spilling from her eyes.

Fresh memories of the little ellies earlier, and now the beauty of Gerhard's images and videos had touched her heart. Gerhard's work was art of exceptional quality and high emotional value. Art and nature always had a profound effect on her. It had to be that, and Kerri's kindness, she reckoned.

"Thank you, Kerri."

Saira put a hand on Kerri's forearm to emphasize her heart-felt words.

"I can't thank you enough. This will save everything."

Kerri didn't respond, other than to pat Saira's hand on her arm. Kerri's smile showed her curiosity about Saira's statement, and her eyes glinted with the suspicion that Saira was thanking her for more than a cameraman.

Moments later, Gerhard returned carrying a tray with tea things and cookies. His presence announced him before he entered the room. Rundu followed like his shadow. As he put the tray down on his desk, Saira looked at his hands. She hadn't noticed them before. Now, she saw they were not only manly hands, but they appeared capable, safe hands, hands that held cameras and created art that touched her heart and soul.

Reality shifted, and she glimpsed beyond who Gerhard

appeared to be. She saw his gentle spirit, his deep loyalty and integrity, his strict moral compass and his artistic soul. It was clear he didn't need the job at Desert Lodge, and it was now evident he did it out of a sense of enjoyment and loyalty to his friends there.

The man standing before her, was the epitome of all she had ever dreamed of, her soul mate. That he existed at all, filled her with a force of love and gratitude she'd never experienced. At that moment, it seemed she'd always known him. She had a sudden weird sense that their connection was stronger even than death itself.

The sound of his voice snapped her back to a reality that left her yearning to return to the other, clearer realm she'd just glimpsed.

"I thought you ladies might like refreshments."

Kerri got up and started pouring the tea.

"Thanks, Gerhard. It's very thoughtful of you. Would you like some?"

"No, thanks. I have a few things to see to. I'll be back soon."

Once again, Rundu's cheetah paws followed in Gerhard's steps across the wooden floor, their sounds growing fainter as they walked away.

Saira drank her tea and watch the beautiful videos. She could feel herself calming down and knew no matter what else happened, her life had changed forever today. It felt as though she'd been split into two people. One lived in her new reality with the strong possibility of reciprocated love from her soul mate. The other, who'd found such a treasure in the desert, filled her with the hope her project could be something extraordinary. Perhaps with it, a new life awaited her. Excitement burned in her chest. But sooner than she'd wanted, they were ready to return to Desert Lodge.

This time, when Rundu accompanied them to the truck, Saira prepared herself to be less trepidatious of him.

Saira felt proud of herself for touching Rundu, even though it was a quick tentative rub behind his ear. His huge purr wasn't something she'd expected to hear, but it relaxed her. When she felt safe, she slid into the back seat again and pulled the door shut.

Feeling much happier about life than she did this morning, this time, she was determined to stay awake all the way back to Desert Lodge. She wanted to enjoy every second of the alien landscape as they drove down the road.

But moments later, her phone pinged. It was a message from Peter.

Has something happened to your cameraman? xxx

Saira frowned.

She texted back.

How did you know? The BBC offered Bill a commission. But I think I've just found someone else. Why? xxx

Almost at once, Peter's next message appeared.

J's been in touch with Max's office. Something about funding from London? But nothing about a new camera operator. Guess he doesn't know you've found one yet. I'll check things this side with my new bestie, Cindy. M is still abroad, and Cindy's still chasing cameramen from Manda's 'retired' list. lol xxx

Saira bit her lip as she thought about Peter's text.

How did Jonathan know about Bill's resignation so soon? Unless...

She leaned forward and tapped Kerri on the shoulder.

"Has Jonathan been in touch with you about Bill's resignation?"

Kerri turned so she could face Saira.

"I haven't seen him today. Bill only told me about it this morning when you were in my office."

Saira nodded and sat back again.

She sent a quick text to Peter.

When did J contact M about funding for a new cameraman? Bill only called Kerri this morning. xxx

Peter's response came at once.

Cindy told me about it last night. Sounds dodgy! xxx

Saira stared at Peter's text before responding.

Nothing about J is straightforward. Sounds dodgy all right. He's up to something. xxx

BY THE TIME Gerhard drove the truck through Desert Lodge's gates, Saira was ready to kill Jonathan. But she'd need every ounce of self-control if she wanted to beat Jonathan at this game she was determined to win.

As though Gerhard could sense her turmoil, he surprised her by being very gentlemanly, as though opening his house to her meant he'd also softened his attitude toward her. He opened her door and helped her down from the truck.

His actions surprised Saira, but what was even more of a shock was the jolt of electricity she felt when he touched her hand.

She looked up to find those intense eyes staring deep into hers, mere inches from her face. Heat rose up her body as her heart knocked against her ribcage. The urge to run away almost overcame her, but she felt frozen to the spot and unable to tear her eyes away from his. His gentle hand on her shoulder burned through her thin top.

But the sudden sound of Jonathan's voice behind her felt as though someone had poured a bucket of ice water over her.

"Oh, there you are. Skiving off again, I see. I need the filming schedule and went to your room. But you'd locked the door. In the future, if you are going to leave the premises, you should let me have a key to your room so I can access the information we need."

Jonathan took long strides to where they were standing. He wore a frown, and his face resembled a thundercloud looking for somewhere to break.

Saira could feel the heat and colors of anger and humiliation mix on her face. She was just about to respond when Gerhard stepped forward and stopped Jonathan's body with his.

Gerhard's voice was a soft, dangerous growl when he spoke.

"That's no way to speak to a lady. And not that you deserve an explanation, but to use your words, she wasn't skiving off. She was out scouting for a new cameraman."

Jonathan's eyes narrowed as he looked from Saira to Gerhard and back.

He sneered his response.

"Since when does Saira need a knight in shining armor? She's always been feisty enough to fight her own corner. I don't know who you are, and I don't care. But stay out of our business."

By this time, Kerri had walked around the truck and joined the party. She placed a placating hand on Jonathan's forearm.

"None of us are trying to interfere in your business, Jonathan. But none of us expected you here, including Saira. As you know, Naomi is the owner. She and I have only ever dealt with Saira and Max before this project started. So, forgive us if we don't understand your involvement here. Naomi and I agreed to work with Saira. We still intend to do so, and when we sign the contract to go ahead with the project, it will be with her. So, Saira is not obliged to share anything with you and certainly not her room key. Our guests have a right to feel safe here, and I'm not sure Saira would feel that way if you had a key to her room."

Jonathan's face had gone pale. The frown between his eyes had deepened, and the set of his mouth showed the intensity of his growing anger.

Saira watched Jonathan. She knew him too well. All the signs were there that he was about to explode. She braced herself for the confrontation, but her heart sang a cheerful song that both Kerri, and Gerhard, had come to her defense. It was more than she'd expected from either of them.

Jonathan pulled himself up to his full height, trying to regain power over the much taller and imposing Gerhard in front of him.

Just then, Khwai and a truckload of safari guests drew up alongside them and stopped in a small sandstorm. Jonathan wafted his hand in front of his face to get rid of the dust and glowered at Saira as he addressed Kerri.

His voice dripped sarcasm.

"Well, let me remind you, I'm still Max's son. This project belongs to MaxPix, and I have seniority over Saira."

He dismissed Kerri when he returned his ire on Saira.

"So, if it suits you, Saira, we would appreciate your presence in the lounge, so you can at least deliver the filming schedule to the crew in person. And you can stop your search for a camera-man. I've been in touch with my dad to request the extra funding for a proper professional cameraman from London. I think we've wasted quite enough time with the locals. It's bad enough that we have to work with a local crew."

Kerri put her hand up toward Jonathan's chest.

"Not so fast, Jonathan. I think it's time Naomi and I came to greet and welcome the crew to Desert Lodge. So, if you don't mind, Saira will accompany us in a few moments after we've spoken in my office, first."

Jonathan said nothing but glared at Kerri before he turned on his heel and stormed off toward the lounge.

As he disappeared around the corner, Kerri and Gerhard both turned to Saira and spoke in unison.

"Are you okay, Saira?"

Saira blew out a breath through pursed lips.

That went better than she'd imagined it would, knowing the fuss Jonathan could kick up. But it was obvious he didn't want to come across as the asshole he was in front of Kerri and Gerhard. Saira just prayed he hadn't messed up her chances of shooting the pilot here at Desert Lodge.

Bloody Jonathan.

Saira looked from Gerhard to Kerri before she spoke.

"I appreciate you both understand the situation I'm in. But Jonathan is right. I've always had to fight my own battles with him."

Gerhard's eyes were bluer and warmer as he nodded to Saira. His large hand enveloped her shoulder in another thrilling squeeze before he walked back toward the truck.

Kerri had called Naomi, meanwhile, and was asking Naomi to meet them in her office as she gestured for Saira to follow her.

EIGHT

By the time Saira and Kerri got to her office, Naomi was already there, waiting for them.

Saira could tell at once from the expression on Naomi's face that Kerri had informed her about the argument with Jonathan. Naomi was sitting in Kerri's chair, her eyes fixed on Kerri's computer monitor. But on seeing them, she turned the monitor around.

Naomi walked around the desk and took Saira's hand.

"I'm so sorry about what happened, Saira. We want all our guests here to feel safe, and I'm appalled to hear you had such trouble with Jonathan Galbraith. I was going to call Max in London, but Luca talked me out of it."

Before Saira could respond, the man on the screen cleared his throat.

Saira couldn't help staring. The man was breath-taking. He looked like an angel and was the embodiment of the romantic hero with his dark hair and eyes, his straight, elegant nose and full, sensual mouth. Yet, Gerhard's tall, muscular figure with his blue-blue eyes and artistic depths popped into her mind.

Naomi smiled and stood aside, gesturing with her hand toward the monitor.

"Saira, this is my husband, Luca."

Then Naomi looked at Luca and gestured toward Saira.

"Darling, this is Saira I've told you about."

Saira nodded to Luca as all three women took their seats in front of the monitor.

So, this was the famous Luca Armati.

Luca's smile and the mischievous twinkle in his eyes made him even more handsome.

His accent carried a soft Italian musicality, which made his lovely voice sound exotic to Saira's ears.

"Hello, Saira. Welcome to Desert Lodge. I am sorry to hear you're having problems with one of our guests."

Saira noticed though Luca's voice was friendly, it carried an underlying tone of authority. She liked him at once and could see how well suited he and Naomi were. Their loving interaction was in stark contrast to the wreckage of her relationship with Jonathan.

Naomi interrupted her husband.

"No, Jonathan isn't a guest here, darling. He's Max Galbraith's son, but he didn't arrive with Saira. He's staying in Windhoek and flying back and forth every day."

Luca nodded and frowned.

"Oh, I see. Still, I am sorry to hear of Jonathan's clash with you, Saira."

Naomi turned to face Saira.

"You're probably wondering why we're all meeting like this, Saira, and why we have Luca on Skype with us?"

She didn't wait for Saira's nod before she continued.

"This situation is slightly more complicated than we could have imagined. Kerri and I want to work with you and MaxPix.

But we had no idea Jonathan would appear in the picture. Luckily, Luca knows everybody."

Naomi and Luca shared a secret smile, and Saira got the impression there was a story behind their smiles.

Luca nodded.

"I don't know Max Galbraith well, but I have come across him at various functions over the years. And MaxPix was involved in one of our Armati supercar ad campaigns several years ago. I'm sure he'll remember me. I'm more than happy to help. If you could let me have his private number, Saira, I'll call him tonight."

Saira's head was spinning. Things were happening very fast in a way she hadn't foreseen. To have the support of these great new colleagues, meant so much. That she'd also come to think of them as friends so soon, surprised her.

Naomi interrupted again.

"Kerri and I only ever contacted you or Max's secretary. She seems to have left, though? There is a new girl, Cindy? But she couldn't give us Max's personal details."

Luca smiled at Saira.

"Just leave the number with Naomi. She'll pass it on to me. It was lovely to meet you, Saira. I'm sorry, ladies, I have to go."

A beautiful smile lit up Luca's face.

"Business is a demanding mistress."

Naomi laughed.

"You mean you prefer to play with cars than with us? Enjoy your time alone, Mr. Armati, because when I get home...."

He smiled, blew a kiss to Naomi, and waved to them, before switching off Skype at his end.

The monitor went dark.

Saira looked at Naomi, and hoped her smile conveyed her gratitude.

"Thank you so much for helping me, Naomi. You've all been wonderful. But I thought you lived here?"

Naomi laughed at the expression on Saira's face.

"I do when I'm in Namibia, but I share a wonderful home with Luca in Modena for part of the year. I've never been able to persuade him to stop playing with his beloved cars. Now, it will be even more difficult as soon, he'll take over the Armati supercar business from his father."

Saira nodded and tried to ban the feelings of guilt from her body that she couldn't follow the plans her parents had for her. She understood Luca's plight.

Kerri spoke as she got up and walked to her chair.

"Yes, and Gerhard was a proper hero today, wasn't he?"

The way Kerri said Gerhard's name made Saira wonder if they were an item. She looked at Kerri's hand and saw her wedding ring. Saira hadn't noticed a ring on Gerhard's finger, but that didn't always follow, did it? An icy hand clamped around her heart and her knees felt weak, though why, she couldn't fathom.

Gerhard had appeared more relaxed with Kerri than the silent man Saira had to deal with in the desert. He and Kerri's intimate conversation in the car showed Gerhard seemed to have no problem talking with Kerri. It would make sense he'd be comfortable with Kerri if they were married. But that's just ridiculous, isn't it? Wouldn't Kerri have introduced him as her husband by now? And what did it matter to her if they were married?

Saira bit her lip and tried to get her wayward emotions under control. Whatever was the matter with her?

Come on, girl. Get a grip.

Naomi's hand on Saira's arm brought her back to the present.

"So, Saira, Kerri and I both look forward to working with

you. We haven't changed our minds about that. But we want to wait until Luca has spoken with Max, and Jonathan is no longer here before we sign the contract with you. We hope you understand."

Naomi's eyes were sincere, and Saira read her honesty there.

She nodded.

"I understand. If I were in your shoes, I'd do the same."

Kerri got up.

"Excellent. I'm glad we all have our cards on the table. Now, let's welcome your crew to Desert Lodge, Saira. The South African film agency that put them together has an excellent reputation, and we asked for the best. They ought to be the cream of the crop."

Saira followed the women on legs that continued to feel like jelly about her thoughts around Gerhard being married to Kerri. She cursed her weirdness with every step.

The din of excited chatter and laughter struck them before they reached the lounge. But Saira didn't expect the room to resemble the classroom of five-year-olds when they entered. Kerri caught a paper plane mid-air before it damaged one of her eyes. Naomi danced around a tall guy who was talking, gesticulating, walking backward and almost colliding with her.

Saira remained standing in the doorway and scanned the room. There was no sign of Jonathan, but Saira knew his games only too well to be complacent about his absence. He'd be waiting somewhere nearby so he could enter the room after them and assert his authority over the group which would include the three of them.

Perhaps a sixth sense of self-preservation made Naomi and Kerri stay near the doorway beside Saira.

As members of the crew noticed the three women near the

door, a gradual silence fell over the room until every face turned toward them.

Saira stepped forward.

"Thank you for gathering here. You might already know these lovely ladies, but allow me to introduce Naomi Armati, owner of Desert Lodge, and Kerri Coetzee, who manages it. They wanted to meet you all properly and welcome you to Desert Lodge."

Saira glanced at Naomi and wondered if her brief speech was enough of an introduction.

But she didn't have to worry because Naomi smiled and stepped forward.

"Hello, everyone. Saira is right. We wanted to meet you. I know a few of you, but I haven't met all of you yet. Desert Lodge is important to us. We want you to feel comfortable while you're working with Saira. All of us have a unique opportunity here to create something wonderful. Not only is it a chance for you to further your own careers, but if everything works out, it will also be great publicity for Desert Lodge. We've never had a film crew working and staying with us before. So, I would ask every one of you to bear that in mind during your stay. There are other paying guests here. We want them to continue enjoying their time with us, and we ask that you respect their time with us."

When Kerri continued where Naomi had left off, Saira couldn't help thinking again what an impressive team these two women made.

"We want you to enjoy yourselves, too. You have access to the same facilities as our guests. But to repeat Naomi's request, we'd appreciate it if you'd respect our guests' privileges. For example, if you see the guests in the swimming pool, please wait until they've finished swimming before you use the pool. The same goes for the spa and the Armati sand buggies. But the safaris are different as we'll arrange safaris for your group only. If you need anything from housekeeping, contact me, and I will sort it out for you."

Naomi nodded in agreement.

"Yes, Kerri is right. We want you to enjoy yourselves even though you are working. Perhaps you might like to revisit us for a vacation and experience Desert Lodge as guests?

"Meanwhile, as Desert Lodge's name is involved in the production of this TV pilot, you need to know our intention is to work with Saira and MaxPix. When Jonathan turned up, we were as surprised as Saira was. We've had no previous contact with him and didn't expect him. We've contracted you to MaxPix. But since we put the team together, we'd ask that you respect our wishes to work with Saira and not Jonathan."

Saira saw the surprise and confusion on the faces in front of her. It made her wonder once again what Jonathan had told them about the project. It appeared Naomi's words were as much news to them as it was to Saira. She hadn't thought Naomi would announce something like that to her crew and could only imagine how Jonathan had already influenced them.

Tony, whom Saira had met on her first day at Desert Lodge, stepped forward.

"But Jonathan is Max Galbraith's son, isn't he? And Max owns MaxPix, doesn't he?"

There were nods and murmurs around the room at Tony's questions.

Naomi held up her hand.

"Yes, it's true. But until Jonathan appeared here, we had only ever dealt with Max and Saira. Max appointed Saira to this project, and we agreed to work with her. Over the previous months, we've built a great working relationship with Saira. We feel she's best equipped to portray Desert Lodge in the way we feel comfortable with. Our contract with MaxPix stipulates Saira working on the show as a condition of it being shot here."

Saira felt surprised and relieved at Naomi's words. Surprised, because until now, she hadn't known they had altered the conditions of the contract. That Naomi and Kerri both supported her being here was a great relief. Naomi couldn't have been more explicit about her wishes as far as the project was concerned.

Saira bit her lip and shook her head.

How would she ever repay these amazing women? Even if Max had wanted Jonathan to lead the project now, he wouldn't be able to do so and continue shooting the pilot at Desert Lodge. Saira knew Max wouldn't want the pilot to be shot anywhere else in Namibia. Max was aware several Hollywood A-listers had chosen Desert Lodge as their preferred Namibian vacation spot. Therefore, selling the pilot would have kudos and be a doddle to pitch. Max would have to accept what Naomi wanted for Desert Lodge. That MaxPix wouldn't want to lose such a lucrative business as the Armati Supercar campaign on top of it, also helped.

Saira blew out a silent breath through pursed lips. She could not have foreseen things taking such a turn.

Naomi looked around before continuing.

"Where's Jonathan?"

"I'm here."

At the sound of his voice, everyone turned to look at Jonathan. As Saira had suspected, he'd positioned himself behind the three women.

Naomi turned and nodded to him.

"I trust you heard what I just told the crew? I'd hate to repeat everything."

Jonathan's face carried a deep frown, and his lips were thin and white, showing the level of his fury. The energy in the room had transformed. Now, it felt pregnant with anxiety and confusion.

Saira's phone rang. She wanted to stay to see what would happen, but taking it out of her pocket, she saw it was Peter. She'd have to take the call.

Holding up a finger, she turned around.

"Excuse me, I'll have to take this."

She nodded to Naomi and Kerri and left the room, squeezing her way past a rigid Jonathan.

As she walked down the corridor toward Kerri's office for some privacy, she heard Jonathan's voice rising in volume and pitch before his feet stomped down the hall. The bang, as he slammed the French doors shut behind him, made her flinch as she expected to hear broken glass. But she breathed out relief when no such sound came.

Saira closed Kerri's office door behind her.

"Hi Peter, is everything all right?"

"Hi yourself."

Saira felt herself tear up for the third time today at the sound of Peter's voice. She had to get a grip.

"What was that commotion in the background, darling?"

Saira had to smile at the curiosity in Peter's voice.

"Naomi just told the crew that she'll only allow the shoot to take place at Desert Lodge if they can work with me and not with Jonathan. It seems to have caused some confusion."

Peter whistled before responding.

"Does Jonathan know?"

"He does now. He appeared at the end of Naomi's speech, and I'm sure he heard what she'd said. I was waiting for the fireworks to begin, but it seems it's over for now. You know Jonathan, though. He never lets go without a fight."

The sound of Peter's laughter was comforting and familiar. A pang of longing for her life in London stabbed Saira's heart.

But Peter seemed not to notice her silence.

"Oh, dear. It sounds as though Jonathan has bitten off more than he can chew this time. And it gets better. Wait till you hear what I have to tell you."

There was a lengthy pause.

"Come on, Peter. Stop teasing me and spit it out."

Peter laughed again.

"What would you do if I told you Jonathan had one of his mates at the BBC contact your cameraman, Bill Furie, to offer him some bogus job just to get him off yours?"

It was Saira's turn to pause for longer than she'd intended.

That was low, even for Jonathan.

Her voice sounded muted to her ears when she responded.

"Bloody hell. I can't help wondering why Jonathan is trying so hard to undermine me?"

"Jealousy, babe. Nothing but jealousy."

Peter had said it before, Saira remembered.

"It's ridiculous."

"I agree, Saira, darling. But it's who he is. You're much better off without him. I'll never know what you saw in him."

Saira snorted.

"Neither do I. Now. But he can be more charming than you can imagine."

Saira was silent for a moment as she contemplated her next move. The situation felt like a chess game. Even though she wasn't stupid enough to let her guard down too soon, as far as she was concerned, the win was in sight. But Jonathan never played by the rules. And neither would she. Not this time.

She couldn't deny it gave her a little thrill to think he'd met people who wouldn't indulge him. It had to be an unfamiliar experience for him.

Since Naomi had been so transparent, Saira felt she could follow suit.

"Could I ask a favor, Peter? Could you send what you just told me in an email and copy Naomi and Kerri, please? And while you're at it, you may as well copy Max on the email."

As Saira walked down the corridor back to the lounge, Gerhard came through the French doors at the opposite end.

Saira stopped in her tracks. Her legs had that weird sensation of being like jelly again, and her heart started hammering against her ribcage at the sight of him.

She swallowed to get better control over her breathing.

"Hi, again. What are you doing here?"

When Gerhard spoke, his voice sounded deeper and warmer than Saira remembered.

"Naomi asked that I introduce myself to the crew as your new cameraman."

NINE

The sudden, shrill scream of the phone next to Saira's bed ended her long, sleepless night.

She checked the time. The neon red numbers said it was six o'clock.

She was about to answer, but hesitated. After all the surprises yesterday, she wasn't ready to face anything else so early in the morning. But the phone's relentless piercing ring that cut through the stillness of the morning added to the heavy headache behind her eyes.

"Hello?"

Her voice sounded sleepy and tired to her ears.

"Good morning, daughter of mine."

At once, tears stood in her eyes at the sound of her father's beautiful baritone voice. But she didn't want him to hear how relieved she felt that he was on the line. He was intuitive and would guess at once something was amiss. Instead, their pleasantries danced around Saira resigning from MaxPix and returning to London as soon as possible. She felt the energy of her father's fears behind his words. That he didn't push the issue filled her with an appreciation for his consideration.

Fifteen minutes later when they said goodbye and Saira hung up the phone, she thought about how much her life had already changed. She almost didn't recognize this Saira who'd landed in the desert only a few days ago. Her life in London seemed already to belong to someone else in another world. The thought surprised her. She'd never imagined herself anyone other than a Londoner. But Namibia had cast its magic spell on her. She hoped it wasn't temporary.

Gerhard came to mind at once. He was a significant cause of her inability to sleep. Yes, the trouble with Jonathan had also contributed to her sleeplessness. As had the extraordinary events of yesterday when her new colleagues had stepped up to help her. But she couldn't rid herself of her constant thoughts around Gerhard. With him in her mind's eye, Saira imagined her father's eyes. She envisioned only disappointment in his and her mother's.

Gerhard was too white, too European.

Saira's heart broke each time she thought about how she could never fullfil her parents' dreams for her. Not only did her career give them cause for concern but also so did the man they had in mind for her to marry, settle down with and have children. That she couldn't conform to their ideals and give them what they wanted for her, was her constant source of anxiety and sadness. She never meant to disappoint them, but it seemed she did so with every decision she made and every turn she took.

When the phone rang for the second time, Saira had no qualms about answering it.

Kerri's cheery voice sounded almost too loud in her ears.

"Good morning, Saira. I hope you had a great sleep. When you're ready, Naomi and I would love to invite you to breakfast this morning. Could you come to my office in about half an hour, please?"

Saira wanted to feel excited, but she was too tired.

Get a grip, girl.

She tried to match Kerri's early morning enthusiasm but felt she failed.

"That sounds fantastic. Thanks, Kerri. I'll see you in half an hour."

Saira put the phone down and stretched before she went to the wardrobe and rummaged through her clothes, trying to find something equal to what she imagined the day would bring. Her limited wardrobe made her decision easy. If yesterday was anything to go by, she'd be winging it, anyway.

As she stood in the shower, hoping the water would wash away the fatigue from her body, her thoughts returned once again to Gerhard. How would she cope working with him on set every day? Why was he occupying her every thought? She'd never experienced such torment before. Her excitement in recognizing him as her soul mate had disappeared like fog in the sun at the thought he and Kerri could be a couple. Saira would never go there. As far as she was concerned, he was out of bounds. Now, her head must catch up.

By the time Saira met up with Kerri and Naomi in Kerri's office, she felt much more herself and in control again.

Staff had turned one corner of the meeting table in Kerri's spacious office into a breakfast area with places set for the three of them. Kerri and Naomi already sat at the table, each with a coffee in front of her. Saira enjoyed the scene before she tapped on the doorframe and entered the room.

The women looked up. Their smiles and energy were electric with excitement.

Saira felt her body stiffen at once as her guard went up. She wanted to be prepared today and not taken by surprise repeatedly, as happened during yesterday's events.

Kerri got up. Her short red curls formed an untamed halo around her head.

"I didn't know what you'd like for breakfast, Saira. So, I asked Chef to prepare a cooked breakfast plus some muesli and yogurt if you prefer it. But we can provide anything else in line with your culture if what we have here isn't acceptable. We have fresh filtered coffee over here and a selection of fruit juices over there."

Kerri indicated toward the sideboard against the wall. Like the wardrobe in Saira's room and Kerri's table, it was fashioned from the most beautiful wood Saira had ever seen, no doubt indigenous to Namibia. Several bowls of food on a hot plate covered to keep in the heat, stood on the sideboard, buffet-style.

Saira had long ago become her own woman, free from any cultural bounds, and the foods she chose reflected it. After she'd helped herself to scrambled eggs, delicious looking sausages, coffee and orange juice, she took her seat at the table. Kerri and Naomi joined her, and the three women ate in silence for a few moments.

Naomi smiled at Saira.

Her eyes twinkled with a secret she appeared to find impossible to contain. She had scraped back her blonde hair into a ponytail, and like Kerri, wore a tracksuit. Saira felt awkward and overdressed but knew Naomi and Kerri would catch up after breakfast.

Saira did her best not to appear impatient. Still, her curiosity had reached almost boiling point to discover why they had invited her to such an early breakfast.

She was about to ask rather than wait for them to put her out of her misery. But Kerri went to her desk to retrieve some papers. She returned to her seat at the table and passed them to Naomi.

Naomi put the papers next to her plate and spoke between sips of coffee.

"Thank you for providing Max's private number, Saira.

Luca called him last night, and they had a long conversation. Luca explained to Max that Jonathan had arrived unexpectedly and wanted to work on the project. Luca told Max we were only prepared to work with you and MaxPix. Max is currently traveling in the Orient and was surprised to discover Jonathan had appeared at Desert Lodge. He agreed that Jonathan's appearance wouldn't threaten your position as project manager and producer, and he promised to recall Jonathan back to the UK."

Naomi checked her watch.

"In fact, Max agreed to contact Jonathan last night. He should already be traveling back to the UK by now."

Saira admired the casual way in which Naomi imparted the important news. She felt Naomi was doing so deliberately to put her at ease. Perhaps her anxiety showed more than she'd cared to admit?

She sat forward as Naomi continued.

"We believe the most significant part of a successful project lies in the relationships between the people involved. Over the past months, we've come to regard you as a member of our team here at Desert Lodge. And a friend.

"Max had his new secretary email us the new contract late last night. It stipulates our conditions, our agreement with MaxPix, and that we only want to work with you, Saira. Max agreed to everything we'd asked for, and so we're happy to sign the contract this morning."

Saira sat back in her chair.

Once again, her head was spinning. She'd envisioned Max replacing her with Jonathan. Now, she realized her anxiety around the issue might have been a contributing factor in her sleepless night.

Kerri had marked each page they had to sign. Saira watched as first Naomi, then Kerri signed their names on every page containing a yellow sticky note.

Then Naomi passed the contract to Saira as she spoke.

"Even though we had agreed to this contract, please take your time to read it over, first, Saira."

Saira nodded and smiled.

"My mother is a lawyer. I've been reading everything before signing it from a very young age. I'm sure you'll understand."

It was clear their meeting was over, and Naomi and Kerri were itching to get back to their respective rooms to shower and get ready for the day. Before Saira left, Kerri gave her a plastic folder to put the contract in. The women shook hands, even though Saira hadn't signed it yet, and said their goodbyes for now.

It was a relief that filming was in sight. Excitement and optimism replaced the tiredness in Saira's body as she walked down the corridor, a new lightness in every step she took. Shutting the French doors behind her, she stood on the sun-drenched patio for a moment and closed her eyes. The scorching sun that burned yellow against her eyelids and the feeling of the weight where she held the contract against her stomach felt like a new beginning, a clean slate.

But the sound of Jonathan's voice cut an ugly wound through the beautiful morning and jerked her back from her moment of bliss.

"There you are. I went to your room, but it was locked. I assumed you were still sleeping. So, I thought I'd wait out here for you."

Saira took an involuntary step backward as she tried to get control over the sudden thudding of her heart.

"What are you doing here, Jonathan?"

His hostility and anger washed over her in bigger and bigger waves the closer he came, threatening to drown and annihilate her completely. Jonathan's narrowed eyes and the sneer around his mouth betrayed the rage he appeared to carry in every cell of his body.

Saira readied herself for the possibility of a fist to her face. It wouldn't be the first. She knew the signs that betrayed his need for an outlet for his anger. But the hand he lifted toward her only grabbed the folder in her arms.

Saira tried to hold on to it, but he was stronger than her.

"What are you doing, Jonathan? Give that back right now."

Jonathan ripped the contract from the folder and started tearing it into smaller and smaller pieces.

Saira put her hands on her hips.

"Oh, don't be so stupid. You know we'll just print another one."

But as she watched Jonathan ripping up the contract, time slowed down. How had she not seen the small-minded, spoilt man for who he was? Though he had the body of an adult male, all she could see now was the frustration of the small, powerless child within him.

Saira felt almost sorry for him.

At that moment, a deep calm came to sit in the center of her body. It came with the knowledge she could never return to who she'd been before. The time for putting up with Jonathan's tantrums was over. The same was true for Max's unreasonable demands, her need to prove her parents wrong, and her ambitions to make something of herself at MaxPix. It was gone in that instant. What had caused it? Had the shock of the emergency landing in the desert prompted her to view herself with more honesty? Did her new colleagues at Desert Lodge, who felt like she'd known them all her life, have anything to do with it? Was it her glimpse into Gerhard's soul yesterday?

Whatever it was, something fundamental had shifted in her. She could breathe out for the first time in her life.

Saira had always regarded herself as a strong woman, just

like her mother. But now she saw with incredible clarity how fear had been the fuel that drove her. The truth stared her in the face through the mirror Jonathan had shown her as he continued his childish behavior.

The realization shifted her reality in that instant. Yes, she would finish the project. She'd come out here to do it for Max. But what if it was all a sign? The problems with the cameramen and now Jonathan tearing up the contract?

It was time to step out of her comfort zone, time to stop being scared, time to follow her own path. This was the last project she'd do that wasn't her own.

She looked up to see Jonathan standing on the pieces of paper at his feet. He'd balled his fists at his sides.

Saira felt even her voice sounded stronger and more confident.

"Do you feel better, Jonathan? What's got into you and why are you behaving this way? I know your father has asked that you go home to London. So, I'm not sure why you're still here? You're no longer needed."

As Jonathan looked up, Saira saw the fury had gone out of his body. He sagged as though he was exhausted.

"I'm sorry, Saira."

Jonathan ran a hand through his hair. Only now did she see it looked lanky and unwashed, a first for him.

"I don't know where to begin. When you left for Namibia, it felt as though you were leaving me. Until that moment, I hadn't realized how much I care for you, Saira."

Saira couldn't decide whether Jonathan was being sincere or playing one of his usual games.

"You have a great way of showing it."

Jonathan tried to smile, but it turned into a grimace, and he stopped.

"I know. I've been an idiot. Don't let me beg, Saira. Come back. I know I haven't always been the best boyfriend."

Saira snorted.

"You mean like those times you slept with every single one of Max's secretaries? And that time you tried it on with Manda?"

Jonathan shook his head and put up his hands in his defense.

"I know, I know. I told you I know I was an idiot. I haven't been the best boyfriend. But please give me another chance. I don't know how to live without you in my life."

"That's why you followed me here? And that's why you got rid of my cameraman?"

Jonathan looked as though Saira had dumped a bucket of snow over him.

"You knew about that?"

Saira's sigh revealed she'd reached the limit of her patience with him.

"I know everything, Jonathan."

Jonathan ran his hands through his hair again.

"I wanted to make you see that this project wasn't as important as us. You left me with no choice."

Jonathan had used that line once too often. Long ago, it might have pulled on her heartstrings, but Saira felt nothing now. His words had no effect on her. Instead, she continued to feel calm and in control.

"That was such an underhanded thing to do, Jonathan. Why couldn't you just talk to me like a normal human being? Why go through all the games?"

Before Jonathan could respond, Saira held up a hand.

"No, don't tell me. I don't want to hear any more of your nonsense. I'm sure you know by now Naomi and Kerri don't want to work with you. That's why Max has recalled you back to London. I think it's best you leave as soon as possible, Jonathan. I'll stay here and complete my contractual obligations with Desert Lodge and MaxPix. Then, I'll consider my future with you and MaxPix."

"Please, Saira."

"Stop it, Jonathan. Don't make this more difficult than it is. You should leave now. You've caused enough damage."

Jonathan stood for moments staring at Saira as though he couldn't believe what had just happened.

He seemed to expect she'd reconcile with him, give in to his demands, and return to London with him. But as the truth hit him and he realized he'd lost, his body sagged even more. For moments, he stood, staring at Saira. When she didn't respond, with a shake of his head, he turned and walked toward the short landing strip behind the house. His pilot was already there, waiting for him in the Cessna.

Only after Saira saw him board the small plane and it took off, did she feel her shoulders relax. She continued to feel the peculiar calm, as though she'd just faced and overcome her biggest fear.

As she walked back to her room, she paused at the swimming pool where several guests were enjoying an early morning swim. They seemed so carefree.

With a slight shock, she realized she felt free too.

She knew then the shift within her had everything to do with the decision to follow her dreams. All of them, come what may.

TEN

Saira blinked as the last of her crew left. Until now, she hadn't realized she'd be sad to see them go. But it was imperative to have a new team who'd have no preconceived ideas about who oversaw the project or remained loyal to Jonathan.

The only member of the old crew who stayed was Shona as she'd become Saira's right-hand person and PA. Saira felt the role suited Shona far better than her original one did, and Shona agreed with her.

As soon as the old crew had left, Saira and Shona went to the lounge to reclaim their headquarters.

Shona stood with her hands on her hips as she looked at the disarray in the room.

"Shall we just rearrange all the tables to their previous positions?"

Saira wondered if Shona's baby pink tracksuit would withstand the heavy work they had to do today. But Saira walked to the nearest table and waited for Shona to take her place at the other end so they could move it.

"Yes, do you agree it's better that the monitors face outward again so everyone can see each other? We don't have time for formal working conditions."

Shona nodded and lifted her end of the table.

They were half an hour into moving the furniture back to their original positions when Kerri popped her head around the door.

"Oh, no. If I'd known you needed help, I could have arranged for some."

She walked into the room, her face a picture of concern.

"You've done loads already. Take a break, and I'll get some guys in here to finish it for you."

She didn't wait for a response from either Saira or Shona. Instead, she tapped away on her phone before she looked up.

"Right, some guys should arrive soon. I've ordered coffee and tea, and that should be here soon too."

She was almost out of the door when she turned around.

"Let me know if you need anything else? Looks good so far."

She grinned and waved as she left.

Though Saira didn't mind rearranging the room again, she was grateful for Kerri's intervention.

As Saira sank into the nearest chair, she noticed Shona wiping beads of sweat from her brow and flopping down into a chair near the door. Mere minutes after Kerri had left, several tall, muscled native guys wearing anti-poacher uniforms entered the room and asked what had to go where. They moved the heavy tables as though it weighed nothing at all. It took just over an hour to reorganize the room to the way Saira felt it would work best, and she couldn't thank her movers enough. She didn't want to think about how long it would have taken with only Shona and her moving everything.

Bloody Jonathan.

After the guys had left, Saira stood in the doorway and checked the results.

"We may as well interview the prospective couples while we're waiting for the new crew to arrive. Let me see who we've got so far?"

Shona's giggle alerted Saira to the possibility of an influx of responses. Her phone pinged, and her eyes widened at the size of the file Shona had just emailed her. Yup, she thought as much. She ran her eye down the list of names.

Shona watched her boss, a slight smile hovering on her face.

"I reckon the ads worked so well because of the promise that the winning couple's wedding would be filmed at the prestigious Desert Lodge. And that Hollywood A-listers had visited the lodge. All the best glossy magazines, South African and Namibian television programs featured it, which also helped."

True to her word, Kerri had arranged for an ongoing coffee service to the lounge. As Saira and Shona took their seats in front of the biggest monitor in the room, a waitress arrived to bring fresh coffee and tea and remove the earlier offerings. While Saira poured milk into their coffees, Shona Skyped the first couple on their list. Both women made notes even though every interview was recorded. Gathering information as quickly as possible meant there would be no need to refer to every recording when they were finished.

As they talked to couple after couple, Saira couldn't help thinking about the mess Jonathan had caused and the time he'd lost them. He'd even delayed getting the contract sorted. Kerri had had to re-print it, and after everyone here had signed it, she'd scanned and emailed it to Max for his signature.

After they'd finished interviewing yet another couple, Saira yawned and stretched her arms above her head.

"I think we're done for the day, Shona. We talked to most of the couples. We deserve a break."

Saira checked the time and realized it was long past the time to stop for the day.

Outside the window, the last of the sun's rays were fast disappearing over the roofs of the guest suites, and lights around the lodge came on to reveal a different, softer side to it.

Saira almost envied Shona's soft lilting voice that sounded as energetic as it did when they first started.

"I loved every minute of today. It was intense."

She slid her pen over the paper in front of her.

"From the couples you'd chosen, we only have four more to interview tomorrow."

Saira got up.

"That's great. I can't believe we got through so many today. Intense is definitely the right word for it. But I'm exhausted. I find the best way to unwind is to swim. Do you want to join me?"

Shona glanced at the window.

"But it's already getting dark outside."

Saira smiled.

"The lights in the pool are there for people who want to swim at night. But don't worry if it's not your thing. Do what you must to relax. Tomorrow will be another full-on day. Perhaps start with dinner?"

Despite Shona's continued enthusiasm, her face was pale and looked pinched. Saira could see the girl was exhausted.

Shona nodded, and Saira gathered her things, leaving Shona to lock up. The young woman had impressed Saira. She'd made a mental note to add Shona to the list of staff members she wanted for her new company.

As Saira left the enormous old house, she stood for a moment on the patio. The little lights on either side of the path that led to the swimming pool and the guest suites, weaved its magic through the dark African night.

She breathed into her belly and blew her out-breath through pursed lips as she allowed her face to turn up to the breath-taking starlight above her.

Yes, she could breathe here.

When she felt ready to move again, she took her time to walk along the path. The night air carried exotic scents and strange noises. The otherness of the ambience felt like a balm she could savor. She continued to take deep breaths and appreciate the still-warm night air. With a slight jolt, she recognized in a part of her heart she'd never met before, a yearning for people and places she had yet to meet. It was an unfamiliar feeling and slightly disconcerting. But it made perfect sense here, where the sky was big enough to consider the fulfillment of all her heart's dreams.

In her room, Saira donned her swimsuit and grabbed a towel. The pool filled the courtyard between the suites. The water enhanced the changes from day to night, almost like a water-feature. As she walked toward the pool, she left her towel on a chair nearby. She slid into the pool, relished the sun-heated water on her skin.

Midway through her second leisurely length, she noticed someone else in the pool with her. She looked up to see Naomi and Kerri swimming toward her.

Kerri's eyes twinkled in the lights.

"We thought we might find you here. Isn't it lovely at the end of a long day?"

Saira returned Kerri's smile.

"Is this how you both relax?"

Kerri shoulder pumped Naomi.

"No, Naomi is a morning swimmer. But she skipped her swim this morning because of our early breakfast meeting. And I thought I'd join you guys while I wait for my husband to turn up."

Saira's heart sank and sped up at the same time. It sank because she didn't love the idea that her worst fear will now be confirmed when it turned out Gerhard was Kerri's husband. And it sped up because she'd be seeing him again soon. How would she escape? She had no reason to do so.

She swallowed before she spoke and hoped her voice didn't sound as strange as it felt to her.

"Oh, does he enjoy an evening swim as well?"

Behind them, Naomi continued to swim powerful lengths one after another. But Saira only glanced at Naomi's prowess in the pool. She felt light-headed that Gerhard and Kerri's relationship would soon be confirmed. How would she face it?

Kerri appeared oblivious to Saira's dilemma.

"Oh, no. But he'll be here soon to pick me up. He's usually far too busy with work for swimming."

Before Saira could respond, Johan's large, tall frame came striding around the corner. When he saw them, he took energetic steps toward them.

His booming voice reverberated off the walls as the acoustics of the pool amplified the sound.

"Here you are. Good evening, gorgeous wife of mine."

He squatted at the end of the pool.

"And how lovely to meet you again, Saira. You must come to spend more time at the elephant orphanage when these two wonderful women give you a moment to yourself."

Kerri swam over to Johan and gave him a kiss. Then she turned to Saira.

"Don't listen to him. If Johan had things his way, everyone would keep the orphans company all day long."

Kerri laughed and splashed Johan. He splashed her right back and jumped into the pool, fully clothed. That they were exceptional friends and loved each other passionately was clear.

Saira couldn't believe she hadn't seen their connection when they'd visited the orphanage.

Johan's clothes floated behind him in the pool. He struggled to get undressed amid a lot of squealing and giggling as he and Kerri continued to tease and splash each other.

Saira watched the couple. A feeling of lightness in her chest had spilled over to the smile on her lips. She wished with all her heart she might experience such a wonderful relationship herself one day.

At once, Gerhard's face appeared in her mind. Even shaking her head to rid her of his image didn't help. He resolutely refused to leave. But she couldn't stop herself from feeling the overwhelming relief that Gerhard and Kerri weren't a couple. She knew it was the reason for her sudden joy.

By now Kerri had helped Johan to remove all his clothes apart from his black underwear and socks. His clothes were drifting all around the pool. It forced Naomi to push the items out of her way as she continued to swim length after length and ignore her wayward friends.

Meanwhile, Johan had dived to retrieve his shoes, and with Kerri's help, they dumped everything on the side of the pool.

Saira smiled to herself.

This would never happen in London. She wondered if Gerhard was this uninhibited. As though her thoughts could conjure him, Gerhard came walking around the corner toward them. He stopped at the edge of the pool, and their eyes met. Again, the earth tilted for Saira, and every hair on her body stood up as a massive jolt flowed between them. She wondered if he'd experienced it, or if it was only in her imagination.

To her surprise, Gerhard smiled and waved to her before he turned his attention to Johan.

"Hello, Johan. I just brought back a truck full of safari guests and heard your voice. How are you, man?"

Gerhard squatted down as Johan swam over to him. While the two men were in conversation, Naomi and Kerri re-joined Saira. Naomi dunked the back of her head in the swimming pool to get her long blonde hair out of her eyes and streaming down her back.

She ran a hand over her head as she spoke.

"I don't suppose you've had dinner yet, Saira? You'd be most welcome to join us in the kitchen. That's where all the staff congregates for meals."

Before she could respond, Kerri placed a hand on Naomi's shoulder.

"Johan and I are heading home, hun. I'm not used to early morning breakfast meetings. I'm bushed."

As they were standing near the men, Gerhard must have overheard them and knew Naomi's invitation extended to him.

"Thanks for the invitation, Naomi. I promised Mother I'd join her for dinner tonight. But it's important to catch up with the project. It would be good to know when you'll need my cameraman services."

Gerhard looked at each of the women as he spoke.

"So perhaps, if you're up for it, we could have another early breakfast meeting tomorrow?"

Kerri exaggerated her groan and tried to pull herself out of the pool before Johan got hold of her arms and hoisted her out.

She grabbed her towel from where she'd slung it over a chair and spoke while drying her hair.

"Husband, we must leave now. I need my beauty sleep. These early morning meetings will be the death of me."

Even though she'd put on a whiney voice, everyone laughed as it was clear she was joking.

Johan gave her a sloppy, playful slap on her bottom as he bent down to collect his wet clothes and shoes.

"Give our love to your mother, Gerhard, and when she feels better, you must bring her over to the orphanage. You know how seeing the ellies always cheers her up."

Gerhard nodded to Johan.

Kerri waved behind her back as she left, and Johan took long strides as he followed his wife around the corner to their truck.

Gerhard was still squatting at the edge of the pool and running his fingers through the water.

Naomi moved closer to him.

"How is your mother, Gerhard? Has the treatment helped?"

Gerhard nodded again.

"Yes, thanks, Naomi. She says she's feeling much better and even got up out of bed, today. Her nurse also confirmed she's getting much better. I'm sure she'll be back to her old self again soon."

Gerhard got up.

"Well, ladies, I'll see you both tomorrow morning. Goodnight."

Saira watched Gerhard's muscular back as he walked away and disappeared around the corner of the building.

Beside her, Naomi let out a long yawn.

"I'm feeling exhausted myself. But I'm heading to the kitchen for something quick to eat. Are you sure you won't like to join me?"

Now Saira knew Gerhard wouldn't be at dinner, she felt happier about joining Naomi and the rest of the staff in the kitchen. Gerhard's presence was too disturbing.

"Sure, I'd love to join you. I'll just put on some clothes. See you there."

The women got out of the pool and went their separate ways.

ELEVEN

The moment Saira opened her door, every phone in her room rang.

She checked her cell. It was Jonathan.

Oh, for heaven's sake.

She threw the phone on the bed and picked up the landline.

Max's voice sounded gruff.

"Saira. I've been calling you all evening."

"Hello, Max. I was with Naomi and Kerri. How can I help you?"

After a lengthy pause, Max spoke again.

"This situation is awkward, Saira. I know the Desert Lodge girls want to work with you. But could you see your way to persuading them differently? Jonathan is still in Windhoek. He's been calling me, and he's distraught. He feels I've let him down by removing him from the project. I don't understand why it's such a big deal to have him there. You two have worked on projects before. Why is this one any different?"

Saira couldn't believe her ears.

The gall of the man.

"I'm not sure there's anything I can say to Naomi and Kerri

to change their minds about Jonathan, Max. His behavior here was appalling. It might be one reason they don't want to work with him. The other, I suspect, is because they'd already forged a relationship with me months before I arrived. They've told me that beneficial relationships are what they're after to make any of their projects work. But they'd never even spoken to Jonathan before he turned up unannounced. Their surprise was as big as mine was to see him here. But it's more than that, Max. Jonathan doesn't understand the wedding business."

Max grunted.

"And you do?"

Saira's sigh told of her recent decision to be more patient with people no matter who they were.

"We'd discussed this before you assigned me to this project, Max. Isn't it why you asked me to come here? I understand very well how brides might feel on their wedding day. As you know, weddings are about brides, no matter their gender. Grooms would like to be more involved, but they're side-lined by the bride, the bridesmaids, the mothers and the mothers-in-law. It can be emotional and traumatic for them. Do you really think Jonathan has the skill and personality to deal with emotional brides?"

Max's sigh told Saira he already knew the answer to her question.

Meanwhile, Saira's cell phone continued to ring and ping as message after message from Jonathan appeared.

Saira glanced at the text messages. She could see from the language he used that he was drunk. The first few texts were pleading. Because she didn't respond, each text after that became more and more belligerent and personal.

She knew how manipulative Jonathan was, and almost felt sorry for Max.

"You surprise me, Max. We both know how lucrative the

wedding industry is. This pilot must be important to MaxPix. I can't understand, therefore, that you'd want to jeopardize it all by having Jonathan throwing his weight around here."

"Everything you said is true, Saira. But it's precisely because this pilot is so important that Jonathan wants to be involved with it."

"May I remind you, Max, that we've already signed the contract with Desert Lodge? We almost didn't get the contract because of Jonathan. One of their stipulations in signing it was that Jonathan would leave Namibia. I was told Naomi's husband, Luca, had had a lengthy conversation with you about their reasons for not wanting Jonathan here. I don't see how I can persuade them otherwise."

In her mind's eye, Saira could see Max with his head in his hands. Jonathan was his only son, and most likely would inherit MaxPix from him one day. Perhaps Max shouldn't have allowed Jonathan to become so spoiled.

Saira shook her head.

She could talk. As an only child, her parents had spoiled her. But they never allowed her to run amok, like Jonathan did. When he didn't get his way, like now, he became unpleasant to be around.

Saira was about to say something more, when a light knock came on the door.

"Please hold on for a moment, Max. Someone's at my door."

Saira went to open the door.

Naomi stood in the doorway. She looked much younger with no makeup, her hair pulled into a ponytail and wearing a sundress with flip-flops.

"I came to check you're all right, Saira. We're missing you at dinner. Your phone was busy, and you weren't responding to my texts."

As she spoke and Saira stood aside, Naomi entered the

room. She glanced at the phone on the bed and the cell phone that continued to ping and ring.

Naomi put up her hands in front of her and backed toward the doorway.

"Oh, I'm sorry. I can see you're busy-"

Saira interrupted her before she could leave.

"I'm glad you're here, Naomi. I have Max on the line, and he's asked me to talk to you about your decision regarding Jonathan's presence here. He wants Jonathan back on the project."

Naomi's frown spoke of the same confusion Saira felt.

Naomi gestured toward the phone on the bed, and mouthed, "Is he on the line?"

Saira nodded.

Naomi walked to the bed and picked up the phone.

"Do you mind?"

"Of course, not. Go ahead."

"Hello, Max. This is Naomi. How lovely to hear from you again. Saira just told me you want us to change our minds about Jonathan's involvement with the wedding project. I'm afraid that won't happen. Your son behaved terribly when he was here. He made Saira's life hell, and he used one of his contacts at the BBC to get rid of the cameraman we'd found so he could take over the project. This is unacceptable to us. If you would prefer Jonathan to work on your pilot, I suggest you find a different venue. Desert Lodge will not work with him. I thought Luca had made that clear to you."

Saira couldn't help feeling impressed with the way Naomi was handling Max. Then, she remembered, despite her youthful looks, Naomi owned Desert Lodge. Naomi was also married to one of the most influential men in the car industry, a celebrity in his own right. Perhaps she'd picked up a thing or two from Luca Armati. Thoughts of Luca reminded Saira that

Max had produced several advertisements for their supercars. It must be a very lucrative contract. Saira couldn't imagine Max going against Luca's wishes and jeopardizing that contract.

At that thought, she felt her chest relax. She hadn't realized until now how the threat of Jonathan reappearing at Desert Lodge had impacted on her. The idea she'd be forced to work with him again filled her with dread.

She messaged Jonathan while Naomi was still talking to Max.

Stop texting me. I'm talking to Max. He's on the other line.

But instead of Jonathan's texts diminishing, their frequency only increased.

When Naomi finished her conversation with Max, she handed the phone back to Saira.

Her voice still carried the energy she used to speak to Max.

"Everything should be clearer now, Saira. I'll be waiting for you in the kitchen. Come join me for dinner there when you're done here."

Naomi left and close the door behind her.

Saira looked at the phone in her hand before putting it to her ear.

"Max?"

"Yes, I see what you mean, Saira. They won't be persuaded. I'll deal with Jonathan. Meanwhile, do the best you can. I'm relying on you now."

After they'd said their goodbyes, Saira stood in the middle of the room for a moment. She hadn't foreseen all this nonsense with Jonathan. And what did Max mean, he was relying on her now? Until now, he claimed he'd been unaware of Jonathan's presence at Desert Lodge. But had he?

Her head was spinning, and she wanted to think it was from hunger rather than the trouble with Jonathan, Max and even Gerhard.

She changed into jeans and a T-shirt and towel-dried her hair.

The silence that fell over her room was a welcome relief after the constant ringing and pinging from Jonathan's messages. Max was talking to him or had persuaded him to stop hassling her.

She left her phone behind on the bedside table and made her way to the kitchen to meet Naomi.

The kitchen was not what Saira had expected. On one side of the cavernous kitchen, the famous Chef and his helpers were busy preparing dinner for tonight's guests and breakfast for the next day's rounds of safaris. On the other side stood the largest, most beautiful table Saira had ever seen. Again, it was made from the beautiful wood she'd seen everywhere in the furniture here. Even more surprising was that the table occupied the entire half of the kitchen.

Several members of staff were having their dinner and sat clustered in small groups around the table. At the head sat Naomi. Saira made her way there.

She slipped into the chair next to Naomi, who looked up and seeing Saira, smiled.

"I see you made it out alive."

"Yes, that was hairy. I'm sorry I had to drag you into the conversation with Max, but I'm grateful you were there to set him straight."

Naomi sat back and folded her arms across her chest.

"It surprised me that Max told you to ask us to change our minds about Jonathan. What a strange thing to do for a man in his position?"

Saira shrugged.

"Jonathan is his only son."

"If you ask me, Jonathan seems very spoiled. Many only

children do not behave like him. Luca is an only child, and I'm one too, albeit adopted."

Naomi leaned forward.

"I don't want to tell you your business, Saira, but you are an accomplished, strong young woman. I know I speak for Kerri and Luca as well when I say we feel comfortable with you heading this project. It would be even better if we could work only with you and not with MaxPix at all. Max's behaviour tonight didn't inspire confidence in me. But unfortunately, we are contractually bound to him."

Naomi touched Saira's arm to emphasise her words.

"This project is important to me, you know. It's been my dream to have a TV series made about Desert Lodge. I feel this is the closest I'll get to see my dream fulfilled, and I'll do everything in my power to help you produce the best pilot and TV series possible."

She let go of Saira's arm and sat back.

"Your new crew will arrive tomorrow afternoon, and as you heard at the swimming pool, Gerhard wants to have a breakfast meeting to discuss his role. I reckon we should have an early night."

Saira couldn't agree more.

She ordered some food, and the women ate in silence before bidding each other good night and going their separate ways.

As Saira walked back to her suite, Gerhard's imposing figure once again appeared in her mind's eye.

It might be an early night, but she had a feeling it won't be as restful as she would have liked.

TWELVE

Saira hadn't wanted to be right. But she'd spent the entire night tossing and turning and punching her pillow.

When the first signs of light peeped through her curtain, she threw the duvet aside and got up.

As she walked to the bathroom, she thought her restless night had something to do with anxiety around the breakfast meeting with Gerhard. But her mind was also still replaying her conversation with Max, which, no doubt, had contributed to her battle with sleep.

Her conviction to leave MaxPix and start her own production company became stronger as each day passed and after each interaction with Jonathan and Max.

To get rid of the excess energy in her body, she went for an early morning swim. Her swimsuit was still damp from the night before, but she didn't care, put it on, grabbed a towel and went to the pool. She could hear someone swimming before she saw Naomi doing one lap after another. Naomi touched the side of the pool, looked up and saw Saira.

Her smile was bright and alive with the adrenaline of her swim.

"Morning, Saira. I see your night was as restful as mine. I bet we both continued our conversation with Max in our minds?"

Saira laughed and nodded.

"Is it that obvious? You're right. His call last night has brought up a lot of questions for me. Don't worry about the project, though. It's all in hand, and I look forward to producing the best pilot possible."

"Oh, I know, Saira. I feel safe in your hands."

Saira slid into the pool, and the women swam for minutes in silence.

When both reached the side, they stopped and wiped the water from their eyes.

Naomi's voice revealed her curiosity.

"How are the interviews coming?"

"They've been great so far. We have four more couples to interview, but unless one of those stands out, I think we've found our couple."

Naomi smiled and seemed delighted with Saira's progress report.

Saira followed Naomi up the steps and out of the pool.

They spoke in unison, "see you later."

In her room, Saira got ready. She couldn't stop the butterflies swirling in her stomach, and her heart started galloping at the thought of seeing Gerhard soon. The full-length mirror told her she looked more than presentable. She'd always loved this look on her. The lilac linen trousers were the perfect happy medium between casual and dressy. Her white short-sleeved top emphasized the beauty of her mocha skin, ebony hair, and deep brown eyes.

Happiness and an aliveness flooded her body, but she wanted to scold herself. Gerhard had affected her in a way no man ever had. There was something about him. The way he looked at her consumed her so she could no longer deny it. A little voice in her head said, perhaps it was just a temporary crush? But the deep conviction in her body laughed at such a silly idea.

By the time Saira got to Kerri's office, Gerhard and Kerri already sat at the meeting table. They had again turned it into a breakfast table. The aroma of eggs and bacon, toast and fresh brewed coffee, pervaded the room and Saira realized she was ravenous.

After exchanging good mornings and pleasantries, the three of them helped themselves to breakfast.

Just as they sat down at the table, Naomi arrived.

"Sorry, guys, hope I'm not too late. Luca wanted a quick catch-up."

Kerri got up

"Everything all right?"

Naomi went over to the buffet on the sideboard and helped herself to breakfast.

"Yes. Now. Saira can fill in the details later, but Max called Saira last night, and I happened upon the conversation. Max requested that we reinstate Jonathan to the project."

Before the others could respond, Naomi continued.

"Don't worry, it's all in hand. Jonathan won't be returning. I made it very clear to Max and to reinforce how serious we are about our decision, I asked Luca to impress it on Max once again."

Gerhard sat back in his chair and looked at Saira as he spoke.

"Well, I, for one, am delighted Jonathan won't be on the project. I couldn't work with him. The urge to hit him would become irresistible."

The women laughed.

Saira could see Gerhard had meant it as a joke, but she wondered if underneath, he was serious.

Naomi took her place at the table. While they ate, they discussed the filming schedule, the time commitment from Gerhard and how it would impact on his time for guest safaris.

Once again, Kerri had drawn up a contract which all four of them signed when they'd agreed on all the points. Now, Saira was the sole representative of MaxPix, there was no need to disturb Max with contracts any further. He had already signed the one that mattered.

All during breakfast, Saira couldn't help stealing glances at Gerhard where he sat between Naomi and Kerri. She wondered if he knew how enormous his presence was. Though relaxed, it was the most animated she'd ever seen him as he contributed to the conversation with ease and humor. His bearing was almost regal. And when his intense eyes rested on hers, she felt the color rise in her cheeks.

Why he should make such a disturbing impression on her, she didn't understand. It had never happened to her before. It wasn't usual for others to intimidate or affect her, because she was used to the movers and shakers in her parents' circle of friends.

When Saira thought about how long and how closely she'd be working with Gerhard, she became flustered all over again. Her heartbeat and breathing increased, and she felt clammier than she should have in Kerri's lovely air-conditioned office.

Gerhard left first because he had to take a group of tourists into the desert for a morning safari.

After he'd left, Saira thought the room felt emptier without him. But she enjoyed Naomi and Kerri's conversation and when she left, she was satisfied with how the meeting had gone.

In the lounge, Shona was already waiting for her. She'd

arrived early and set up everything in front of the big monitor for interviews with the next couples.

"Morning Shona. Thanks for getting everything ready. Our new crew will arrive this afternoon. Everything must be in place by the time they get here. I'm guessing our next couples are ready for us to talk to?"

Shona nodded and handed Saira the relevant documents.

When they'd finished interviewing all four couples, Saira glanced at her watch. To her surprise, it was already lunchtime. A thrill of delight went through her body. Not only had they finished all the interviews, but they had also chosen the first three couples in order of preference and contacted the first on their list. The selected couple had been ecstatic. They'd agreed to adhere to the short notice agreement they had to sign at the application stage. Saira had to repeat details several times as their eagerness to arrive the following day, had them thinking about packing and flights.

Saira went through the list with Shona and discussed every-thing that had to happen once the couple arrived. The dress was the first thing to sort out, and Shona had already arranged with a bridal company in Windhoek to send sample dresses to the lodge the next morning via Cessna.

Saira appreciated Shona's efficiency anew, and that she could act on her own initiative. Saira felt comfortable leaving Shona in charge as she went to the Lapa for lunch when the younger woman insisted on having hers at her desk. Saira understood it. Hadn't she done the same thing during her first year at MaxPix? Shona had the same drive and enthusiasm Saira had. In fact, the younger woman reminded her of herself at that age.

Saira gathered her bag and phone. Walking along the little path to the Lapa always made her feel as though she was on holiday. She stood in the queue with the other guests waiting at the buffet groaning with dish after dish of mouth-watering food. With a jolt, she realized Gerhard was standing behind her. As she turned around to face him, once again, she couldn't help the tremor when seeing how tall he was. He stood so close, their bodies almost touched. Again, butterflies swarmed in her stomach as electricity flowed between the two of them.

His voice made the little hairs on her neck stand up.

"Shall I shoot a few opening shots around Desert Lodge after lunch? I have all my equipment ready in the truck."

The way the sound of his melodious voice stroked her skin, made Saira wish he felt the same about her as she felt about him. What did she feel?

She shook her head to clear away the thoughts that wouldn't leave.

Even though they were at lunch among other people, when he looked at her and spoke to her, it felt as though they were the only two people in the world. He mesmerized her. She found herself unable to tear her eyes away from his and noticed he seemed to have the same problem.

When she didn't respond at once, he touched her elbow. Once again, electricity shot through her entire body at his touch. She looked down at his beautiful hands that created such stunning art and remembered the fantastic images and videos she'd seen at his home.

Thoughts of his home reminded her of something Kerri and Naomi had said the previous evening.

"When you spoke about your mother at the pool last night, it appeared she was unwell? Is she better now?"

Gerhard kept his hand touching her elbow as they moved along toward the front of the queue.

"Thanks for asking, Saira. She was unwell. But she is on her way to recovery now."

The way he said her name made her shiver.

His touch and his nearness, though exciting and disturbing, felt as though she'd come home. It was an odd sensation to feel so safe with someone she hardly knew. The entire world was but a blur. The only reality was him standing so near her.

When they'd been served, it made complete sense that they'd seek a small table away from everyone else. While they ate, the conversation flowed, but even the silences never felt awkward with him. His intense eyes and the way he held her attention was overwhelming and addictive. She didn't want the lunch to end. From his body language, it seemed he felt the same way.

Saira's heart sang.

When they finished their lunch, Saira texted Shona to let her know she was scouting for filming locations around the lodge with Gerhard.

As they walked to his truck so he could retrieve his photographic equipment, he kept his hand on Saira's elbow. Despite having no control over her teenage-like tendencies in his presence, their physical connection felt perfect. She didn't want him to remove his hand.

He'd parked his truck behind the big old house, a little further away under the shade of a massive tree. Gerhard opened the door, but before he reached in to retrieve his equipment, he turned to face Saira.

His eyes intense, his voice was a husky whisper as he said her name.

Gently, he placed his hands on her shoulders and drew her to him. She did nothing to resist when he bent his head toward hers.

Her body tingled all over. She couldn't breathe.

His lips felt far softer than she'd imagined and more earthy than she'd ever experienced. His kiss ignited such sudden passion in her, she wanted this man with all of her being. She couldn't imagine ever wanting another.

His first kiss was as soft as a butterfly's wings, barely brushing her lips with his, giving her the chance to stop if she didn't want him to continue. That he was so considerate of her melted her. His light kisses made her insides quiver. When she didn't pull away, his kiss grew more ardent. The kiss intensified until her ears rang, and she felt drunk on the passion his mouth drew to the surface. She slid her arms around his waist into a tight embrace, leaning into his muscular body. When his tongue connected with hers and the taste of him flooded her senses, Saira couldn't suppress the groan that came from deep inside her.

Gerhard crushed her against his body, and she felt his need for her pressing hard against her.

When, reluctantly, they pulled apart, their breathing rapid, she saw reflected in his eyes the fire that threatened to consume her. The flare of his nostrils told how close he'd come to losing control. Somehow, it was even more exciting to know she was the reason that drove him so close.

He'd awakened a fire in her she had no idea was there. She wanted him. It was as simple as that.

His voice was gruff and couldn't hide his desire.

"My God, Saira. You're the most beautiful woman I've ever seen."

Saira didn't trust her voice to speak. Her entire body felt ablaze, and she had to fight the intense, almost uncontrollable need to be with him.

High above them, a drone flew. The sound, reminiscent of a mosquito, irritated at the edge of her mind.

THIRTEEN

The few hours Saira and Gerhard had spent alone together went by too fast. That they'd filled their time with secret smiles, long lingering looks pregnant with passion, the brush of hands or hips or lips, made it even more unbearable to part.

Saira was more than impressed with how fast Gerhard worked. He introduced her to spots around Desert Lodge, which he felt would make the perfect backdrops for the required shots. It was obvious he knew the place well and felt a great fondness for it. But everywhere they went, the irritating sound of a drone far above them, marred the tranquility of the place somewhat. Saira imagined it was all part of the anti-poacher efforts and did her best to ignore it. It wasn't too difficult in Gerhard's overwhelming presence.

Before they were ready to part again, it was three o'clock, and Shona texted to alert Saira to the arrival of the new crew.

Saira placed a hand on Gerhard's arm.

"Would you like to join us in the lounge? That way, the new crew can meet us all at the same time."

Gerhard paused for a moment.

"Sure, why not? My next safari isn't until later this evening."

Saira couldn't help herself.

"How late?"

Gerhard's slow smile spread over his face as he understood the meaning behind her words. His eyes softened with desire.

"Wouldn't you rather wait until I'm back from the safari? It would give us more time."

Saira bit her lip and stroked the hairs on his forearm.

"I suppose I could."

Gerhard put his equipment down on the ground and grabbed her shoulders.

"God, Saira. You drive me wild."

He looked around to make sure nobody saw them before he crushed her to his body once more and claimed her mouth with his.

His kiss stole her breath and blanked her mind. She felt they were floating weightless in a universe of their own.

As though both came to their senses, they parted.

Saira admired once again the sexy way his nostrils flared while she tried to get her breathing under control.

Gerhard picked up his equipment again.

His voice was a growl when he spoke.

"I'll just put these in my truck. See you in the lounge."

He took long strides away from her and disappeared around the corner of the building.

Saira stood still for a moment and tried to get control of herself before she sauntered to the French doors that led into the corridor to the lounge.

She found Shona standing near the doorway, a bunch of folders in her hand. She was passing them out to the new crew members as each person walked past her into the room.

Saira noticed the recent crew members were older than the previous crew was and seemed more serious and professional. They still had their luggage with them as they hadn't been assigned their rooms yet. Everyone had claimed a chair and monitor for themselves. When Shona saw Saira, she handed over the folders with their CVs and profiles. Saira stopped next to Shona as she leafed through their details.

"I'm glad to see you have everything sorted, Shona."

Shona's voice was soft, her eyes filled with sincerity.

"I appreciate your trust in me, Saira. I'm enjoying my new role, and I like fresh challenges. Mary, your new assistant director, seems nice. I have a feeling we have the perfect team this time."

Shona's knowing smile revealed she'd had her reservations about the previous crew, even though she'd worked with some of them before.

When everyone had taken a seat and had a folder in front of them detailing their work schedule, Saira welcomed them and explained a little about the project.

She was still talking when Gerhard entered the room. Like her, he seemed to have control of himself again. But they couldn't help sharing smiles and glancing at each other, perhaps more than they should have done. Neither cared if anyone saw it but were aware, they should keep their relationship professional for now.

Saira introduced Gerhard as their cameraman, and after a brief discussion of what he'd need from them, he left. But while Gerhard had been talking, Saira had sent Shona to Kerri's office to let Kerri and Naomi know the new crew had arrived.

The women's timing, as usual, was impeccable because just as Saira had finished briefing the team, Shona followed Naomi and Kerri through the door. Saira introduced them and left them to welcome the new crew to Desert Lodge. Meanwhile, she got on with some much-needed admin work. She was aware of Naomi and Kerri welcoming the new team and that they gathered their luggage when the speeches were over, so they could check into their rooms.

After everyone had left, Saira leaned back in her chair. She allowed her exhaustion to wash over her. What a day. Despite being bone-tired, her body tingled from happiness with how everything had turned out.

The sharp rap on the door snapped her back to reality, and she opened her eyes.

Before she could respond, Kerri opened the door.

"Fancy some dinner?"

Saira checked the time. How was it already six o'clock?

"That would be lovely. Are you joining us tonight? Naomi invited me for dinner in the kitchen last night. It was delicious."

Kerri smiled, walked into the room and sat down opposite Saira.

"No, we'll be having dinner in the Lapa tonight to welcome the new team. Chef has prepared a barbecue as only he can. Johan will also join us as he loves Chef's food. I'm afraid mine don't compare."

Kerri laughed at her own joke.

Saira had admired the couple the previous evening. It was easy to see they loved each other. She wanted to ask how long they'd been married, where they'd met and did they have any children, but she felt she couldn't get that personal so soon.

Instead, Saira joined in Kerri's infectious laughter, appreciating the woman's sense of humor.

"In that case, we might enjoy more delicious dinners from Chef as the wedding party arrive tomorrow morning. I'm guessing their guests and entourage will accompany them."

Kerri wiped laughter tears from her eyes.

"Yes, Shona has already arranged everything with me. She's turning out to be an excellent PA, don't you think? We might want to keep her here after you've gone."

Saira smiled but could feel her frown deepening at the same time.

"I was thinking of offering her a position myself."

Kerri tilted her head to one side as though she was contemplating a conundrum.

"You mean with MaxPix?"

"Perhaps."

Saira knew she could trust Kerri and Naomi. But she needed to figure out things for herself, first, before she talked to anyone else about her plans for her future and her dream of setting up her own company. Kerri's question was an excellent one. It brought up the issue that had plagued her ever since she'd visited Gerhard's house, she now realized.

Where should she base herself?

Gerhard's gorgeous eyes popped into her mind's eye. Now she'd found him, could she let him go again? Thinking of him caused the butterflies in her stomach to flutter around. She did her best to suppress her excitement at seeing him again later tonight. Better steer clear of thoughts about Gerhard if she wanted to remain in control of herself.

She changed the subject.

"Will Naomi be joining us as well?"

Kerri smiled and nodded.

"Yes, she will. And we're in for a treat, as Luca has also arrived earlier this afternoon. I don't know if you heard his jet? That thing is something to behold. He rarely arrives here until a few months later. But he wanted to be here at the start of the filming."

"Sounds like it will be a party?"

Kerri laughed again.

"You can say that again. When Johan, Luca and Gerhard get together, it always turns into a party."

"Oh, will Gerhard be joining us as well?"

Kerri laughed harder.

"You just try to stop him. They're like the Three Musketeers."

Saira's heart sped up and sank at the same time.

She wondered if her private time with Gerhard would still be possible. It didn't sound like it. She had to get away before her disappointment showed on her face.

"Well, in that case, I should have a quick shower and get changed as I feel sticky from the heat and traipsing around Desert Lodge today looking for locations to film."

Kerri looked Saira up and down.

"You look amazing. Nobody would know. But I understand how you feel. I've had a shower myself a little while ago."

Kerri got up.

"Right, I'll see you later in the Lapa. We have reserved the entire Lapa for the film crew and us. We'll allow no other guests in there tonight. But it might be a significant promotion for us anyway, because I'm sure they'll wonder what the fuss is all about."

FOURTEEN

As Saira stood in the shower, the memory of Gerhard's kisses made her quiver again. Her body screamed for release from the tension that had built up throughout the afternoon.

It wasn't difficult to visualize and feel Gerhard's arms around her and his intense kisses on her lips that craved for more. As though of its own volition, her hand reached to touch her private pleasure. It didn't take long for heavenly release to wash through her body. But it only intensified the desire to be alone with him. She had to work through the grip of the need that wouldn't let her go.

What had he done to her?

She felt uncharacteristically insatiable.

Saira dried herself and towel-dried her hair as she rummaged through her clothes. She'd brought little on this trip and no real party clothes. She settled on her orange floaty dress and gold sandals. It wasn't too dressy, but still gave the impression she'd tried. She applied minimal makeup and grabbed a light summer scarf in case it got chilly later.

Her phone caught her eye, but she left it in the room. She'd be with everyone who might want to reach her tonight.

As her hand touched the doorknob, her heart thumped in her chest at the thought of seeing Gerhard.

Oh, for goodness' sake. What was the matter with her? She wasn't seventeen anymore. Now she thought of it, she couldn't remember feeling this way ever before, even at seventeen.

She took a deep breath, instead, and opened the door.

The sounds of people in party mode and the delicious aroma from the barbecue reached her at once.

She closed the door behind her and walked around the swimming pool to the Lapa. It was clear some crew members were old friends, and they were making new friends with others they'd met for the first time this afternoon.

The Desert Lodge staff had transformed the Lapa from its normal exoticness into a feast for the senses. Fairy lights decorated its straw ceiling and three walls, and the glow from the floodlit swimming pool filled its open side. Light music thumped from speakers in all four corners. Enormous pots of swaying desert grasses stood in each corner. Displays of tiny, multi-colored desert succulents in sweet little pots ran along the center of the table that stretched the length of the Lapa. The arrangement had been achieved by pushing the tables together to form one long table where everyone could see and interact with everyone else.

People stood around in small groups of twos and threes with drinks in their hands. Waiters and waitresses in smart black and white uniforms offered drinks and canopés among the party-goers.

As Saira looked around for someone she knew, Naomi appeared in front of her.

"Welcome to the Lapa, Saira. I'd love you to meet Luca. If you'd follow me?"

Naomi led the way, and Saira followed her to the end of the bar where Johan, Kerri and Luca were deep in conversation.

With his inky hair, dark eyes and Italian good looks, Saira thought Luca was even more beautiful than on Skype. But although she admired him, his undeniable beauty seemed alien to her, whereas Gerhard resonated with everything in her. It was ironic, she thought. That Luca was charismatic and warm was clear. Gerhard came across as austere, private, and introverted. But now Saira knew he only appeared that way upon first meeting him. In reality, he was a passionate, empathetic artist who only gave the impression of the outdoorsy action man.

She was still thinking about the differences between Luca and Gerhard when Johan's voice boomed around the Lapa as he caught sight of Saira and Naomi. Making a space for them, he beckoned them forward.

"There she is. Good evening, Saira. Come meet my friend, Luca. I know you've already spoken on Skype, but it's great to have him here in the flesh."

Luca's voice was like chocolate to Saira's ears. He took her hand and his smile enveloped her in warmth.

"Welcome to Desert Lodge, Saira. We're so happy you're here. It has been my wife's dream for a while now to have a TV series shot here. Again, I'm sorry you had such problems with Jonathan and Max. We will do what we can to make things easier for you."

Luca let go of Saira's hand and snaked an arm around Naomi's waist, pulling his wife close to him. When Luca looked at Naomi, Saira saw the depth of his love for his wife.

Luca spoke while continuing to look at Naomi.

"Naomi has worked so hard. She deserves every happiness coming to her."

Johan raised his glass.

"Hear, hear."

Meanwhile, Kerri had ordered a drink for Saira. It surprised her that Kerri knew what she liked to drink.

As though Kerri could read Saira's mind, she smiled and tapped her finger against her nose.

"I know everything."

At first, Saira laughed. Then she wondered what else Kerri might know.

Saira refused to feel embarrassed about kissing Gerhard earlier in the day. They were both adults. If Kerri had seen them, so be it.

As though mere thoughts of him could make him appear, Saira felt Gerhard behind her.

Again, Johan raised his glass.

"Hey, Gerhard, man. You made it. We were wondering if your safari group had abducted you. Kerri told me they were a group of young ladies from Japan on tour in Namibia. They might all have fallen for your blue eyes and German good looks."

Johan laughed uproariously at his own joke.

Gerhard smiled and took the can of beer Kerri offered. His eyes found Saira's, and he winked at her before he raised the beer.

"To good old friends and to making gorgeous new ones."

Everyone in the circle clinked their glasses against his beer can before they took a sip from their drinks.

Saira wondered if it was her imagination, but she thought she'd seen a quick glance between Kerri and Naomi when Gerhard had winked at her. Perhaps she was just sensitive. She thought no more of it and followed the others to join the queue for the food.

Déjà vu ensued when, in the queue for the buffet once again, Gerhard stood behind her. He was standing very close to her. The heat from his body seared through the thin material of her dress. When he bent his head toward her ear, a shiver of anticipation ran through her body.

His voice was just above a whisper, so no one else could hear what he was saying.

"I hope you'll forgive me, Saira. It seems we must take a rain check on our plans for tonight. When Luca arrives at the lodge, dinner always turns into a party."

His breath on her neck sent more shivers through her body, and goosebumps formed all over her skin.

She turned her head toward him, her eyes seeking his.

"I understand. Kerri had warned me. And I believe everything happens for a reason."

Gerhard tilted his head as his eyes devoured hers.

Once again, he leaned toward her neck and whispered in her ear.

"I don't think I can be patient for an opportunity to present itself, to be alone with you."

To emphasize his words, he trailed a soft finger down her arm.

"Things are more convenient at my home. How would you like to join me for lunch there tomorrow?"

Saira's breath caught in her throat at his touch. She didn't know how she'd cope having to wait until lunchtime tomorrow. But she would not throw herself at him. She was a lady, after all.

She looked down, not trusting her eyes to betray her, and nodded.

"That sounds lovely, Gerhard. But what about your mother?"

Gerhard's hand slid to her neck, and he brushed her hair away from her ear. She liked the intimacy of the gesture. It made her feel special, and she smiled to herself. It seemed he couldn't stop himself from touching her. She had clasped her hands together in front of her to stop herself from reaching out to him. She understood his torment only too well.

"My mother is still too unwell to join us for lunch. But would you join me?"

Saira still didn't trust herself to look him in the eye. She bit her lip and nodded.

He rested a possessive hand on her shoulder.

"That's great. Is there anything, in particular, you'd like for lunch?"

Saira was about to say she'd like *him* for lunch. But the heat of her blush spread into her cheeks at the thought of being so forward with him.

Her voice sounded rushed and heated to her ears.

"I'll have whatever you want."

Gerhard's hand squeezed her shoulder tighter, as though he wanted to convey his desire through his touch. It worked. She felt it. They wanted the same thing.

FIFTEEN

The sudden, shrill scream of the phone jerked Saira out of her dream into reality.

She grabbed it to silence the sound that shattered the stillness of the early morning.

"Good morning, Saira."

Shona's voice sounded far too awake this early in the morning.

Saira checked the time. The red neon letters on the alarm clock showed six-thirty.

"What are you doing up so early? Don't tell me you're already in the lounge?"

Shona giggled.

"No, I'm still in my room. I thought I'd better call you straight away. I've just received a message from Vicky."

Saira's heart sank. She sat up in bed and shoved another pillow behind her back.

"Don't tell me there's a problem already? What did she say?"

"There is a problem, but I don't think it's a biggie. She messaged to let us know there's been a delay with their flight from Cape Town, but they'll arrive later today. I thought we should let Gerhard know because he'll only waste his time waiting around for them at Windhoek airport."

Saira's sigh reflected her relief.

"Okay, it doesn't sound like a disaster. What time will they arrive?"

"I'll text their itinerary in a moment, but it looks like they'll get here around twelve-thirty. Do you have Gerhard's number?"

The first thing through Saira's mind was her lunch meeting with Gerhard. They'd have to postpone it. The bitter taste of disappointment hit the back of her throat.

"I have to call him about something else, anyway. I'll let him know about the new schedule. Just text the itinerary over as soon as possible. I'll pass it on to him at the same time. Have you informed Kerri, so she's prepared for the change? And the wedding party would probably need lunch the moment they arrive."

Shona's response came at once.

"Not yet, but I'll send the itinerary to everyone, including Mary, Naomi and Chef."

"We're talking about Mary, the new assistant director, right?"

"Oh, yes. Sorry, I forgot there's another Mary on the new crew. Yes, I mean Mary McCormack."

Shona's work ethic, her ability to think on her feet and deal with things fast as they came up, impressed Saira again.

"That's great, thanks, Shona. Anything else?"

"No, that's it for now. I'll meet the new crew in the Lapa for breakfast in an hour and pass around the handouts you asked me to arrange. They seem a brilliant team as most of them have worked together before. I'll make sure they're ready to meet you at nine-thirty. Need me to do anything else?"

Saira paused for a moment and ran through a mental list of

everything she wanted to achieve that day. Without Shona's help, it might all be overwhelming. Gratitude welled up in her for her new personal assistant.

"That's all for now, thanks, Shona. You're doing a fantastic job, by the way. See you later."

Saira put the phone down and performed several yoga stretches beside the bed.

Moments later, her cell phone pinged as Shona's text with the new itinerary for the wedding party arrived.

Saira looked at the phone and cursed under her breath. The amended timing would mess up their schedule. But wasn't it typical of life?

Her father's voice rang in her mind's ears.

"It's not the size of the challenge, but the way you deal with it that matters."

In the scheme of things, this wasn't a biggie, to use Shona's expression.

Saira scrolled through her contacts and rang Gerhard's number. She sat cross-legged, leaning against the headboard with a pillow behind her head as she waited for him to answer.

His voice sent a thrill through her body as though he was touching every part of her.

"Good morning, Saira. Miss me already?"

She closed her eyes, but the action only intensified the image of him in her mind's eye. The flirtation so clear in his voice reminded her again they wouldn't be having lunch later today. No harm in flirting, was there?

"Good morning, Gerhard. After your kisses yesterday, it's difficult not to miss you."

She thought she might as well be honest and open with him from the beginning. The beginning? What was she thinking? How could she begin anything here? But Gerhard was already so much a part of who she'd become.

Oh, hell. Why stress about something she seemed to have no control over? Live in the moment, she reminded herself.

She almost shook her head to get rid of the pesky thoughts flying around in there.

"But that's not why I'm calling. I know you're probably getting ready to go to Windhoek to collect the wedding party?"

"We definitely have to talk about the other situation at some point, and I look forward to seeing you at lunch to discuss it further. Though, to be fair, I must warn you. I believe little discussion will happen over lunch."

Gerhard's voice and words ignited excitement and desire in Saira.

"Well, that's why I'm calling. The wedding party has been in touch to let us know there's been a delay at their end. They'll arrive at twelve-thirty today. You'll want to reschedule flying there to collect them. Otherwise, you'll spend longer at the airport than you need to. Unfortunately, it also means a rain check on our lunch date."

Gerhard paused before he spoke again.

"Okay, thanks for letting me know about the wedding party. I'll rearrange my schedule, but I'm disappointed we must postpone our lunch date. I was looking forward to seeing you. Do you think we can reschedule it as soon as possible?"

Saira felt her heartbeat increase at his words. She lowered her voice.

"I'm disappointed too, Gerhard. And yes, let's rearrange as soon as we can."

She'd never been so upfront with anyone before, certainly not with Jonathan, even after she'd known him for a year. But she wanted to honor her decision to herself, to remain as open and honest with Gerhard as she'd started. Besides, if such a thing as love at first kiss existed, this was pretty much it for her.

Gerhard's sigh revealed his frustration.

"I'd say we could have dinner, but with Luca here... It always turns into a party, and we're expected to attend."

Gerhard's voice sounded dark with pent-up desire. It did things to Saira.

"I'll find a way for us to be together soon, Saira. I can't wait to hold you in my arms again and feel your soft lips on mine."

Saira's breath caught in her throat at his words. She'd never yearned for anyone more.

He changed tone, and she knew it was as much to save himself as it was for her.

"Right, gorgeous woman. I'll see you later."

After their goodbyes, Saira sat with the phone in her hand for moments before she got up.

A brisk swim should rid her of pent-up energy. She put on her swimsuit and grabbed a towel.

Once again, she met Naomi doing serious laps in the pool. After they said their good mornings, the women swam in silence.

Saira wasn't as strong a swimmer as Naomi and didn't even try to keep up with her. Instead, Saira counted twenty-five laps and then got out.

As she walked away from the pool. She heard Luca's exuberant voice greet his wife before he jumped into the pool and joined Naomi.

Not for the first time, Saira thought their lifestyle ideal. It had to be nice to have two such distinct places to call home, to spend part of the year in each. It had to make life enjoyable.

The thought led to one about sharing two countries with Gerhard.

What was she like?

As she finished her shower, a waiter had already delivered her breakfast. Better to have it in her room today as she was working through her schedule and getting everything ready for her first official work meeting with the new crew.

The work absorbed them all, and the morning flew by in a blur. The new crew was a marvel. Each person knew what they needed to do and was more than capable of executing their duties. Their input raised the standard of the work overall at once. They impressed Saira. She felt the anxiety brought on by working with the previous crew, and Jonathan, fall from her shoulders as the rest of the morning progressed.

At twelve-fifteen, Kerri came to collect her. They joined Naomi under the massive old camel-thorn tree behind the main house to await the wedding party's arrival.

When Naomi noticed Saira smiling at her inability to stand still, a broad smile spread over her face.

"I can't help feeling excited. It's the start of my dream come true."

She turned to Kerri.

"Do you remember our Skype conversation when I first moved to Modena?"

Kerri nodded and joined in her friend's excitement.

"Yes, I remember you telling me you wanted a TV series to feature Desert Lodge."

Naomi clasped her hands in front of her.

"Then, it was just a dream, one I never imagined could come true."

She turned back to Saira.

"I feel passionate about Desert Lodge. We have something wonderful to offer, and I want the entire world to see it. Here, we straddle the modern world and a time gone by. No one can ever get it back, but we all crave a time that feels slower and more comforting. It isn't available in very many places around the world anymore. We offer that. Here, people can get off the merry-go-round, even if just for a week or so. From the letters and cards we've received from guests who'd stayed with us, it's clear people yearn for it. I'm sure it's the best kind of medicine to cure all sorts."

Naomi's words put Desert Lodge in a unique light for Saira. But now Naomi had said it, she had to agree. Again, Saira wished this was her project instead of MaxPix's. There was so much more here than just shooting a wedding reality TV show set in an exotic location. Max was missing a trick for sure.

Saira touched Naomi's arm to emphasize her words.

"I'll make the best pilot I can. This place is more than impressive, Naomi. I understand why Hollywood A-listers come here for their vacations, and I agree, it's worthy of world-wide recognition. It has the old-world charm of an Africa of long ago and modern customs and facilities your guests would expect. It all makes for an attractive package. Plus, you have one of the best chefs in the world working here. I was wondering when the bride has her treatment in your spa facility, could we film there too?"

Naomi's eyes widened as she contemplated Saira.

"That's a brilliant idea, Saira. I hadn't thought of it. But yes, you have my permission to film there. Kerri will arrange everything with the staff."

Before Saira could respond, the drone of a large Cessna plane grew louder. All three women looked up and saw the plane circling, getting ready to land on the short landing strip created for smaller aircraft to use.

Saira's heart started thumping in her chest at the thought of seeing Gerhard as soon as the plane landed. How would she hide her feelings from everyone here? The better question was, why would she want to? Still, it felt right that she did.

Several members of staff had also joined them to wait for the plane to land. Saira thought they looked very professional in their black and white uniforms as they waited to take the guests' luggage to their suites. It added to the status of the lodge.

Moments after the plane landed, Saira spotted Gerhard's tall figure walking around the aircraft. He opened the door and extended the steps so his passengers could disembark. Both sets of parents, the best man and several bridesmaids followed the bride-and-groom-to-be down the steps.

Saira followed Naomi and Kerri as they walked toward their guests and welcomed them to Desert Lodge. Naomi introduced Saira as the film producer and director. She explained Saira had chosen them from all the couples who'd applied. Naomi also motioned for Gerhard to join them and introduced him as the cameraman who'd be filming them.

Gerhard stood so close to Saira she could feel the hairs on his arm touching her. Once again, she experienced the buzz of a current jumping between them. Once again, she had that strange sensation of being in another universe, alone with him. The surrounding voices appeared far away.

Meanwhile, Kerri had arranged for the members of staff who collected the guests' luggage to help check them into their suites and rooms.

Gerhard excused himself to see to the plane. But not before once again trailing a soft finger down Saira's arm and whispering in her ear he was looking forward to seeing her later. His voice, so low and near her ear, sent tingles through her body.

She waved to him as he reached the aircraft, then turned and, on shaky legs, followed Naomi and Kerri back to the main house.

Kerri's voice cut into Saira's thoughts that wouldn't let go of Gerhard.

"We'll give our guests a few minutes to sort themselves out and meet in the Lapa for lunch. Chef has prepared a light lunch for everyone. I hope you and the crew will join us there, Saira?

That way, the bridal party can meet the team. What do you think?"

Saira nodded.

"I agree. It should put the bridal party at ease when filming begins. Thank you, Kerri. I'll collect them en route to the Lapa."

Saira walked away with a spring in her step. Her heart sang. All was well in her world.

SIXTEEN

When Saira and the crew turned up at the Lapa, the bridal party was already there, drinks in hand, chatting and laughing. She thought the word "party" described them perfectly. They were a diverse, rowdy, outgoing bunch. Saira wondered if the Namibian beers they appeared to enjoy so much was a good idea on their empty stomachs.

The contrast between the bride's side and the groom's side was stark, and Saira wondered how that would affect the couple's married life.

The groom's milky-white English parents were reserved and stood to one side with his best man. Their faces wore expressions of forced happiness and uncertainty about how to behave in this situation. It was clear they felt more than uncomfortable.

Though the bride's parents didn't appear as rowdy as the younger members of the bridal party, the mother's excited, raised voice mingled with the other, loud and exuberant sounds. Their accents were unfamiliar to Saira's ears. She had to listen carefully when asked a question. But she admired the exotic, unique tones of their caramel skin, their dark, crinkly hair and dark bright eyes. It would be interesting to see what Vicky and

David's children would look like. Perhaps that was why she'd chosen this couple?

At the thought of blended couples, Gerhard sprang to mind. He was one, she was another.

She saw him standing at the bar.

Because he was tall and gorgeous, not to mention yummy, several bridesmaids had cornered him against the bar. They appeared to be regaling him with tales of their eventful journey to Namibia that morning.

When he saw Saira, he turned pleading eyes on her and mouthed, "help me," over their heads.

Saira couldn't help giggling at the sight of Gerhard's imposing figure being held captive against his will. But she found his resolve to remain polite against such odds, impressive.

Saira tore her gaze away from him and found the bride and groom. Now they were here, Vicky seemed less anxious than Shona had reported earlier in the morning. Vicky's radiant smile and eager eyes grew more animated when she spotted Saira. She waved and dragged her fiancé behind her as she made her way toward Saira.

Saira lost the start of her sentence among the babble of the other people in the Lapa. Vicky had spoken before she'd reached Saira. "... excited to be here... David and I will do whatever you want. We want the TV show to be fabulous because we'll be featured on it. I mean, isn't it just the best record to have of our wedding?"

Vicky glanced at David for a moment, adoration in her eyes, before turning her attention back to Saira.

"Do you want us to rehearse something?"

Saira smiled.

She'd come across such enthusiasm before. It always came from inexperienced actors and film subjects, a sign they'd watched too many documentaries about making movies and imagined the process was the same.

Behind Vicky, David rolled his eyes. He shrugged his shoulders at Saira in apology as a pained expression inhabited his face.

She felt almost sorry for him. But it was obvious he knew Vicky well, and whenever he looked at her, Saira could read the love in his eyes for his fiancé.

As they talked, Saira steered them toward the buffet area so they could at least get some lunch. She realized food was the last thing on Vicky's mind. But her poor fiancé, even paler than Saira imagined he usually was, looked as though he was about to faint from hunger.

Yes, she needed to brief them. But now was not the time.

Just as Saira had hoped, Vicky's parents appeared. Vicky's mom was even more animated than Vicky, and that was saying something.

She clutched Saira's hand.

"The first thing is to get the dresses sorted, don't you agree? And that includes the bridesmaid's dresses, and I'm assuming the TV company will pay for it all, including the dresses for the mothers?"

Saira felt her smile becoming fixed. She'd had to deal with this type of bossiness before and wouldn't tolerate it on this shoot.

She extricated her hand from the woman's grip.

"There's nothing for you to do or worry about. We've taken care of everything, and we'll inform you when you're needed for anything, including dress fittings. Now, why don't you enjoy lunch and meet the film crew while we all have the time to mingle. Once filming starts, you won't be able to talk with them."

Saira's words reminded her of Jonathan's shenanigans and

how she now had even less time to film the pilot than before he showed up and messed up everything, including her crew. She swore in her mind.

But Vicky knew her mother and confirmed Saira's estimation of her that she was a bright girl. As Vicky steered her parents away, she talked about the food, how lovely everything was and how excited she was they'd chosen her for the shoot. She felt sure the TV people were professionals, nothing for her mother to worry about. It appeared to work as her mother allowed her daughter to distract her.

David continued to move along the queue with Saira.

"Thanks for your understanding, Saira. Vicky's mom can be a handful, not unlike Vicky, and not everyone understands their passionate natures. But that's just one reason I love Vicky so much."

David glanced toward his fiancé, his eyes soft with love for her.

Saira nodded.

She was about to say something when a bridesmaid approached. The woman hooked an arm through David's and leaned her head against his shoulder. For a moment, Saira wondered if they were siblings because apart from their coloring, she was a stunning, darker female version of David.

David turned toward Saira.

"You've met Michelle this morning, Saira? She's Vicky's oldest friend. They've known each other since before school. Michelle's family will arrive tomorrow for a brief vacation before the wedding."

Michelle continued to lean against David while he spoke, and Saira got the distinct impression Michelle liked him more than a brother-in-friendship.

Saira castigated herself for her cynicism.

"That must be wonderful, Michelle. I've lost touch with all

my friends from school. It must feel as though you and Vicky are sisters?"

Michelle giggled and continued to hold on to David's arm.

"Oh yes, Vicky and I are very close. We've always been. And now she's given me a gorgeous new brother."

Again, Saira wondered if there was more going on between David and Michelle as they glanced at each other when Michelle said the word "gorgeous."

David patted her hand on his arm.

The impression of a forbidden intimacy between David and Michelle had startled Saira.

As she looked up, Gerhard beckoned her to join him. Relief flooded her body. She made her excuses but had to stop herself from running to Gerhard. She couldn't stop her face from breaking out into a massive smile as she walked toward him. For now, Saira banished from her mind whatever weird thing was going on between David and Michelle.

As Saira got close to Gerhard, he extricated himself from the company of bridesmaids surrounding him, said the director needed him.

Gerhard took her elbow and steered her ahead of him, away from the bar toward the pool. Once again, she felt the thrill at their physical contact. But he was unaware of it or did a better job of hiding it.

"Thank you for rescuing me. I didn't want to be rude to the girls, but they are persistent. Plus, they continued to speak in Afrikaans, and my Afrikaans isn't that great, despite having been born here."

Saira had never given thought about the different languages people spoke here. From the decorations in Gerhard's home, she'd assumed he was European and therefore bilingual in English and another European language. She'd guessed it had to be German. But now, she realized she might have been wrong.

He must have seen the questions in her eyes because he stopped and turned to her.

"I hope you don't hate the Germans. You may have guessed from my home, my ancestry?"

"I'm not in the habit of hating an entire nation. I don't think I could hold you responsible for the actions of a madman long ago, who wasn't even German by birth, if that's what you're referring to?"

Gerhard's intense eyes locked on hers and his smile, perhaps because he didn't give it often, made his face even more handsome. His smile opened him, showed the warmth of his personality and the beauty of his soul. Again, it reminded Saira that an artist lived inside his strong, muscular body.

She didn't want the moment to end, but Kerri appeared and ushered them to a table where Naomi and Luca sat. As Saira took her place at the table, she noticed that people in groups had remained separate, almost as though in their own little tribes. It was something she'd seen often and had always wondered about. Her theory was they felt more comfortable that way because they could speak in their tribe's shorthand. But she'd always enjoyed seeking out unfamiliar people to talk to and fresh experiences. Perhaps that's what made her so different from her parents.

Lunch, for her, turned out to be less about food and more about her excitement at Gerhard's presence next to her.

During coffee, Shona approached and knelt at Saira's side

"Would you like to brief Vicky and David about the filming? They've been asking."

Saira smiled.

She'd have to teach Shona.

"Don't worry about Vicky and David, Shona. I'll deal with them for now and if I'm not around, refer them to Mary. Has Vicky been badgering you?"

Shona's shoulders relaxed, and her smile revealed her relief.

"Oh, thank you, Saira. Yes, you're right. Vicky has been asking me repeatedly to let them have the filming schedule. I wouldn't give it to her without your consent."

As proud as Saira was of Shona's fantastic work ethic and organizational skills, she had to remember how young the girl was. It was Shona's first time being a PA.

Saira laid a comforting hand on Shona's forearm.

"I've experienced such behavior before, Shona. It happens when people get overexcited. But it can make our lives more difficult. For now, I want you to concentrate on your tasks and schedule. If Vicky approaches you again, just redirect her to Mary or to me. We'll deal with her for now. A time will come when I must ask you to be the go-between, but that's further down the line."

As Saira spoke, the lights came back on in Shona's eyes, and her eager smile showed her gratitude for Saira's understanding.

Beside her, Saira could feel Gerhard's eyes following Shona as she walked away.

He turned to Saira.

"You have a winner there. If I were you, I'd hold on to her. Naomi and Kerri might steal her from you."

Naomi's golden-bell giggle showed she'd overheard Gerhard.

"Gerhard isn't wrong, Saira. Kerri and I have been admiring Shona and several other members of your capable, helpful new crew. If I were you, I'd start my own company and employ these guys before someone else nabbed them."

Saira's heart skipped a beat. She knew Naomi was only joking, but her words were too close to Saira's dream. Was it a sign?

Kerri got up and pushed her chair under the table.

"Well, on that note, I'd better go do all the jobs I'd have given to Shona."

As everyone around their table joined in the laughter, Saira noticed Luca had been watching her.

His eyes held a mischievous twinkle when he realized she shared their brand of humor.

His voice teased further.

"I don't know... All that red hair will have the temper to go with it. She could prove trouble down the line, so better to leave her here with us, Saira."

As she laughed at Luca's joke, she watched her more mature, new crew mingle with the bridal party. They were making easy conversation, and she was grateful things had turned out so well. She felt she was justified in her belief that things happened for a reason.

Out of the corner of her eye, she noticed Michelle leaning into David, laughing near his face. On his other side, Vicky's frown, thin lips and darkened face showed a storm was brewing.

SEVENTEEN

The disturbing feeling all was not well with the bride and groom had followed Saira around all afternoon like a nasty odor. Despite that, she did everything on her list.

The alarm alerted Saira to her meeting with Vicky and David. She collected her papers and went to their suite. As usual, Kerri had arranged for coffee during the session. A waitress bearing coffee arrived at the same time Saira did. On her heels came Mary, racing to the meeting, her brown curls like a halo around her head, her habitual slight frown between her eyes.

At Saira's knock, David opened the door at once. She wasn't sure if he'd opened it for them, or if he'd been on his way out. From his bearing and the energy in the room, Saira guessed the couple had continued arguing. Michelle's actions at lunch seemed the apparent cause.

Saira stood still for moments, admiring her surroundings. She'd thought her suite beautiful and spacious, but the bridal suite was almost twice the size. It wasn't so much a suite but resembled an apartment. Beautiful furniture decorated with a distinctive African flavor, lived in the space. One entire wall comprised massive floor-to-ceiling glass sliding doors. They were open and gave onto a patio that led to a private garden and a small pool.

When Vicky, who'd been sitting under an enormous sun umbrella on the patio, heard Saira and Mary, she came in and closed the sliding doors behind her.

The waitress deposited their coffee things on the coffee table in the lounge area. Saira couldn't help admiring the way the light reflected off the surfaces of the hardwood side tables. It gave her a powerful sense of the exoticness and otherworldliness of this country.

Once the waitress had left, Vicky poured coffee for everyone.

"Thank you for making our meeting private, Saira and Mary. Everyone else is excited and wanted to be involved. But some things are private and should remain that way."

She flicked an accusatory glance at David.

David said nothing and accepted his cup of coffee from Vicky.

Saira wondered if she should intervene and decided against it at once. Weddings were fraught with anxiety, and she'd had enough of her own to deal with recently.

Whatever was going on with David and Vicky, she was sure they'd work it out. They seemed so in love earlier. She didn't think it was an act. But it was normal to expect a few temper tantrums. It was their wedding, and a day that would change their lives forever. It had to be stressful. Saira reminded herself to remember it when she briefed them, and later when filming began. It was easy to forget they were real human beings going through a life-altering experience. She had to remember they weren't only subjects she directed to create the best, most riveting TV programs possible.

She put her coffee down on the small table beside her chair and sat forward.

"Right, this needs to happen..."

Saira presented the storyboard she'd worked on with her visualizer. Vince was a genius, and Saira hoped the couple appreciated his work. When she'd finished, Mary filled in the details. But David and Vicky only listened and nodded. Saira explained she and Gerhard had already chosen the best locations around the lodge for the shoots. She stopped several times to allow them to say something. But as they stayed silent, she continued to outline the schedule, suggested outfits for each shoot and who else should appear in the shoots. Even when Mary handed over the program she'd printed out for them, they said nothing, accepting the printout with a nod.

Not that Saira had ever wished anything bad on anyone, but perhaps it was the best thing the argument had curbed Vicky's over-the-top exuberance from earlier in the day. That the couple seemed unable even to look at each other during the meeting, tugged at her heartstrings. She hoped they could sort themselves out before filming started.

Saira felt relieved the meeting went so fast. She couldn't wait to get out of the thick atmosphere. Mary stayed behind to go through everything step-by-step and answer their questions. However, Saira doubted there would be any. As she closed the door behind her, for once, she embraced the heat of the sun that chased away the gloomy darkness of the couple's argument.

She checked her watch. Her next meeting with the Spa manager and Kerri was sooner than she'd realized. But she stopped at the pool for a few moments. The water looked inviting as she stared at it before continuing on her way.

Near the corner, the sound of a woman's giggle followed the unmistakable sound of Gerhard's voice. Saira couldn't hear his words, but his soft, calm voice sounded as though he was in the middle of a conversation. His voice sent thrills through her body. But the pleasure was short-lived as the woman's giggles expressed seduction and sounded suggestive.

Saira stopped in her tracks. Should she avoid them? Perhaps she should walk around on the other side of the guestrooms.

What was she-twelve? How silly. It would mean being late for her meeting.

Despite wishing otherwise, her heart continued to hammer in her chest.

At once, she found herself paralyzed. The shock of the realization she'd fallen in love with Gerhard had ground her to a halt. She wanted to argue with herself, but her body wouldn't lie. Her pulse throbbed throughout her being, her hands felt clammy. Black spots appeared before her eyes. Her legs gave way and she sank down into a squat so she could get a grip. She wouldn't give in to the sudden out-of-control weakness that had come over her.

Love? Really? Is this what it felt like? The feeling was overwhelming, uncomfortable, scary. This wasn't what she'd wanted, nor had she looked for it.

Gerhard had said nothing to show he felt the same way she did. She'd be leaving after they'd completed the pilot. What was the point of starting something with him, anyway? They came from different worlds. It was impossible.

The girl's giggle came again and sliced through Saira's heart.

Get a grip.

They weren't in any kind of relationship and certainly nothing romantic or exclusive. They'd only shared a few kisses. That was all.

Saira touched her lips.

But while it might have been only kissing for him, for her, it had been an earth-shattering experience.

What was she thinking?

If he wanted a fling with someone else, it was his choice. She couldn't do anything about it.

Saira shook her head.

She didn't need complications in her life right now. She'd just got rid of Jonathan. The thought of Jonathan brought on a sudden rage of indignation that burned in her chest. But the fire turned into pain, far more agonizing. It gripped her heart in both hands at the sudden, stomach-punching fear that Gerhard may not return her love. What would she do, then?

Come on, girl, she admonished herself.

She was a fighter, she'd get over it and move on. That's what she'd do.

Saira got up, pulled her shoulders back, straightened her spine and prepared to march past the couple. But she couldn't ignore them. She plastered a smile on her face and waved as she walked by, but didn't trust her voice, so said nothing.

The shock of seeing Gerhard leaning against the wall with Michelle in front of him, she knew, showed on her face despite her best efforts.

Michelle was smiling up at Gerhard, her hand on his chest. Her body rested against his, her curves fitting around his groin and hip.

The smile on his sensual lips reminded Saira how soft his lips were on hers when he'd kissed her, and how those same soft lips aroused such desire and turbulent emotions in her.

She felt like running, escaping, but fought to keep her composure and put one foot in front of the other. Her steps felt awkward and jerky to her. Her heart throbbed in her ears, and the world swirled in front of her eyes. Unshed tears burned behind her eyelids.

She wouldn't cry. She wouldn't cry.

Her entire body was shaking.

As though from underwater, she heard Gerhard's voice.

"Saira! Wait!"

He grabbed her arm to stop her.

"It's not what it looks like."

Saira couldn't look at him, but he put a finger under her chin.

"I came to find you, and she sidled up to me. She means nothing. You must know that. I don't play those kinds of games. I wasn't playing with you."

Saira waited until she knew the anger had burned away the shock and hurt in her eyes before she looked up at him. She wanted to say something, to hurt him, to dismiss him. But the look of distress in his eyes floored her. She knew she couldn't do it.

It took tremendous effort, but she slowed her breathing even though her heart still felt as though someone kept on kicking it.

She would continue her decision to be open and honest with him.

It took a monumental effort to keep her voice calm, and she lowered the ends of her sentences. It was a tactic she used in meetings dominated by male colleagues.

"I like you too, Gerhard. But I must leave when we've finished the shoot. What then?"

He stroked her cheek and tucked a stray hair behind her ear. His eyes looked far away into the distance for a moment, as though he contemplated her question.

But he turned his intense gaze back to her before he spoke.

"Why don't we deal with it when the time comes? Why don't we forget about it for now? It's an entire month away. Lots can happen before then."

"I don't want to be a fling for you, Gerhard."

"I've never regarded you as a fling, Saira, not for a single minute from the moment I saw you."

She heard the truth in his voice and tried to process his words, but her mind was reeling with what he could mean.

Kerri's happy, bright voice snapped them both back to reality.

"There you guys are. I thought I'd rescue you from Vicky and David if you needed rescuing so we can get to Rose. But I can see you didn't need me. Come on. Rose only has half an hour for us before her next client arrives."

Kerri appeared oblivious to what had just happened between Gerhard and Saira. Kerri linked an arm through each of theirs and marched them off toward the Spa.

Behind them, Saira heard a snort and the slap of flip-flops against the concrete as Michelle stomped away, and almost collided with Mary, as she stormed off to her suite.

Gerhard had heard it too, because he looked at Saira over Kerri's head and lifted his eyebrows as if to say, "Oh, dear, someone's pissed off. Oh, well."

If Mary had sensed anything, she kept it to herself and fell into step beside them.

At the Spa, the receptionist, who looked to Saira like a gorgeous obsidian princess, glanced up when they walked through the door. She smiled, got up and led the way to the manager's office, her long braids swaying at her back. Her delicate hand gave a light tap on the door.

At Rose's "yup," she opened it and stood aside.

Rose was busy on her computer but looked up as they entered, a welcoming smile spreading over her dark-skinned face.

Saira had an immediate sense she'd be in safe hands with Rose whatever Spa treatment she chose.

Rose moved around her desk with uncommon alacrity in someone of her size. She continued to smile as she invited them to sit down on the comfortable-looking chairs in the lounge area against the far wall.

The ambience in the Spa impressed Saira as much as Rose's psychic skills did when she frowned and pursed her lips.

"Trouble in paradise?"

She'd addressed the question to Saira.

"With the bride and groom? I suspect so, yes. How did you know?"

Rose tapped a conspiratorial finger against her nose.

"I think everyone saw Michelle's claim on David at lunch. It was only a matter of time before that bomb went off."

Rose snorted as she laughed, her ample bosom wiggling up and down with mirth. She wiped her eyes with a tissue she extracted from her bra before she spoke again.

"Welcome to the Spa, Saira and Mary. I should say, welcome to Gerhard too."

Her smile was coquettish as she addressed him.

Saira almost shook her head. What was it with women and Gerhard? Did he mesmerize them all the way he did her?

His absent-minded nod in Rose's direction spoke of his obliviousness of his effect on the female of the species.

Rose's eyes lingered on his face for moments, as though she was reading his mind before she faced the women again.

"We see all sorts here. But this is the first time I've seen a best friend deliberately trying to disrupt her friend's wedding. Jealousy is such a nasty old thing."

Rose giggled again.

Saira tried to smile. But it was difficult to talk about Michelle after what she'd just witnessed between the girl and Gerhard.

Rose's comments reminded her she'd do whatever she could to make Vicky's wedding day special. Why did women have to be so cruel to one another? It had always befuddled her. But she'd have to monitor Michelle. Better still, get one of the younger, single male crew members to watch her. Maybe she'd go after him and stop causing mischief elsewhere.

The thought prompted Gerhard's words about the girl meaning nothing to him to ring through her mind again. It was also a reminder it was futile to begin something with him. There could be no beginning. It would only lead to genuine heartache for her and after seeing the tenderness in his eyes, perhaps for him.

Saira stopped trying to stay present after she'd presented the storyboards for filming in the Spa.

Gerhard had sat down next to her. His arm and leg touched hers and his nearness played havoc with her emotions.

But Kerri and Mary were blessings, as was Rose. They talked enough for a small nation. The meeting went by in a blink. Rose offered a guided tour, and Saira couldn't help being impressed by everything in the Spa. It was luxurious enough to cater to a famous, high-paying clientele used to this. Saira wanted to believe the aromatherapy odors helped to calm her turbulent emotions and she was almost sorry to leave the cool calm of the Spa.

Outside, the heat of the late afternoon once again surprised Saira.

Would she ever get used to it?

On their way back to the main building, they stopped for moments by the pool to watch guests enjoying the water. Some were lying on sunbeds under enormous umbrellas, and waiters were taking and delivering drinks orders. The bridesmaids from the wedding party sat together and it was obvious they'd had quite a lot of alcohol already. Their excited voices echoed off the water and the buildings as they chatted and laughed.

Saira sensed rather than saw Gerhard spotting Michelle at the same moment she did. Michelle wore the smallest bikini

Saira had ever seen. It left nothing to the imagination, and from the way she behaved, it was clear she was after some male attention. Several young male German guests had joined the girls and contributed to the party atmosphere.

As though Gerhard wanted to reassure Saira again that Michelle meant nothing to him, he held her elbow in his warm hand. His touch was comforting, felt secure, and despite trying to resist it, sent tingles through Saira's body.

Kerri waved and smiled at the girls.

"That reminds me... Now Luca's here, dinner becomes a party every night. I hope you'll join us again tonight, Saira? Mary, you'd be very welcome, too."

Saira had heard the "party" phrase a few times now. It sounded like fun, but she hesitated only for a moment.

"Thanks for the invitation, Kerri. I have several phone calls to make and work to catch up on, so if you don't mind, a rain check?"

Mary took her cue from Saira and declined before walking away back toward the main house and the film crew's HQ.

Kerri's voice was sincere.

"Sometimes, I forget you're here to work, and you're not just a friend. But please join us whenever you can. Don't wait for an invitation."

Saira felt Gerhard's gaze on her and cursed the blush that spread up her neck under his scrutiny.

His voice was low and melodious.

"Perhaps you would join me for a pre-dinner drink, instead, Saira?"

The wink Kerri gave her as she walked away, made Saira wonder if Kerri had been aware of the tension between her and Gerhard all along.

Gerhard took Saira's hesitation to mean she needed more persuasion.

He checked his watch.

"You haven't been on a safari yet, have you?"

She shook her head.

"I could take you to the waterhole now. There won't be any other safaris yet, and you'll see some wildlife. We can have our drinks there. I'll bring you back safe and sound, I promise."

His face wore such a sweet expression. How could she refuse? Plus, they could do with being alone, to soothe away what happened with Michelle.

"Okay, but I have to get back. I need to call MaxPix before they shut for the day."

He put two fingers over his heart.

"I promise. I'll just go get the truck ready. Meet you outside the kitchen."

As Saira watched, Gerhard took long strides around the building. She wondered if she'd made the right decision. But getting away from the lodge for a while, could be useful. It could put things into perspective again.

EIGHTEEN

Saira deposited her workbag and laptop in her suite and texted Shona her whereabouts. Then, she walked around the main building to where Gerhard was waiting for her in the safari truck.

He took her breath away. He was so handsome as he sat there, his arm resting on the open window. Saira couldn't help thinking he looked almost regal.

When Gerhard saw her, he came to open the door for her. His chivalrous behavior reminded her of her father's respectful manners. She couldn't imagine Jonathan ever doing something like opening a door for her. She would have frowned on it before. But to Gerhard it seemed such a natural gesture, Saira understood it had to be part of his upbringing and culture.

As he got into the truck beside her, Saira felt the faintest note of doubt creeping into her mind. Being alone with Gerhard was perhaps not the wisest thing she'd done this day. But he did nothing to make her feel uncomfortable. Instead, he talked about the meeting they'd just had with Rose and enquired after the bride and groom following Rose's comments earlier. As they spoke, he started the truck and drove toward the gate that took them into the desert. Saira felt herself relax as they traveled in companionable silence. There was nothing in Gerhard's bearing that demanded conversation, and she was grateful for it. It allowed her to feast her eyes on the desert landscape.

It appeared desolate, but she knew life was all around them. Several large camel-thorn trees accommodated massive birds' nests, and Saira delighted at seeing the tiny birds flitting in and out of their multi-nest complexes. How clever they were. How did every single little bird find their own nest in such a big clump of dried grasses and twigs, she wondered?

Ahead of them, along the never-ending straight track, the sun dipped toward the horizon. The blue of the sky morphed into colors resembling the fires crackling in the barbeque pits Chef lit each night. They passed one orange-red dune after another that appeared massive against the deepening fire colors of the sky.

Saira gasped when a line of dark-green trees appeared. The contrast was spectacular.

Gerhard pointed to the right of the trees.

"Oh, good, we're just in time. Look past that large tree there. Can you see the giraffes?"

Saira's eyes followed his finger. She sat forward in her seat. Seeing giraffes on the telly was one thing, but quite another to see them so close-up. She didn't think being close to wildlife would be this exciting. But now they were approaching the waterhole, and she could see the animals drinking there, the otherness surrounding them hit her full force.

She raised her phone and zoomed in to take a few photographs to send to her parents. She knew her father would have loved this. As they drove closer, many more animals came into view. The zebras, with their short, braying sounds, had always reminded Saira of Africa whenever she'd heard the sound on nature programs. But here the sound was even lovelier. The kudus with their massive horns stood near a herd of much smaller springbok. Saira felt proud of herself for recognizing most species. It was good to know watching wildlife programs had taught her something and weren't only a way to deaden herself after arguments with Jonathan.

Gerhard drove to a structure intended for the safari trucks from where the occupants would have the best view of the waterhole. He stopped at the best spot. While he went to get their drinks from the back of the truck, Saira stayed sitting forward on her seat. She rested her arms on the dashboard and felt the world shift as she became absorbed watching the animals at the waterhole.

When Gerhard presented her drink, she was surprised it was her favorite. He must have seen amazement flickering over her face.

He winked at her.

"Kerri knows everything and always makes sure every guest has their favorite drink. It includes you."

He clinked his beer bottle against her glass of non-alcoholic ginger beer and offered her snacks from cute Tupperware bowls.

Saira focussed on the animals at the waterhole because Gerhard's presence made her heart kick in her chest and her palms sweaty.

Now and then, she put her glass down and picked up her cell phone to take more pictures. Why hadn't she thought of bringing a proper camera? But she wasn't the world's best photographer. She pressed the video button on her phone to capture the giraffes. The way they spread their front legs so they could drink was almost comical, but for their majestic bearing.

Despite the different species at the waterhole, everything seemed peaceful. Not for the first time, Saira thought how humans could learn from animals about cooperation and living together in harmony. In the branches above their heads, little doves cooed, the sound further emphasizing the tranquility of the place.

It felt as though Saira had escaped to a different planet, one where time moved slower, and stress was unheard of.

Only Gerhard's nearness distracted her. She didn't think he could hide the enormity of his presence, even if he tried. He seemed oblivious to it and the effect he was having on her. He'd placed his arm along the top of the seat and rested his hand on her shoulder.

She was both grateful to him for acting on their mutual desire for physical connection and surprised at how right it felt.

Now and then Gerhard would break the silence by pointing his beer bottle toward something and telling her interesting facts about an animal or nearby plant or tree.

But every time he looked at her, the intensity of his eyes ignited a fire inside her. It dawned on Saira they were alone. The thought seemed to occur to Gerhard at the same time.

He put his beer down and took her glass, putting it on the dashboard. Then he faced her.

"Saira."

His voice said everything in that one word.

With his hands on both her shoulders, he pulled her toward him, giving her the chance to move away or stop him. She did neither. It was impossible to tear her eyes away from his. And when his lips brushed over hers, she felt herself sigh and closed her eyes, preparing to give herself over to the yearning he had unlocked in her.

His kiss was light at first, his lips again as before, like

butterfly wings, barely touching hers. His hands held her as though he was holding something precious. As his kiss deepened, she felt her body igniting as though he'd struck a match inside her. She returned his kiss with as much ardor as he had triggered in her.

When they broke apart, both sat panting, and Saira felt herself drowning in the darkened pupils of his eyes. But she also read surprise there, the same wonder she'd experienced that this wasn't just a kiss. This was a melding of their souls. She recognized it and knew he did too. She placed a finger on his lips, not wanting him to speak, not wanting to break the magic of the moment. Her heart was thumping throughout her body, and she fought to get her breath under control again. But she couldn't contain the smile that spread over her face. She'd never felt happier.

When Gerhard picked up his beer, she noticed his hand was shaking, and the bulge in his trousers confirmed she wasn't the only one aroused by their kiss. But as their eyes stayed locked on each other, their desire was clear. They'd forgotten the animals and the waterhole.

Then, they heard the unmistakable sound of another safari truck approaching. Saira smoothed down her hair, retrieved her glass of ginger beer and moved away from Gerhard.

When the other truck parked next to theirs, Gerhard raised his beer and Saira her glass in greeting, but they stayed only long enough to finish their drinks before Gerhard started the truck.

"I'd really like a lunch date as soon as possible, Saira."

Would she ever get used to the way he said her name?

But the kiss had robbed her of her voice, so she nodded.

As they drove back to Desert Lodge, Gerhard held her hand. He steered the truck with his thigh and pointed with his free hand to things she might find interesting. But she found it hard to concentrate on anything other than him.

Each time he looked at her, he squeezed her hand as though he wanted to remind her of the heat between them. As if she needed reminding. The taste and smell of him had infiltrated her mind. The thrill of his tongue against hers filled her with a desire she'd never experienced before.

But the moment they stopped outside the lodge's kitchen, Saira felt the tension seeping back into her body.

She checked to make sure they weren't being observed. Then, she leaned toward Gerhard and gave him a quick kiss on his mouth before getting out of the truck and walking away as fast as she could.

It wasn't just a case of beginnings with him, was it? It was also the knowledge that he could burn her, destroy her if she'd let him. No, better to concentrate on work.

As Saira walked around the corner of the building, she almost collided with Kerri who was rushing in her direction.

Kerri's face looked like thunder but lit up when she saw Saira.

"Thank God you're here. It's pandemonium."

Saira stopped in her tracks.

"Why? What happened?"

Before Kerri could respond, Naomi came up behind them carrying a disturbed look on her face. Mary came close on her heels. They stopped when they saw Saira.

Naomi turned to Kerri.

"I think it's best we talk in your office, don't you think, Kerri?"

She looked at Mary as she spoke.

"Thank you for your quick thinking, Mary. You're a marvel. But we should meet with Saira by herself for now. Would it be okay if we called you, should we need you?"

"You know where I am."

Saira watched Mary walk away and thanked all the gods of the universe for someone as competent as her new assistant director.

Kerri led the way through the French doors and down the corridor to her office. Saira followed behind the women, her mind a maelstrom of thoughts. Something had obviously shaken Naomi and Kerri. Saira knew it had something to do with the bridal party and most likely, Michelle.

When they opened the door to the office, they found Luca sitting behind Kerri's desk, deep in conversation with his manager in Modena.

He held up a finger as the women stopped in front of the desk.

"Si, Roberto, I agree. Can you action that? I will be back in..." He looked at Naomi, "... another week."

They seemed to operate via telepathy, Saira thought.

Saira checked the time on her phone to make it less obvious that's what she was doing and cursed under her breath. She'd miss the opportunity to make her calls to MaxPix. She'd just have to speak to Manda and Peter and get everything done that way.

Luca finished his Skype call and sat back in the chair.

"Ladies, how lovely all three of you came to see me."

His eyes held that mischievous glint Saira knew was part of his makeup.

Naomi went to stand behind her husband and snaked her arms around his neck.

"Mr. Armati, would you give us some space? We've hit a snag with the bridal party."

Luca held Naomi's hands where she'd crossed them over his chest.

He looked up at her.

"Again? Maybe someone is trying to tell you something about this group? I expected them to have behaved better than they have. It should be an honor that Saira had chosen them for the filming here, but they don't seem to understand or acknowledge it."

Naomi rested her chin on his head.

"But all sorts can happen when people get married."

By his smile, Saira could tell there had to be a story behind his and Naomi's wedding.

"Let me know if I can help?"

Naomi nodded and kissed his ear.

"You're my superhero, Mr. Armati, but I think we've got this. Thanks for the offer, though."

Luca got up, put an arm around Naomi's waist and kissed the top of her head, her forehead, eyes, nose and mouth.

"Right, Mrs. Armati. In that case, I don't know of anyone better to sort out the mess than you. I'll leave it in your capable hands together with the lovely Kerri and our new friend, Saira."

He winked at Saira as he left the room and closed the door behind him.

Naomi sank down in the chair Luca had vacated. Kerri sat down opposite Naomi and invited Saira to take the chair beside her.

Saira looked from one to the other. She couldn't read their faces.

Kerri turned to face Saira.

"Johan heard the commotion first. It took him and the best man to pull them apart."

Saira knew who Kerri meant.

"Michelle and Vicky?"

Naomi and Kerri nodded in unison.

Naomi leaned forward and put her elbows on the desk.

"I've never seen such a catfight. It would have been funny if it wasn't so serious."

Saira could feel Kerri's control collapsing as giggles escaped her mouth. Naomi was doing her best not to join in the laughter. Saira saw Naomi was biting the insides of her cheeks to maintain professionalism.

"I mean, hair was flying. And it wasn't extensions."

By now Kerri was stomping her foot and tears were streaming down her face as she roared. Her laughter was infectious, and soon all three women collapsed in their chairs as they gave themselves over to fits of hysterics.

When everyone could breathe again, Saira got up and started to pace as she spoke.

"The picture you painted is hilarious, I have to confess. But the situation is serious. We haven't even started shooting anything yet and for things to deteriorate to this extent doesn't fill me with confidence that everything will run smoothly once we do. Michelle is the culprit here. I'm surprised Vicky hasn't sent her on her way yet."

Naomi pressed the buzzer on Kerri's desk. She ordered coffee before getting up and walking over to the lounge area to plop down in a more comfortable chair. Kerri followed and took a seat on the sofa. Saira joined them.

Naomi put her hands behind her head and stretched her long legs out on the coffee table in front of her.

"I don't want to interfere, Saira. But as the producer and director of the pilot, if I were you, I'd either have a serious word with Vicky or I'd send Michelle back to Cape Town. Apart from making an exceptional pilot, we'd like to provide the best experience for guests at Desert Lodge. We want it for Vicky and David too. As we have invited them here and they aren't paying for anything, perhaps the decision to send Michelle back won't affect her relationship with Vicky. It will make for a better filming experience for everyone else. What do you think?"

Saira hesitated for only a moment.

"It's an idea. Since Michelle has caused so many problems already, I don't think we need to treat her with kid gloves. We don't want to be rude, but she doesn't deserve our sympathy."

As she spoke, Saira took out her phone and texted Shona to type a letter confirming Michelle was no longer needed. They would return her to Cape Town first thing in the morning. Kerri followed Saira's example. She texted a lodge administrator to arrange a return flight for Michelle to Cape Town and organize a room at a hotel for the night, plus a pilot to take her back to Windhoek tonight.

Saira sat back against the sofa.

"I can't thank you guys enough for all the help you're giving me."

A soft knock at the door announced the delivery of their coffee. At Naomi's command, a blonde waitress entered.

Saira did a double-take as the girl's hair was the same colour as Naomi's but they shared no other features, so not family, then. Saira wouldn't have been surprised. It seemed so many members of the same families have worked at Desert Lodge for years. It bode well for future projects with them.

The waitress poured their coffee, handing out the cups and offering cookies before leaving.

Naomi spoke over the rim of her cup.

"Saira, you feel to us as though you're a member of the Desert Lodge family. We'll always support you, however we can. We want you to have the best time here, so you'll return and make many more TV series set here."

Even though Naomi was smiling through her words, Saira heard the sincerity and ambition in Naomi's voice. She understood it at once. Didn't she feel the same about her dream?

As though Naomi could read her mind, she put her cup down and focused on Saira.

"Kerri and I have been discussing you. I hope you don't mind?"

Saira smiled and shrugged as if to say, "isn't it natural?"

"I know we have seen no footage yet. But it impresses us the way you're managing things, and we wondered why someone as obviously gifted as you would work for MaxPix? Wouldn't you rather want your own business?"

Saira's breath caught in her throat. Could she trust her new friends with her secret?

Kerri took Saira's hesitation as confirmation.

"I knew it. It's your dream. You're far too capable to be working for someone else. As you know, we've been in touch with Max, and have had a telephone relationship with him for months. But if Jonathan is any sign of what Max is like, we cannot imagine you working for someone like that for long."

Saira smiled despite her misgivings.

"Well, you're both right. But it's my secret. I should have known women as astute as the two of you would see it. This pilot was supposed to prove to Max I could do something amazing. I wanted to prove to myself I was ready and capable of starting my own production company. I don't have the kinds of contacts Max has and so felt I'd have to finish the pilot first before I'd have proof I could strike out on my own. But as time has gone on, and I know I've only been here a few days, I wish this project was my own instead of MaxPix's."

Saira sat back and lowered her eyes.

There. It was out. There was no turning back now. She had shared her dream out loud to near strangers. In her book, once you verbalized something, it was your destiny to fullfil it. Hadn't her parents always impressed that same sentiment on her?

She felt rather than saw Naomi and Kerri glance at each other as though they were proud of guessing correctly.

Naomi poured more coffee for them.

"Well, Saira, you may not have the contacts Max has, but we have some of our own. Several Hollywood A-listers have already come to stay here, and they included not only movie stars but also directors and producers of film and TV."

Saira was aware her eyes had widened as she looked up.

She'd considered none such offers of help from Naomi and Kerri. But hadn't they just proved they'd help when she needed it? By helping her, they'd help themselves promote Desert Lodge to the world to make it an exclusive global vacation destination. She understood their thinking.

As though Naomi didn't see Saira's look of surprise, she continued.

"Also, don't forget Luca. The connections that man has are incredible. It's because of him we've had such success here already and had visits from movers and shakers from all over the world."

Saira blew out a breath through pursed lips as she considered the implications of Naomi's words.

Yes, Luca could come in useful when the time came to break the contract with MaxPix. What? Breaking her contract? She couldn't believe she was thinking these thoughts, that her dream might come true and so soon. Perhaps it was time.

She squared her shoulders and took a deep breath.

"There is the contract with MaxPix."

Naomi's thoughtful frown lifted.

"Luca has one of the best lawyers in the world who is his best friend working with him at Armati. I'm sure he'll sort it out for you. It shouldn't be a problem, not after Jonathan tore up the contract, and we had to reprint it. We have it on CCTV."

Saira felt the excitement build inside her chest at the thought her dream could come true alongside Naomi's.

"That's such a generous offer, Naomi. Thank you. I've never gone back on my word before, and I've never broken a contract before. Could I think about it?"

Naomi nodded.

"The offer is there if you're ready. We'd love for you to become a permanent member of the Desert Lodge family. But only if it works for you."

Saira put down her coffee, a frown forming between her eyes.

"If we think along the lines that this project might become my own, I think it's too small as it stands now. I can make it wider. We'll need more couples. But I don't want to take up all your paying guest rooms for the bridal parties."

Kerri, who'd caught on fast, turned to face Saira.

"That's a brilliant idea, Saira. I don't know if you've noticed how large our staff accommodations are? Even with your crew, there are still plenty of rooms available. Perhaps you haven't had a reason to go there? I used to live there myself before I married Johan. Most of our staff members live nearby with their families, so they need not stay on the premises. We can accommodate a few more bridal parties using staff accommodation. The rooms are as big as self-contained apartments, and we could put the bridal parties separate from your crew."

Saira nodded.

"That would be hugely helpful. And I think we'd need to move David and Vicky's bridal party there."

It was Kerri's turn to nod.

"I agree. We can't show favoritism toward one couple."

Saira and Kerri took their phones out again and started texting to get everything underway.

When Saira looked up, she found Naomi watching her, an enigmatic smile on her lips.

"What?"

"See? We make a formidable team already. Luca, Johan and Gerhard may be the three male Musketeers around here. But they'd better watch out for the three female musketeers."

Naomi raised her cup of coffee. Kerri and Saira did the same, clinking their cups together.

It tasted of victory. But Saira couldn't help wondering what battle they'd won.

NINETEEN

Michelle wasn't the type to leave without a fight. Saira knew that. She also knew Michelle hadn't read the letter from her office because when she got to her room, she found only Vicky and David's response under her door.

Vicky's feminine handwriting on the back of the letter communicated their gratitude for Saira's help with the problematic Michelle situation. The smudge on the note made her think Vicky was crying when she wrote it. Saira believed Vicky's sadness about losing a bridesmaid and her words about how much she'd wanted her best friend to be a part of her wedding. But she didn't blame Saira for returning Michelle to Cape Town, and Saira thought she read relief between the lines.

Saira put the letter on her dressing table and texted Vicky to ask if she'd heard from Michelle.

Saira's phone pinged almost at once with Vicky's text response.

No idea where she is. Been to her room, texted and called, but no response. Might be with the German guys? Vx

A soft knock on Saira's door announced her dinner had

arrived. She opened the door and allowed the waitress to serve her dinner at the dining table.

As she ate, Saira responded to all the other emails awaiting her attention. Then she sent detailed emails to Manda and Peter asking for their help with things at the London office. Emails sent, Saira sat back in her chair.

Now, apart from Peter and Manda, two more people knew of her dream. But Naomi and Kerri had sworn to keep her secret until she was ready to reveal it, and she trusted them.

How many times had she heard or read somewhere that life could change overnight? She'd always assumed it meant weddings, births or health problems, accidents and death. It never occurred to her that life could change without such trauma.

Her mind was buzzing with thoughts of her future. How weird that she felt no loyalty to MaxPix anymore? She had known it for some time. She'd only been here for days, but her life in London already felt as though it had happened to another Saira in another lifetime.

Yes, perhaps email was the best way to deal with the London office meanwhile. Phone calls could drag her back into that world, and now she wanted, more than she'd imagined, to put it behind her.

Until today, until her conversation with Naomi and Kerri, she hadn't noticed how unhappy she'd been at MaxPix over the last year. She'd assumed her feelings were Jonathan's fault. But he'd only been a part of the problem. The biggest part, her dream, had lived unfulfilled in her heart all this time.

Her audible sigh sounded like a kind of song as she stretched her arms above her head.

It felt good knowing she had such wholehearted support from Naomi and Kerri even before she started her own company. Things were fast progressing in the right direction and Saira couldn't help feeling the excitement bubbling up within her body.

Thoughts of Michelle only resurfaced when her phone pinged with Kerri's text to alert Saira that the bridal party's move was about to happen. She finished her meal, grabbed her phone and key and pulled the door shut behind her.

It was common courtesy, Saira felt, to be visible during such things as moving her talent around. She wouldn't need to help. Desert Lodge's staff was some of the most professional she'd ever come across. They swarmed like desert ants as they moved everyone and everything over to the staff quarters in record time and with minimal fuss.

Moving David and Vicky went almost as Saira imagined it would, were it not for her mother.

Vicki's mother was another matter. She'd called everyone, from members of the film crew to Mary, Shona, Saira, Kerri, Naomi, the staff at reception and even Rose at the Spa. Her aim was to vent her frustration at being moved from a perfectly good suite to something she deemed far below her standards. That she hadn't seen the room yet, held no argument with her.

Saira walked faster toward the raised voices amplified over the pool. It was a genius idea to have the pool in the square and the guests' suites surrounding it. Getting closer to the suites where the bridal party had stayed, the voices became louder and more hysterical.

For goodness' sake, what now?

Through one door, Michelle and Vicky were having a screaming match. Their words were getting more and more personal. Meanwhile, a hapless David stood in the doorway. Mary stood behind his shoulder, ready to help should they need to separate the women again like they did earlier.

Next door, Kerri stood facing Vicky's mother, who was sitting on the bed. The woman's face was blotchy and red, and her shoulders shook as tears streamed down her face. Her voice had reached the high whiny notes of someone who wanted her way and planned to get it, no matter what.

"But it's not fair. We're the victims here, and no one is helping us. Isn't the customer always right? You're supposed to be the manager. Why can't you see reason? Don't you realize without us there isn't anything to film? You need us more than we need you."

Saira stepped forward, but one look at Kerri's face told her underneath Kerri's steely control, she was mad as hell. Instead, Saira watched as the bride's mother pleaded, cajoled, manipulated, yelled and stomped her feet like a toddler. She had a significant influence on Vicky, who'd had her own fiery outbursts when the staff came to help with their move. Both women made sure everyone knew they were being downgraded.

Saira wondered what vexed them most, the move or that they were no longer the only bridal party in the pilot. Either way, she should have filmed this, she thought.

Then she smiled. Nope, that would be a whole other show.

Meanwhile, nothing Vicky said could convince Michelle that Vicky hadn't ordered her away after their hair-pulling fight earlier in the day. Vicky tried to convince Michelle the TV people did it. Michelle wouldn't listen to Vicky and instead, continued her tantrums, using her new-perceived victimization as a weapon against her distraught friend.

But Saira read the relief on Vicky's face when Michelle stormed off with her bags swinging in every direction. She didn't glance back as she raced toward the landing strip where a Cessna was waiting to take her to Windhoek. The girl's arrogance and extreme entitlement reminded Saira of a female version of Jonathan.

Saira had to smile when Kerri, fresh from her victory over

Vicky's mother, walked by and whispered in her ear, "Apple, tree, close..."

Saira's patience and kind-heartedness only stretched so far. It was a lesson in extreme ungratefulness if ever she needed one. These people were staying at Desert Lodge for free, dammit. What more could they want? The screaming and yelling sessions did her head in. Enough was enough.

After they'd moved everyone to their new suites, Saira asked Mary to gather the bridal party together in the Lapa.

Saira had to slow her breathing. She needed to maintain her professionalism as director and producer and reminded herself to drop her voice at the end of her sentences to establish further authority.

When everyone had gathered, she looked at the faces surrounding her, many of whom were sulking.

"I understand you feel slighted because we had to ask you to move out of the paying guest suites and into the staff accommodations. Your new accommodations are enormous, and we're confident you'll be very comfortable there. I'd like to remind you that you are at a venue where guests, including Hollywood A-listers, pay enormous amounts of money to visit. We have paid for your dresses and suits for the wedding. Your meals and drinks here are free, and you have enjoyed several safaris into the desert for free. This is a unique opportunity not afforded everyone. I also understand we upset you because you will no longer be the only bridal party featured in the pilot. May I remind you we never promised you'd be the only party? You'll feature along with three other bridal parties as part of a television pilot that we will sell around the world. The others will join us tomorrow morning, and everyone will stay in the staff accommodations. No one will get preferential treatment even though you've already received it.

"So, my question is, since you all seem so unhappy with the

arrangements, is this project still something you want to take part in? Or would you prefer to return to Cape Town, so you can arrange your own wedding the way you want?"

Saira felt she had nothing to lose being upfront with these people. It might make her life more relaxed if they left. She remained silent as she watched the effects of her words. If it weren't so serious, it would be funny.

Realizing they might lose the benefits Saira had mentioned, the transformation on Vicky's and her mother's faces was almost comical. Both women became flustered and flushed.

Their words tumbled over each other.

"Oh, no, we're very happy with-"

"It's wonderful that other brides will get this opportunity to-"

Saira stopped listening to them. But she noticed their broad smiles didn't reach their eyes. Vicky's mother raised her eyebrows so high they were in danger of disappearing into her hairline.

Saira knew they would have bragged to friends and family back home about their awesome and unique opportunity. To return with their tail between their legs would be too much to bear for their fragile egos.

But Saira had decided. She wouldn't tolerate any more bull from anyone. She'd already wasted enough time on unreliable cameramen, Jonathan's nonsense and a rebel crew. It was time to get tough and get to work. That this pilot might be the first for her own company further helped to put things into perspective.

Before anyone could say anything more, she put out her hand, her fingers splayed in a definite stop sign.

"Right then, if you stay, please liaise with my assistant, Shona, for anything including your schedules for rehearsals and shooting over the next few days. The nicer you are to her, the more likely she'll be to help you. Thank you."

Saira left before she got dragged into more drama. As she walked toward their HQ in the lounge, Saira texted Vince. They'd have to come up with a new storyboard and visuals before tomorrow morning.

It would be an interminable night.

TWENTY

Kerri was a marvel.

By the time Saira crawled bleary-eyed from her bed, Kerri had already installed the recently arrived bridal parties in the staff accommodation.

Kerri's text had awoken her. It said, *see you in my office for a quick breakfast meeting before filming starts at ten. Everyone's excited.*

Saira dragged her exhaustion into the shower where she hoped the water would wash away the aches from tensed muscles. It seemed to work. After being pelted by the large rain shower, she felt more like herself again. She stepped out of the shower, draped a towel around her body and another around her hair.

She'd just finished getting dressed; linen trousers and a sleeveless T-shirt when a knock came at her door. It wasn't Kerri's usual sharp rap, and it wasn't the soft, hesitant knock of her regular waiter.

Saira peered through the peephole.

Gerhard's proud profile was striking against the blue sky behind him. His straight blonde hair had flopped over his forehead, which gave him a dreamy, sexy look. He appeared to be watching someone in the swimming pool while he waited for her to open the door. It was an opportunity to admire his straight, aristocratic nose and luscious lips. But his attraction wasn't only physical. It was the man, the soul that lived inside such a magnificent specimen of manhood, that did crazy, exciting things to her heart.

Saira glanced at her image in the mirror next to the door and smoothed down her hair, still damp from the shower. Her pulse was throbbing in her neck, and a swarm of butterflies took off in her belly. Thoughts of being tired flew away. Excited to be alone with him, even for these few minutes, replaced any tiredness. She pinched her cheeks to bring a little color into her face, ran her hands down her clothes, then opened the door.

"Good morning, Gerhard. What a lovely surprise to see you here so early."

Despite doing her best to appear calm, Saira felt the heat rising into her face. The blush traveled to her hairline and heated her scalp as Gerhard's intense blue eyes roamed over her body and fastened on her mouth. She remembered only too well the feel and taste of his lips. The memory had seared itself into her mind and senses.

Gerhard scanned the area to make sure they weren't being observed, then took a step inside the room and kicked the door closed behind him. He grasped her shoulders and pulled her into his body, his lips obliterating any other thoughts in her mind. As his tongue joined hers and his kiss deepened, a delicious warmth spread through her body. It invaded her belly and moved into her core, making her legs feel like jelly.

Gerhard's groan into their mouths coincided with hers. The sound brought them back to reality, but as they pulled apart, their eyes stayed locked, and they received the same message of desire and need for each other.

It cost him, she could see, but Gerhard took a step back and leaned against the door.

"Damn, Saira, you make me lose control. I've never met a woman like you. You're everything I've ever wanted. You're mine."

His voice was hoarse with desire and passion, and his nostrils flared in that sexy way Saira loved so much.

She took slow breaths as she fought for control over her breathing. Her body was aflame. Gerhard's powerful hardness, as much as his words, had burned itself into her. She couldn't think straight.

"Well, that was some good morning kiss. Wanting you this much is pure torture, but I'm glad you feel the same way. You make me lose control too, you know?"

She blew out another breath, smiled at him and fanned herself. She knew that making light of what she felt, what they both felt, was a way to deal with her feelings and ground herself.

"We have to get ready for breakfast with Kerri and Naomi."

It took all her willpower to turn away from him. She collected her bag, phone and keys. But as she walked back to him, toward the door, he grabbed her hand.

"Saira, I mean it. I won't play with my emotions or yours. The way I feel about you has not only surprised me but has also taken me by surprise. Our work here is impeding what we both want. I understand it's best to maintain a professional relationship while we're working on this project, I understand that. But I'll wait and make it worth your while to do the same."

She held his hand and looked deep into his eyes before responding.

"Well, in that case, you may be happy to hear your feelings and intentions are reciprocated."

He drew her toward him again, but this time, it was deliberate and gentle. He held her against his body for a moment, his hand cupping the back of her head.

Saira closed her eyes. Against her ear, his heart was still galloping in his chest, and she smiled at the thought she was the cause. She allowed the feelings of safety and coming home to invade her. It felt so right with him. Of course, she'd wait.

When she stepped away from him again, they unlinked their hands and smiled at each other.

The creases at the outer corners of Gerhard's eyes revealed his happiness.

"I guess we must put on a front of being only professionals. For now."

Saira continued to smile into his eyes.

"Yes, I agree. For now."

The lightness in Saira's chest felt as though sunlight had broken through the bruised clouds of her past. She recognized the feeling as happiness, a happiness she'd never experienced before, certainly not with Jonathan. The novel sensation wanted to bubble up inside her, fly free. But she wanted to hold it close, savor it like her favorite dessert.

Why, then, did something niggle at the back of her mind? But she knew why. The words they'd both spoken, "for now," felt too much like a temporary thing, a fling. And she was not interested in a fling with Gerhard. His words and behavior left no doubt in her mind he wasn't looking for something temporary either. Her heart skipped at the thought of what it could mean.

But what of her parents? How would she even broach this relationship with them? Hadn't she already put them through enough anxiety about her choice of career? The difference was, she could change a job. A career didn't have to be permanent. But a relationship was another matter, at least for her. She suspected Gerhard felt the same.

As she walked beside him, past the swimming pool, past the Lapa toward the French doors that would take them into the body of the main building, Saira's thoughts remained around her parents. She couldn't help remembering the parties at her parents' home where they'd introduce her to various young Indian men from good backgrounds. The parties were a regular occurrence, following the same pattern. She could always predict who'd be the lucky man. It would have been amusing had it not been so heart breaking.

Gerhard's beautiful hand caught her eye when he opened the French doors and stood aside for her to go in ahead of him.

"A penny for your thoughts? You seemed miles away."

"Oh, I'm just thinking of my parents. I guess I miss them. We see each other at least once a week when I'm in London."

Gerhard put a hand on her shoulder to make her stop.

"You're close to them?"

"As their only child, I guess we've always been close. I know I'm lucky. It's unusual to have such a wonderful relationship with such great parents. But they both still work very hard in their professions. I was thinking how lovely, but most likely impossible, it would be for them to see Namibia. I've come to love it here."

Gerhard tilted his head to the side, eyes narrowed.

"But... I feel a but coming? You're wondering how they'd react to us, aren't you? I'm sorry, Saira, I hadn't considered our relationship might not gain their approval. It never occurred to me that perhaps you'd have to marry within your own culture. But I assumed because of Jonathan-"

Saira held up a hand to interrupt him.

"Oh, no. Yes. I mean, my parents would prefer me to be with someone of my culture and background. But they never objected to Jonathan, even though they didn't like him. I'm sure they'd never stop me being happy with whoever I choose. They disliked Jonathan because he was and is, an ass."

Gerhard threw his head back and laughed.

"I can't disagree with your parents. I think I'd like them, and I hope they'd like me. Perhaps they could visit you here if the pilot succeeds and you return to film the rest of the series?"

"It would be great, and I know they'd enjoy Desert Lodge and Namibia. I'd love for them to visit now, but I'm not sure they can arrange it so soon."

At the other end of the corridor, Kerri poked her head around her door.

"There you are. Come on, guys, breakfast's getting cold and time's running out."

Gerhard smiled and lifted his eyebrows at Saira in a gesture that said, "oops, they've caught us."

He closed the French doors behind them and together, they continued down the corridor toward Kerri's office.

Saira's head was spinning. Did he imply the m-word? Not the right time to think of it now. But something to compartmentalize, savor, for later when she was alone.

Even before they'd reached Kerri's office, the breakfast smells met them. The first aroma that hit Saira and made her mouth salivate was that of freshly ground coffee.

Already seated at the table were Naomi, Luca and Johan.

Johan's voice boomed as Saira and Gerhard entered the room.

"There you are. We thought you got lost."

His remark was none too subtle, made Saira laugh and blush at the same time.

Gerhard's snort revealed he shared the same sense of humor.

"I see all the Musketeers are here. I knew about the three

male Musketeers, but I can see we've gained female counterparts. Together, we should make a formidable team."

He winked at Saira, went over to the buffet and helped himself to breakfast. Luca and Johan spoke over each other as they agreed with Gerhard and expanded on the Musketeers topic. Saira was waiting for the "all for one and one for all" quote and smiled when Johan said it. Gerhard ignored their banter but took a seat at the table beside them and ate in silence while they continued to tease him.

Saira got coffee and treated herself to scrambled eggs and bacon. She'd have to watch her weight or swim more after such breakfasts, she reckoned. She took her plate and went to sit opposite Gerhard. For moments they ate in silence. Then, Johan, who had arrived first with Kerri and had finished his breakfast, pushed his plate aside.

He took a sip of coffee, leaned back in his chair and looked from one face to another before resting on Saira.

"Saira, I know this filming malarkey is your jam, but I'd like to make a suggestion. Luca and I always try to educate people about the plight of the desert elephants in Namibia. It's our mission to highlight the problems with poaching. It's one reason Luca has invested so much in the drones, which makes watching for poachers far easier."

Saira noticed all eyes were on her, and she wondered if what Johan had to say was something they'd all agreed on beforehand. It raised the importance of his announcement in her mind.

Johan linked his hands behind his head and continued.

"I don't know if Kerri told you about our wedding?"

He glanced at Kerri and Saira read his love for his wife in his eyes and smile.

"A very special ring bearer attended our wedding."

He focussed his attention on Saira again.

"Our guests went crazy for her. I thought it might be an excellent idea for you to consider using her or one of her sisters in your pilot."

Saira pushed her plate away, sat forward with her elbows on the table, curiosity relieving her of her appetite

"Go on."

"Well, I don't know if you know the story about the orphaned elephant named Naomi?"

Johan glanced at Naomi and Luca.

"I believe it was finding ellie Naomi that sealed the deal for them."

Johan laughed at his own joke.

"They don't allow guests on anti-poacher raids here. But somehow, Luca had persuaded Naomi he was different, that he wouldn't get in the way. They found the tiny ellie, who stood traumatized at her mother's dead carcass after the poachers had removed the tusks. After they got her into the back of the truck, they brought her to Desert Lodge and called me. I came to assess her and named her for Naomi.

"It's always heart breaking to see these tiny elephants grieving and mourning for their mothers. How traumatic to be introduced to death at such a young age. At the orphanage, we do what we can for them to help heal their broken hearts.

"But ellie Naomi stole everyone's heart she met. She's quite a character. So, when Kerri kindly agreed to spend the rest of her life with me, I couldn't imagine a better ring bearer than ellie Naomi."

Kerri, who'd been listening to her husband, leaned forward, tears glistening in her eyes.

"I had no idea Johan planned to use Naomi to be our ring bearer. It was a lovely surprise. Especially as my best friend..."

Kerri shoulder-bumped Naomi,

"... couldn't be here for our wedding. She was busy galivanting in Italy with her new husband. Who could blame her? I guess little ellie Naomi made up for it. Remind me to show you some of our wedding piccies later, Saira. You'll see how adorable ellie Naomi was."

Saira was only half-listening to Johan and Kerri's memories of their wedding day.

In her mind's eye, Saira could already see the tremendous impact having the ellie would make to the pilot.

When she spoke, her eyes glittered from the excitement she struggled to conceal.

"That's an incredible idea. Thank you so much, Johan and Kerri. It would definitely bring the exotic into our pilot even more than I could, by filming at Desert Lodge, which is fascinating enough already. I'll let you both have the item-by-item schedule so the ellie won't have to hang around too long while we set up the shoots."

Johan dropped his hands onto the table.

"That's very considerate of you, Saira. If you didn't suggest it, I would have insisted on it.

"On the whole, the ellies love attention. Too much social stimulation isn't the best thing because we'll release them back into the wild when they're old enough. But meanwhile, I'm hoping by featuring in the pilot, it would help raise their plight wherever you sell the program in the world."

Saira mimicked Johan's body language, sat back in her chair.

"I see your point about raising their plight, Johan. But I must confess, from a purely selfish perspective, it's a brilliant idea and will enhance what we do here."

Luca pushed his plate away and took a sip of coffee before he joined the conversation.

"I love the idea, Johan. When we discussed it last night, I thought it was brilliant then, and I think it's excellent now.

"I'm also wondering, Gerhard..."

Luca leaned back in his chair to address Gerhard from behind Johan's back.

"... it just occurred to me that another magnificent idea might be to have Rundu here. What do you think?"

Saira's heart skipped a beat. She wasn't sure how she'd feel with the cheetah around. Then she remembered Gerhard would be on site the whole time as their cameraman.

Gerhard looked at Saira through narrowed eyes, a wicked smile curling around his sensual lips.

"If Saira can handle Rundu, I'm sure he'd be delighted to join me at work."

The amusement she saw in the others' eyes told her that her smile was more of a grimace, but she was determined to be brave.

"Well, since you'll be on site the whole time, I'm sure Rundu's presence won't be a problem. Again, it's another brilliant idea, thank you, Luca. It will make for wonderful shoots with these two animals."

Johan sat forward and leaned his elbows on the table.

"Well, ellie Naomi has grown since then. We can still get her to pose with the brides and grooms, but I reckon we need to bring along one of the smaller ellies for the ring bearer role. It will be more impactful."

The logic in Johan's argument wasn't worth quibbling about.

"That sounds fantastic, Johan. I'll leave it all in your hands. You know the ellies, and you know which ones would suit us and help sell the pilot best."

Kerri looked around the table, got up.

"Right, that's our meeting concluded, and breakfast finished. Can you all leave my office now so I can get on with some work? It sounds as though we're taking things to another level and it's exciting but will make for more work for all of us."

Saira had to smile at the excitement she saw in Kerri's eyes and noticed her body was almost vibrating with it.

Everyone got up. Luca and Naomi left with their arms around each other. Johan gave Kerri a loud kiss on her mouth and a playful slap on her bottom before leaving the room.

Saira pushed her chair back.

"Come on, Gerhard. Let's go. Kerri has mountains of work to do, and it's our fault."

Saira smiled at Kerri, hugged her and walked around the table, grabbing Gerhard's hand on the way, pulling him toward the door.

Gerhard appeared to like her rough treatment of him. He slid his arm around her shoulders and marched her through the door and down the corridor, singing a song from Oklahoma Saira hadn't heard in ages.

Oh, what a beautiful morning. Oh, what a beautiful day.

He had an excellent tenor voice, and she watched his face as he sang. Why had she ever thought he was a rude, brusque oaf? Every time she thought she'd figured him out, he surprised her.

She joined in the chorus as they walked through the French doors into the brilliant Namibian sun.

Oh yes, and so it begins. What a beautiful day, indeed.

TWENTY-ONE

Saira touched the headboard and pointed her toes. She loved how the stretch put her in touch with every part of her body, a body still vibrating from Gerhard's fiery kisses last night. If they continued like this, she might explode from sexual frustration, and she imagined, so would Gerhard.

What were they, in school?

But she smiled to herself at the knowledge things would soon change. The past three weeks had been pure torture to be so near him daily and yet unable to consummate their desire for each other. Their stolen kisses here and there teased and tormented. But they'd agreed their professional relationship had to come first. However, Saira suspected by now everyone was aware of the heat between them. They could hardly hide it.

She turned her head toward the window, where the sun peeped through the tiny crack in the curtain. It seemed surreal that they'd been shooting the pilot for three weeks already. If she allowed herself to think about it, she was sure her head would spin in both directions. The amount of work she and her team had accomplished was staggering. If they carried on this way, they might miss the deadline by only a few days instead of weeks, as she'd feared after Jonathan's interference.

Naomi and Kerri's support had been crucial. Even Luca had surprised her. Despite him being torn between Italy and Namibia, his curiosity and desire to support Naomi meant he'd stayed to watch the proceedings.

Saira's sigh revealed the level of her contentment. She couldn't deny how good she felt they'd already accomplished so much. Neville was a brilliant editor. Saira had experienced excitement and sadness in equal amounts at the thought of having to hand over the final edit to MaxPix. But she couldn't dismiss the contract.

She threw the duvet aside, sat on the edge of the bed and glanced at the clock's neon red numbers. Seven o'clock. Time to get up.

Undressing and dropping her pajamas on the bed, she went to take a shower. Shampooing her hair, she thought about the schedule for the days ahead. Two weddings today, two weddings tomorrow. She'd wanted the weddings filmed in real-time, but boy did that put pressure on everybody.

Naomi and Kerri had suggested the biggest, baddest party for the crew when the filming was over. Saira couldn't blame them and was grateful they also felt the team had done an impressive job. They were the best crew she'd ever worked with, and she'd already been thinking about how to keep them for her own company, even though it was still just a dream.

Switching off the shower, she grabbed a towel and raced to answer her phone's insistent ringing.

Shona's excited voice was on the line.

"I thought you'd be in the pool. I was just about to check."

Shona laughed at her own eagerness.

"Thought I'd give you the heads up. The hairdressers and

makeup artists have arrived and are having coffee in the kitchen."

One-handed, Saira patted herself dry as she listened to Shona and then laid the towel over her head until she had the use of both hands with which to dry her hair.

"Thanks for letting me know. Has Gerhard arrived yet?"

"According to Kerri, he's on his way back from a sunrise safari and should be here in about ten minutes. The crew is having breakfast in the Lapa."

Saira used her free hand to open the wardrobe and drawers, pulling out clothes as she listened to Shona.

"I know the first wedding is only at two, Saira, but you wanted film footage of the bride getting ready? You still want that?"

Saira jumped on one leg, trying to get her foot into her pants.

"Oh, yes. It would make no sense having footage of the couples before the wedding and then not having any of them getting ready. See you in the Lapa in five. Could you herd the hairdressers and makeup artists there too, please? That way we'll all be in one place when Gerhard arrives, and we can start straight away."

"Sure. Techie extraordinaire, Mike and his team have already set up lights and equipment in the room we'll be using for the getting-ready shots."

Saira thought again about how lucky she was to have Shona and such a dynamic dream-team working with her on this important project.

"Excellent. Later."

Because of her limited fashion choices, dressing each day had been easy. Her functional, semi-smart wardrobe was comfortable. She towel-dried her hair while looking at her image in the mirror. Her navy linen trousers and matching sleeveless

T-shirt with the pink flamingo on the front were perfect for today. Plus, she'd been told navy complimented her light mocha coloring, and she had to agree. Her hair had grown a little longer than she liked to wear it, but it meant her hair was now wavy rather than curly. She ran her hands through her hair to loosen and elongate the waves and to make sure it was almost dry. Everything dried fast in the Namibian heat, including her hair. She applied minimal makeup and satisfied she'd done the best with her appearance, grabbed her bag, keys and phone before marching out the door.

Saira arrived at the Lapa at the same time as Shona, who trailed hairdressers and makeup artists. Following behind them came Naomi and Kerri walking on either side of Gerhard. They appeared to be in the middle of a serious conversation.

But Saira saw the excitement showing in Naomi's eyes and knew this was another of Naomi's dreams come true. The rigmarole Naomi had gone through to become a registrar so she could officiate at the Desert Lodge weddings herself was inspirational. Saira knew the couples getting married over the next two days, appreciated that Naomi would marry them. It seemed to give extra validation coming from the owner of such a prestigious lodge. A shrewd marketing move, Saira thought.

As she looked up, her eyes locked with Gerhard's. She felt heat spreading throughout her body and for a moment, had trouble breathing. How could she forget his heated kisses last night when he'd accompanied her to her suite? Beneath the kisses, were the promise of so much passion. The situation between them was becoming ridiculous. They were consenting adults, and she was in love with him. From what he'd said and shown her, she had to believe he felt the same way—another reason to look forward to next week. Then, they'd only have the editing and production to complete.

A thrilling in her belly made her gasp a little as she imagined them together. She could almost feel his hands all over her body, and she shivered with the pleasure of it.

Gerhard was moving toward her as though he was being pulled by a magnet. He stopped mere inches away from her. Before his eyes fixed on hers again, they traveled over her body and came to rest on her lips.

"You look lovely as always, Saira."

Would she ever get used to the way her name sounded in his mouth?

"You don't look so bad yourself, Gerhard."

She blinked to rid herself of the pictures of them together in her mind.

"Are you ready for the main events?"

Gerhard moved closer and cupped her elbow in his large, warm hand. Sparks licked her skin at his touch.

"I've been ready since the moment I saw you, Saira."

An involuntary giggle escaped her.

"I'm talking about the weddings, silly."

"So am I. Ours."

Saira's heart pounded against her ribcage. Did she hear him right?

Gerhard must have felt her stiffen under his hand because his eyes showed immediate concern. She could see he thought he'd offended her.

But before either of them could say anything, Kerri arrived like a whirlwind of energy.

"Right guys, are we ready to get the show on the road? Techie Mike told me everything was in place. Would you like to check it for yourself, Gerhard?"

He continued to look at Saira as he answered Kerri.

"Yes, I was just trying to persuade Saira to come with me."

Kerri placed a hand on each of their shoulders and pushed them ahead of her.

"Right then, let's go. Time isn't our friend."

She marched them through the crowd, toward the French doors. Flinging open the doors, Kerri steered Saira and Gerhard down the corridor to the office that had once belonged to Naomi. Now, the staff had transformed the room. All the paraphernalia of a top-notch beauty salon was on display, ready to be used. Mike and his team were already testing and re-testing equipment, making sure the lights were all working, and there was enough space for everyone who needed to be here. Saira couldn't help the excitement building inside her as she watched her team getting ready.

This was it. This was the start of her dream.

She watched as Gerhard went to check every camera angle. He ensured everything was set up correctly, that the x's where people were supposed to stay, were in the right places.

Satisfied, he looked up at Kerri.

"Can we get those who'll work here into this room, please?"

Without a word, Kerri texted Shona to get everyone to the beauty room.

"I'm still sorry we couldn't offer something at the Spa, Saira. But as we've booked it out, this room was our next best option."

Saira touched Kerri's arm to reassure her.

"This room is wonderful, Kerri. This is a much bigger room than the ones at the Spa. And the light through these lovely large windows is perfect."

Kerri nodded, satisfied she'd done the right thing to offer the room.

As they waited, she made sure there were enough champagne and glasses for the brides, the mothers and the bridesmaids to enjoy while they were being pampered.

Saira stood to the side and watched as everything happening with expert precision. This shoot felt by far the most professional she'd ever attended. Magic was about to happen here. It already pervaded the air around them.

Saira had full confidence that Gerhard understood the tone of the shots she wanted. It was essential to pull the viewers into the room, and although they'd be watching the show, she wanted them to feel as though they were here. She wanted the excitement and anticipation to reach out and touch the hearts of the viewers.

A cacophony of excited female voices grew louder as the women followed Shona to get ready.

Saira waited until everyone was in the room before she encouraged them to be as natural in front of the cameras as possible. She knew it would happen sooner than they could imagine and would give them half an hour to get used to the cameras being so close to them.

Meanwhile, she couldn't keep the smile off her face as she watched Kerri making small talk and pouring champagne. Hairdressers and nail artists worked on nails and pedicures.

Saira jumped a little when Gerhard appeared next to her, his arm touching her shoulder.

"It's exciting, isn't it? Our first project together. I hope it won't be our last, Saira."

His blue eyes bored into hers as he said her name.

She loved that his thoughts reflected hers. She'd been thinking along the same lines and wondered how she'd approach the subject with him when the time came. How would their working together affect his life and work in Namibia? She couldn't help worrying about it.

Gerhard appeared to read the concern in Saira's eyes. He lifted her hand and kissed her fingers.

"But let's discuss it at a more appropriate time, shall we?"

Saira nodded as Gerhard continued.

"Johan has texted to say the ellies have arrived, and they're ensconced in the stables behind the hangar. Do you want to see them?"

But just as Saira was about to respond, they heard the heavy-footed, fast treads of Johan's footsteps as he approached. Their heads whipped toward the door as he marched into the room. He saw them and rushed over, agitation clear in his widened eyes.

Trying to whisper, his voice broke.

"Guys, we have a problem."

As though Kerri could sense her husband's distress from across the room where she'd been chatting to their guests, she arrived at his side and touched his arm.

"What's wrong?"

Johan took several deep breaths. He gripped Kerri's hand and turned to Gerhard.

"You put Rundu in the small stables, didn't you?"

Gerhard put an arm around Saira's shoulders and drew her into his body, as though by doing so, he was protecting Rundu. She could feel his heart thumping against his ribcage and knew his actions were unconscious. For moments, she worried what others would think, but then berated herself. Even though the cheetah's presence had made her feel uncomfortable, Rundu was Gerhard's baby. He clearly cared for the animal. Something was obviously wrong with Rundu.

Gerhard's voice sounded guttural with dread.

"Yes. Why? What's happened?"

Johan pulled a hand through his hair and again took several breaths before he spoke.

"Well man, he's not there. I went to check on him to see if he needed water, and even though the stable doors were closed, when I opened them, he wasn't there. The room was empty. He's not some kind of Houdini, is he?"

Saira noticed Johan's weak smile as he tried to make light of the situation.

But the hard muscles in Gerhard's body tensed.

"No, he's not. Let's go."

He grabbed Saira's hand, and she allowed him to pull her after him as he followed Johan and Kerri from the room.

TWENTY-TWO

Nothing was as empty as space previously occupied by someone we love, Saira thought, even a much-loved animal.

She stood in the doorway as Johan and Kerri followed Gerhard into the small stable that should have contained Rundu. Not only was the space empty, but it felt cold without Rundu's presence.

Saira wouldn't have thought it of a cheetah.

She noticed Kerri watching her husband, at a loss for once to help.

Johan paced while running his hand through his hair.

"Someone had to come in and take him. But who would do such a thing? And how? We were at the other end of the stables unloading the ellies. I can't believe we wouldn't have heard or seen someone coming in here."

Johan's voice sounded hoarse with remorse and desperation.

Gerhard leaned against the wall, his head in his hand.

"I thought he'd be safe here. I was thinking of bringing him with me, he's tame enough. But it might have freaked out everyone who doesn't know him. I couldn't risk it. Not with so many people around."

He pulled away from the wall and faced Johan, his hands by his side.

"I'm not blaming you, Johan. Please don't blame yourself. But I think you're right. It smacks of a professional job."

Luca and Naomi arrived, looking frazzled. In typical Italian style, Luca kissed Gerhard on both cheeks and hugged him tight.

"We'll do everything we can to get Rundu back, I promise, mio amico. I'm so sorry. It was my suggestion to involve him in the filming. We've spent so much time, effort and energy on anti-poaching efforts. It feels like this is in retaliation for some of the work we've done. Whoever took Rundu must know how much he means to you, to all of us. He grew up here."

The pain in Gerhard's eyes was raw.

"No, Luca, don't blame yourself. I put Rundu in here. I did this to him."

Kerri went to Gerhard and snaked her arm around his waist to console him.

Naomi touched his arm as she looked up at him.

"Gerhard, don't do that to yourself. No one could have known this would happen, including you. Luca is right. We'll do everything we can to get him back as soon as possible."

Gerhard looked from Luca to Naomi to Saira, where she'd remained standing in the doorway.

His eyes were darker than Saira had ever seen them.

"Thanks, guys. I know you, and all the guys in the anti-poaching squad will do everything you can."

He rubbed his hands over his eyes and let out an audible breath, squared his shoulders.

"Let's go. We have a wedding to shoot. I trust you guys with my life. I know you'll find him."

He walked toward Saira, took her hand and left the stable with a last backward glance.

Saira felt the tension in his body and squeezed his hand.

So much for hiding their feelings. Hadn't Gerhard just announced it by his actions? Saira waited for a reaction from the others, but none came, and Gerhard led her back toward the main building.

Kerri ran up to them from behind and slipped her arm through Gerhard's. Saira mimicked her actions, drawing his arm through hers on her side. It was probably better to appear supportive in a friend sort of way.

Back in the beauty room, Shona and the inimitable Mary appeared to have everything under control. No one else seemed aware of the crisis, and things had progressed. Hair was being done, nails were being painted, pedicures were waiting to dry, and champagne had been drunk.

Saira thought the champagne and its effects may have something to do with the relaxed atmosphere that met them as they entered the room.

Gerhard went over to techie Mike and checked the footage. He seemed satisfied, and Saira saw him give a thumbs-up to his team. All the same, Gerhard moved a few cameras around and continued to shoot from several angles.

Saira couldn't help admiring Gerhard's ability to focus on the work at hand when his mind had to be on Rundu. The man had formidable powers of concentration.

Meanwhile, Kerri had arranged for drinks and refreshments. The waiters had placed everything on the sideboard in the morning. Now, waiters arrived with food and laid out a delicious buffet lunch for everyone present.

Saira noticed Gerhard filming people dressed in white toweling robes, as they helped themselves to the food. She loved the informality of the shots. In her mind's eye, she saw the last cut and how great it all fit together. Edits made her think of Neville, and it surprised her to find him sitting in the corner. He was scribbling notes on a pad as he made editing decisions while he watched the filming. He seemed to know in what sequence Gerhard would set up his shots. Saira had never seen an editor working in quite this way before, but it made perfect sense because of the restrictions and restraints on their time.

Again, she cursed Jonathan under her breath for the time he'd cost them.

As Saira watched, she made brief voice notes to herself on her phone and dreamed again about having this team working for her in her own company.

Beside Neville, Vince sat at a small table, scribbling the next sets of storyboards as fast as he could. Saira watched them for moments before turning her attention back to Gerhard. The only minor thing that gave away Gerhard's stressed frame of mind was the tiny tick in his jaw.

On one side of the room, the team had built screens. The smart lighting design team had rigged the lights in such a way that the flimsy material covering the screens obscured the bride and her bridesmaids as they got dressed. The glimpses of their bodies through the screens were alluring. Tall vases with wavy African grasses and white lilies decorated the area around the screens and made it look even more romantic.

While some people were still having their lunch, others were already getting dressed, and Gerhard's team was filming them all.

Neville would have fun editing all the different footage, Saira thought.

She looked up as Johan and Luca followed Naomi into the room. From the look on their faces, they had no good news regarding Rundu's whereabouts. Saira glanced at Gerhard, but he seemed absorbed in his work. Instead, she joined the friends at the buffet.

Her eyes asked before she did.

"I can see from your faces you don't have good news yet? Did you find any signs near the stables that could help to track Rundu down?"

Johan was piling sausages onto his plate, but he glanced at Saira as he spoke.

"That's what's so weird. It appears Rundu's vanished into the ether. There are no tracks. But perhaps it's not surprising, as the ground in front of the stables is extremely hard. If it were sandier, we could find tracks. But too many vehicles had come in and out today using that stretch of the road, and that makes it difficult to find any unusual car or truck tracks or Rundu's spoors. Whoever took him, may even have tranquilized him, and carried him out. I've spoken with Khwai, who, as you know, is the best tracker at Desert Lodge, and I would venture the entire Namibia. If he can't find Rundu, no one can."

Johan looked crestfallen, and Saira got the impression he'd give anything to be out there with the anti-poacher squad looking for Rundu. But one look at Kerri told her it was Kerri's wishes that he ate something first before going off again. It made sense why he was piling food onto his plate and eating as fast as he could, not bothering to find somewhere to sit down.

Saira knew Johan wanted to support Kerri. She could see how torn he was. Her heart went out to him.

But Kerri understood her husband, and while Saira watched, Kerri touched his arm and whispered, "It's okay, honey. After lunch, you go. Do what you must do. You need not be here."

The way Johan's shoulders went from slumping to straight revealed his relief.

Meanwhile, Luca had joined Johan and stood beside him with his plate of food, refusing to leave his friend's side during lunch and continuing to offer supportive words. But Saira knew

Luca wouldn't be able to help Johan after lunch. Luca would never leave Naomi at this stage.

Once again, Saira felt gratitude swelling in her chest for these fantastic friends and colleagues. They made her think no matter what challenges they faced, they would succeed, together.

As she glanced at the time, Shona appeared at her side.

"It's time for everyone to get to the wedding site. Khwai got in touch before he left with the others to look for Rundu. He's arranged with some waiters to drive the guests to the site instead of the guards. Already, several trips had taken guests there. Now, we're ready to take the bridesmaids, Naomi, Luca, the extra camera equipment and Gerhard and his team. I've already informed Gerhard, and they're ready to go. Mike has set up the technical equipment at the site this morning, and he'd left two of the grips there to guard it against wild animals attacking anything."

Saira smiled and nodded.

"Thanks, Shona. Yes, Mike told me what they'd done. I'm impressed with everyone's commitment and efficiency on this project. And I love the idea that all the weddings are taking place on the same site where Naomi and Luca, and Kerri and Johan got married. It seems appropriate that our weddings should be there too. Who can resist a desert wedding? There are so many beach weddings. But I've not seen many taking place in the desert. I'm sure our audiences will fall in love with the exoticness of it all. I love how hard everyone has worked to make our site so stunning. The plants and roses from Desert Lodge's gardens and the arch where the ceremony is to take place is the most romantic thing I've ever seen."

It was Shona's turn to nod and smile.

"I couldn't agree more. One day, when it's my turn to get married, I'd love it to be here."

"We'll make it happen. All you have to do is to find the right guy."

They laughed at Saira's words before she fell into work mode again.

"I've asked Kerri to stay with the bride and her parents, and I know Mary has arranged with a member of our team to stay with the wedding truck to take them to the site when we give the go-ahead."

Saira had never worked with an assistant director like Mary before. The woman was a force of nature. Mary was another member of Saira's dream-team she'd earmarked to work in her company when the time came.

Mary and Shona led the bridesmaids out of the room. Their heels clicked down the corridor, through the French doors where the next bridal party and their guests had congregated. They applauded as the bridesmaids stepped into the Namibian sun that seemed to cast a blessing of its own on them.

Saira returned to the room. She took a last look around to make sure everything and everyone that should be gone, had gone. Then, she left and bounced through the kitchen, the shortest route to the trucks, where she joined Gerhard, Mike and the team to drive to the wedding site ahead of the bridesmaids.

As they drove nearer to the site, Saira smiled at the colorful dresses of the guests, so stark against the red sand dunes.

Kerri had asked several staff members to help with ushering duties. The European staff were in their black and white uniforms, but several members of the native staff had dressed in traditional Herero costume. They looked not only colorful but also regal. Genius idea.

Saira reminded herself to thank Kerri for the inspiration. She made a quick voice note on her phone. They should do more of this at the next weddings.

Everyone was in place. The bridesmaids stood in front of the congregation. The best man was fiddling with the rings in his pocket, and the bridegroom was mopping his brow. But all heads turned when the decorated wedding vehicle arrived, and they watched as Kerri helped the bride and her parents to step down from the truck.

Saira couldn't help the tears that slipped from her eyes as the San choir's beautiful voices sang from beneath a cluster of dark green trees nearby. She watched with pride and excitement how Gerhard and his team continued to shoot the wedding ceremony from many angles. Some guys operated handheld cameras, others wielded heavy film equipment, and one of Gerhard's team flew a drone that filmed the proceedings from above.

Once again, she noticed Neville sitting at the back scribbling on his pad. She knew she'd have the edits by next week. The man was a marvel.

Saira scanned the faces surrounding her. They carried looks of joy and awe. Satisfaction rose inside her. It was precisely the reaction she wanted to inspire in viewers. If everyone's response here showed what she could expect from viewers, she was sure the pilot would be successful.

Naomi, looking rather more like a high priestess than a registrar, did a fantastic job of marrying the couple and too soon, the ceremony was over.

Saira hadn't thought she'd enjoy the wedding as much as she did. But even more astonishing, she was looking forward to the rest of the weddings with enthusiasm. When she saw the animated expressions on her team's faces, she realized they felt the same.

Her eyes found Gerhard's tall, straight figure. He was moving backward as he continued to shoot the couple walking down the carpeted aisle. Rose petals that guests threw at the couple, fell on him and stuck to his blonde hair. But she couldn't read his expression. A slight frown of concentration appeared between his eyes.

Again, she wondered if she'd heard him correctly before? Did he really say what she thought he'd said about taking their relationship forward? His words had caught her off guard. Marriage, even though expected of her, wasn't something she'd thought of for herself, at least not soon. It seemed something far away, something she would have to sacrifice for, something she'd have to give up her career for and an enormous part of herself.

Would marrying Gerhard be a sacrifice? It didn't feel like it. Instead, the thought of spending the rest of her life with him filled her with excitement. It was a future she'd never imagined for herself.

The sounds of the San choir clapping, stomping their feet so their ankle bracelets jingled while they sang a joyous song, combined with the couple's laughter. Their jubilation pulled Saira back into the present.

The couple had forgotten the cameras. Their happiness was palpable. Shared joy had transformed them into being even more beautiful than they were at the start of their wedding ceremony. They smiled at each other, at their guests, waved and boarded the decorated convertible truck that stood ready to return them to Desert Lodge. Gerhard followed and got in the truck, sat opposite them and continued to film their beaming faces. The drone operator followed Gerhard.

Saira and the rest of the team, including Naomi, Luca and Kerri, got into the next truck and overtook the bride and groom to get to Desert Lodge before them. Kerri had arranged a champagne party for each couple and their guests in the Lapa following their weddings. She wanted to get back as soon as possible to make sure everything was running according to her plans, especially since most of her staff were at the wedding.

Everyone was looking forward to the big party Kerri had scheduled for Sunday evening after they'd married all the couples. She'd invited everyone, and excitement about the party had overtaken even the paying guests at Desert Lodge. For now, though, each wedding party would have a chance to enjoy a get-together with their friends and family. Saira thought it was perfect and again, she felt lucky to be part of such a great team.

TWENTY-THREE

Driving up to the big old house that made up the main building of Desert Lodge, Saira saw Johan's towering figure. He was sitting at one of the wrought-iron tables under the porch outside the kitchen. The way he held his body, she could see he was waiting for them.

Saira closed her eyes, and even though she wasn't the praying kind, she prayed it was good news about Rundu. But the foreboding feeling in the pit of her stomach said she was wrong.

Johan, who'd been reading something on his phone, looked up when he heard the drone of their vehicle approaching. He got up, and by how he slumped his shoulders, Saira knew her gut instinct was right; it wasn't good news.

Although they'd overtaken the wedding truck, Saira knew the newlyweds and Gerhard weren't too far behind. But she couldn't see them when she glanced back. It wouldn't be useful for anything to upset Gerhard. There were still more weddings to film.

As soon as their truck stopped, she jumped down and

rushed to Johan. Kerri, Luca and Naomi followed on her heels, as eager to hear Johan's news as she was.

The crew member with the handheld camera who'd joined them on the truck also got down. He disappeared around the corner of the building. Saira knew he'd film the newlyweds as they arrived and walked to the Lapa for their champagne celebration.

She reached Johan first, took his elbow and steered him toward the kitchen door, looking over her shoulder to make sure the others were following. As they stepped into the kitchen, Kerri suggested they have coffee here and talked away from the guests and the crew. Saira felt grateful for Kerri's sensitivity. She appeared to understand only too well it wouldn't be a good idea to put more stress on Gerhard. Everyone depended on him.

When they sat down at the table, a waiter served coffee and offered freshly made chocolate chip cookies. Everyone watched Johan as he took a sip of his coffee.

He put his cup down and cleared his throat.

"Well, it's very perplexing. We still don't understand who could have taken Rundu. We also don't know how they did it. Khwai had been through the place with the thoroughness of a wise tracker. But even he couldn't find a single spoor that showed Rundu had left the stable. His food and water bowls are still there, and whoever took him, left his soft toys behind Gerhard had brought to keep him occupied. But of Rundu himself, there is no sign or spoor. We've also checked the footage from the CCTV cameras Auntie Elsa had had installed outside the kitchen a few years ago. It happened when poachers tried to steal ellie Naomi-I'm sure you guys remember? But Rundu's stable is just outside the camera's range."

Johan looked at the surrounding faces. The way he lifted his right eyebrow revealed his thoughts before he spoke the words on his mind.

"So, some opportunist was very lucky to find Rundu and took him, or someone who knows Desert Lodge well, and knew how to miss the cameras, had taken him."

Luca leaned his elbows on the table and steepled his fingers together under his chin.

"Or... Could it be someone's been following Gerhard? Who would be his enemy? But maybe there is such a person, si? If someone was looking for a cheetah, surely they would have taken Rundu from Gerhard's home? It's too much of a coincidence if you ask me. Whoever took Rundu had to know Gerhard would bring him to Desert Lodge today, and who knew that, other than us? This sounds personal to me. Sounds like someone has a grudge against Gerhard and I'll bet they've been following him. When they saw him putting Rundu in the stables, they took their chance."

Naomi nodded. She'd been watching her husband as he spoke.

Now, she turned her attention to everyone else.

"I agree. It feels like that to me, too. But I can't imagine who could have a problem with Gerhard. He's a little curt when you first meet him, but he has a heart of pure gold when you get to know him, a real softie. And he's done so much for so many people."

She turned to Johan.

"But you mentioned Khwai couldn't find any spoor? Where is he now?"

"Ah, yes. That reminds me-Khwai has taken one of Rundu's soft toys and has gone to see if the hunting dogs can find him that way. I wasn't sure it would work because dogs usually avoid cheetahs. But then I remembered those dogs are tough. Khwai once cornered a wounded lion with them. So, finding Rundu shouldn't be a problem for them. If anyone can find that cheetah, it's Khwai. I've asked that he wait until the wedding party is in the Lapa for their champagne celebration before bringing out the dogs. We don't want to frighten the guests."

Johan's laugh at his own joke sounded forced, but it broke the tension, somewhat.

Everyone whipped their heads toward the noise at the door when Shona burst into the kitchen.

"Here, you all are!"

She stopped in her tracks when she saw their strained faces.

"What happened?"

Saira indicated for Shona to take a seat next to her at the table. She brought Shona up to speed on the Rundu situation and swore her to secrecy.

Two frown lines deepened across Shona's forehead, showing her level of distress at the thought someone had abducted Rundu.

"I'm sorry about Rundu, and I'm glad that such an amazing tracker as Khwai is out looking for him. I've heard so much about him, and I'm sure he'll find Rundu soon. I mean, if he could find a smoke signal in the desert...?"

She looked around the table for agreement from the others.

Saira nodded.

She remembered how impressed she'd been with Khwai's skills. Guests and members of her crew who didn't know him said they'd suspected he had magical powers to have found her and Gerhard at their broken-down plane in the desert.

But Saira noticed the way Shona's eyes shone and the trouble she had concealing her smile. It showed her mind had already moved away from Khwai and his abilities.

Shona's voice revealed her excitement about the real live tame cheetah and ellies nearby.

"How exciting to have animals in our show. I didn't realize that's why they're here. Why didn't we use them at the first wedding?"

Saira explained she'd discussed it with Mary and Gerhard. But they'd agreed it was wiser to have a clean run first before introducing the animals. The couples could pose with ellie Naomi and Rundu afterward.

Saira didn't want to think the thought, but it deposited itself unbidden into her mind-if they found Rundu in time.

Kerri glanced at her watch.

"Right, guys. It's time we get back to our duties. Naomi and I will pop into the Lapa to congratulate the newlyweds. You lot scatter."

Everyone smiled at Kerri's command.

She got up and draped her arms around Johan's neck from behind and kissed him on top of his head.

"Don't worry, honey. I'm sure Khwai will help you guys succeed. Just keep looking until you find Rundu, okay?"

Naomi followed Kerri's example and got up. With a last air kiss at Luca, she followed Kerri through the middle door. Saira knew the women would walk down the corridor through the building out the French doors at the other end. It was the easiest route to the Lapa.

She nodded to the men before she and Shona followed in the other women's footsteps through the middle door to the beauty room.

The level of activity resembled that of the morning. The exceptions now were that the next bride and her entourage were being pampered. Gerhard and his team were busy filming and seemed not to notice when Saira and Shona entered the room. But Saira saw by how he moved his body, he was aware of her presence.

She resisted the overpowering urge to go to him, to touch him, to comfort him. But she didn't want to upset him further about Rundu's disappearance. Instead, she watched as Shona put on an Oscar-winning performance of being cheerful and professional.

When the waiters brought in new refreshments, replacing those from earlier on the sideboard, Saira walked up to Gerhard.

"You haven't had a proper break yet. I think it's time you took one. I know you've scheduled a kind of rotation with your team, but I feel it's essential that each of you take a longer break now. It's almost five o'clock. It's been a long, hard day and we have another wedding to shoot. Come, have something to eat with me?"

Her fingertips skimmed over his free hand, and again, she felt the thrill of heat between them.

Gerhard looked down at her, his eyes softening despite the tension frown lines between his eyebrows.

"That's the best offer I've had all day. You're right, we've arranged a rotation system, and each of us has snatched a few minutes' break here and there. But I agree, we should take a longer break before the next wedding. I'll organize it with my team. Stay where you are. I'll be right back."

He glanced at the food being brought in as he went to talk to each of his team members. Saira saw them synchronizing watches and swapping positions, so each camera remained staffed. She couldn't help smiling at the thought they looked like they were in some kind of spy movie.

Then Gerhard took long strides as he walked back to her. He surprised her by taking her hand and leading her out of the room. She'd expected them to load up on food at the sideboard with everyone else. But Gerhard continued walking up the corridor to the kitchen. He must have called ahead because as they entered the kitchen, Chef handed them a picnic basket.

"Where are we going, Gerhard? There's no time for a picnic."

Gerhard said nothing. Instead, he winked and smiled at her

and continued to lead her out of the kitchen. They turned left. Saira had never gone that way. They walked around the building, through a gate and into a stunning little secluded garden she'd never seen before. Gerhard steered her toward a tiny summerhouse and invited her to sit down on a bench in the shade.

The heat seemed concentrated in this compact space. With it, the aromas of the plants and flowers surrounding them were intense and exotic to her nose. Saira glanced around at the stunning red and orange desert flowers that grew at the edges of the small lawn in front of the summer house. Bees and cicadas tried to out-buzz each other, and little doves cooed in the branches of the trees behind them. The experience was almost surreal. From here, they couldn't see or hear any of the excitement of the filming or the first wedding party's celebrations in the Lapa.

But Gerhard's presence was too distracting. Saira couldn't look away from him. She watched as he opened the picnic basket and offered her a delicious-looking sandwich on a plate. The bread smelled so fresh, she had the impression Chef must have just baked it. But before Saira took a bite, Gerhard poured ginger beer into two tall glasses. Not only was the picnic a lovely surprise, but Saira couldn't help being impressed that he'd remembered her favorite drink.

Gerhard offered her a glass and clinked his against hers before taking a sip. His sigh sounded contented as he leaned back against the bench's backrest, his free arm trailing along its edge behind her.

"This is nice, isn't it?"

Saira was oh-so aware of the warmth coming from his arm behind her neck. She swallowed the sip she took and felt as though she was swallowing down her sudden racing pulse, too.

She tried to keep her voice level and as natural as possible.

"It is, and it feels like a celebration. What are we celebrating?"

He turned to her, his blue eyes intent on hers as he took another sip.

"I'm celebrating meeting you, Saira. You've been on my mind every day since I first met you. And I want to celebrate you for the rest of our lives together."

Saira's heart hammered so hard against her ribcage, she wondered if he could hear it.

She watched in a daze as he put his glass down near his feet, took the plate and drink from her hands and put those in the picnic basket. Then he took her hands in his.

She licked her lips and shivered at his touch and saw his pupils dilate at her reaction to him.

"I mean it, Saira. I'm serious about you. We both know we have something rare, something special between us. It doesn't come along often. I don't want to regret it for the rest of my life if we don't follow through. Do you?"

His voice was so soft, so sincere, so intimate, it sent tingles through her entire body, and her heart swelled with love for this beautiful man.

Saira swallowed at the sudden lump in her throat.

No one had ever spoken to her like this. No one had ever looked at her like this. Until this moment, she hadn't known she'd craved such attention. This experience confirmed for her it was something she wanted more of, and she wanted it from Gerhard. Yes, their physical attraction was undeniable. But what she felt for him was profound. The relief to know he felt the same, was enormous. Every fiber of her being told her if she didn't pursue this with Gerhard, she would always regret it. There would be no one else. How could there be? No one else would ever compare.

There wasn't a thing she didn't love about him. Yes, he was

physically attractive. But she loved his heart, his kindness, his compassion, his honesty, his passion for this desert country where he lived, and his artists' soul. But mostly, she loved that he felt like home.

She tried to still her galloping heart and find the right words to express the enormity of what she felt.

"I feel exactly as you do, Gerhard. Who knew this existed in the world? We're blessed and I don't want to let it go, either."

Gerhard cupped her face in his hands and his soft kiss pulled her into a vortex of yearning.

They moved closer to one another as though drawn by an invisible force. His kisses deepened, and as their tongues became a duet, their passion ignited them both.

He smelled of the plastic from the cameras he'd been working with all day. The desert smells mixed with the familiar soft fragrance of his aftershave. That, and his kisses, made Saira feel dizzy with desire.

It took tremendous effort, but she gently pushed him away.

His eyes flew open, and she read his confusion there.

"As much as I love kissing you, Gerhard, now isn't the time to get carried away. We only have half an hour, and I'm concerned that you eat something and have the energy to film the next wedding."

Gerhard sat back. His sigh told of his relief when he understood her words.

"Oh, if that's all you're worried about, then let's eat. I think I'll need energy later for more than filming a wedding."

He winked at her as he handed back her plate with the delicious-looking sandwich and glass of ginger beer. Then he helped himself to the rest of the sandwiches in the picnic basket.

Saira laughed at his exaggerated eagerness to get the meal over and done with. She knew he was teasing her but suspected he was famished. It had been a grueling day. And it wasn't over yet. But she didn't want to spoil the moment, so mimicked him as she chomped down on her sandwich and chewed as fast as she could, pretending to compete with him. She couldn't stop giggling, though, and noticed how his eyes continued to hold a mischievous twinkle. The grin that spread over his face didn't show any sign of disappearing anytime soon.

Gerhard finished his meal before her. He continued to smile at her, his eyes dancing with serious intentions, as he placed his hand on her thigh. His hand felt warm and somehow familiar on her leg. It sent heat into her core. It was a good thing she'd been sitting down because the desire he'd awoken through his kisses still thrummed through her body. What was he doing to her?

Gerhard pretended not to notice her reaction to his touch and gave her thigh a squeeze.

"I'm serious, Saira. I don't want to ever let you go. It's a torment to wait longer to be with you."

Saira swallowed the last bite of her sandwich and took a sip of her drink while she thought about what to say. Then, she realized if she and Gerhard were going forward with their relationship, she had to be herself with him. It would be a challenge, she knew. It wasn't in her nature to let her guard down, but then again, she'd never felt this safe with anyone apart from her parents.

Well, there was Peter... friends counted, didn't they?

But Saira didn't think her relationship with her friend held any relevancy over this soul connection she felt with Gerhard.

She put her glass down.

"I feel the same. It's been torture being so close to you all this time and unable to-"

Before Saira could say anything more, Gerhard's hand moved higher up her thigh and skimmed her private pleasure.

She watched him doing it and knew he did so on purpose but couldn't hold back the gasp the fire of his touch elicited.

A slow, sexy smile curled around his sensual lips.

"I see. Glad it's not only me then. What should we do about it?"

"What did you have in mind?"

Gerhard stared off into the distance for a moment, as though he was contemplating her question.

He turned those blue-blue eyes back on hers again.

"Do you think after the second wedding when everyone will congregate in the Lapa for the champagne party, they'll miss us?"

"But I thought while Luca was here, evenings alone was out?"

"Saira, don't torture me. I think we've spent quite enough evenings with Luca. I'll come to your room half an hour after we arrive back from the desert."

Saira didn't trust her voice, so nodded.

Her heart was beating so fast she feared it would pop out of her chest. She couldn't stop thinking about what it would be like to be with Gerhard in that way. But from deep inside her, she called up the control to wait until the evening before pursuing more pleasures with Gerhard. Instead, she leaned forward and put their empty plates and glasses back inside the picnic basket.

Gerhard stood, pulled her to her feet. His hand on the small of her back pressed her against his body. She loved how they molded into each other. His hardness pressed against her stomach. His eyes were wild as he threaded his fingers through her hair and kissed her as though his life depended on it. But just as suddenly as he'd started, he stopped.

He pulled away and stared deep into her eyes.

"God, Saira. You drive me wild. I can't wait for later."

She loved the hardness of him against her body and nestled further into him, resting her head on his muscular chest for a moment. His heart pounded against her ear as fast as she imagined hers did.

Gerhard smiled, bent down to pick up the picnic basket, took her hand and led her back toward the kitchen.

"This wedding will be difficult to get through. Let's get it over with. I don't suppose we could hurry them up, somehow?"

Saira loved this light, humorous side of him as much as the more sincere, passionate side.

As they came around the corner, they saw Johan, Khwai, a group of anti-poacher guards and several enormous dogs around the stables.

Gerhard stopped in his tracks.

"Are they doing what I think they're doing?"

Saira felt his body stiffen and hoped the reminder of Rundu's disappearance didn't disturb Gerhard too much. She sensed how much he wanted to approach the group. But she admired his willpower. Instead, he continued to walk to the kitchen. He opened the door for her, put the picnic basket on the table and waved their thanks to Chef.

Gerhard's graceful movements looked as though it was a dance. Saira couldn't tear her eyes away from him. She couldn't wait for them to be together later. But also because the reminder just now about Rundu's abduction concerned her.

Back in the beauty room, concentrating on work seemed impossible. But things appeared to run smoothly.

Once again, Saira couldn't help feeling grateful for her fantastic team.

What could go wrong with them around?

TWENTY-FOUR

The wedding site was even more beautiful and picturesque than earlier in the day. The sun sat low on the horizon and had shredded the pale blue sky with its unique red, orange and pink magic. Tall wooden poles surrounded the site. Large iron bowls at the top, in which fires danced with joy appropriate to the occasion, further enhanced the magical ambience. The massive red dunes around them had cast mysterious shadows among the chairs the guests already occupied. Excitement flowed from them almost like the waves of mist over the dunes in the morning.

The tiniest ellie Saira had ever seen followed Johan up the aisle. The gasps of surprise and pleasure from the guests surrounding her mirrored her own. Johan led the ellie to stand beside the bridegroom and his best man. The baby elephant's tiny trunk curled this way and that and touched Johan's hand as though he needed reassurance from someone he knew and trusted.

Perhaps because it was their second wedding of the day, or more likely, because of the ellie, Saira felt everyone seemed far more relaxed at this wedding than at the previous one.

As the bride arrived, the choir of San singers sang their beautiful wedding song again, swaying rhythmically as they did so. All the guests turned to watch the bride walk up the aisle beside her father. Her eyes widened, and her smile broadened when she noticed the tiny ellie who was their ring bearer.

Saira saw Gerhard and his team were filming more of the guests' reactions as they watched the ellie.

In Saira's mind, she could see how these shots would fit into the pilot. Johan's suggestion to have such an adorable ring bearer at the weddings, was inspired and perfect. She felt almost sorry for the first wedding party that they'd missed the ellie magic. But she knew they'd get their turn to pose with both ellie Naomi and this tiny one.

Once again, newly appointed registrar, Naomi Armati, impressed everyone as she did a superb job marrying the couple who'd written their own vows.

Saira made a note. She'd love their own vows when she got married to Gerhard.

What? Did she really just think about marrying Gerhard? She couldn't believe her thoughts had gone in that direction almost without her permission. But even more surprising, she didn't think writing their own vows was a weird idea. She'd so often heard when it was the one, the commitment wasn't an issue. Only a few weeks ago, commitment to anyone, let alone marriage, wasn't something she'd contemplated. Now, committing to Gerhard seemed natural and inevitable. It wasn't something to contemplate. How quickly things changed.

Saira's heart skipped a beat as she watched the newlyweds walk down the aisle behind the ellie. She could feel Gerhard's eyes on her, and as she looked up, found him staring at her. He was so handsome as the last rays of the sun burned through his hair, giving him a heavenly halo around his head. But there was nothing angelic in the smile he gave her. It was wickedly sexy and carried promises of passion. The thought of how hard he was earlier, how his body felt against hers, made her squeeze her legs together. Her arousal had been building since their heated kisses in the summerhouse and the promise of more to come. It was easy to see from how he held himself, Gerhard felt the same.

Saira found the challenge of remaining calm and pretending everything was okay more testing than she'd imagined she would. It took genuine effort on her part not to rush everything and everyone and get them to the Lapa. She was hoping to at least have a shower before Gerhard arrived at her suite.

But she cursed under her breath that things never went to plan. It seemed somehow, everyone needed her. Mary wanted to have a word about several ideas she'd had. Shona needed some advice about how to deal with temperamental hair-dressers, and Neville wanted to know if she'd attend the edits later in the evening. Kerri asked if she'd like to join them for dinner.

Shitshitshit.

With as much tact and charm as she could muster, she dealt with everyone and then excused herself, saying she had a headache and wanted an early night. No one seemed to mind, and Saira suspected everyone craved the same after the busy day. It was a given that tomorrow would be even more hectic, and everyone was looking forward to letting their hair down at the party afterward. They needed it after the intense work over the past few weeks. No one wanted to be too tired to enjoy it. Saira also knew today was far from over for many members of her team. They still had a lot of admin and editing to do. But she knew they didn't need her looking over their shoulders. She knew they appreciated her trust in them enough to let them get on with it.

By the time she reached her suite, it was much later than

she'd arranged to meet Gerhard. But there was no sign of him yet. Excellent. It meant she could have a quick shower before he arrived. But she cursed under her breath as she fumbled with the key. Her hands were clammy and shaking.

Gerhard gave her a little fright as he unwound himself from the shadows on the other side of her door. He enfolded her into his body from behind and took the key from her hand. It was a little unfair, she thought, how he opened the door so easily. But he distracted her as he pressed himself against her, and walked her into the room, kicking the door closed behind them. She could feel his body shaking from desire and the effort to control himself. That he wanted her this much heightened Saira's arousal. It was both unexpected and powerfully erotic.

The moment the door closed behind them, Gerhard grabbed her, spun her around, cupped her face in his large hands and kissed her with such passion, she felt her head spin as though she was drunk. He pulled her into his body in such a way, there was no mistaking his intentions. But Saira put her hands on his chest and pushed away from him a little.

Again, she experienced that wildness in his eyes as he opened them to stare at her.

His voice was hoarse with desire.

"Don't you want this?"

"Of course, I do, Gerhard. You know, I do. But I want a shower. I am so sticky and sweaty, and I don't want it to be your first memory of me."

Gerhard held onto her shoulders, dropped his forehead to hers and sighed his frustration.

"I understand. Perhaps we could shower together?"

Saira wondered if she'd ever get used to that look in his eyes. She nodded, took his hand and led him to the bathroom.

Once there, a sudden shyness almost overcame her. But Gerhard had no such inhibitions. He reached for her and started undressing her, kissing her lips and body as he peeled off each piece of her clothing. The most Saira could do was to open his shirt and run her hands over his magnificent chest. She'd wanted to do it for so long and now, feeling his hard muscles beneath her hands, he was everything she'd imagined he would be. He overwhelmed her, and she could do nothing more than receive his kisses. She shivered as his skilful hands stroked all over her body, awakening her, claiming her.

When she stood naked, Gerhard drew away for a moment, but still held onto her hands as though he needed the contact and couldn't bear to be apart from her for even a second. His hungry eyes roamed over her body. The action was so shocking and so bold, it ignited such heat in Saira, she wanted to forget the shower.

She'd never seen such naked desire in anyone's eyes before and loved the way his nostrils flared as he ran his hands down her shoulders. Cupping her breasts and rubbing her rigid nipples between his thumbs and forefingers, he kissed her neck, her jaw, her mouth. It was difficult to distinguish the individual pleasures as everything blended into a vortex of sexual stimulation. Her body felt on fire. His hands were everywhere, gliding lower over her stomach, and lower until his middle finger found her private pleasure.

His pupils dilated almost black, and he moaned as he pushed his finger inside her.

"Oh, God, Saira, you're so ready for me."

He removed his finger, and she whimpered at the sudden withdrawal when she yearned for him there.

But she couldn't tear her eyes away as he lifted his finger to his nose and inhaled her scent. His eyes stayed on hers as he licked his finger. A fiery sigh escaped his mouth, and he moved back toward her, inserting two fingers this time.

She gasped at the pleasure and the fuller feeling inside her.

As he moved his fingers in and out of her, his thumb found her most sensitive spot. Saira's knees bent, and her legs opened wider as though of their own volition. The washbasin behind her caught her as she leaned back.

She didn't recognize her voice and had no control over the sounds that escaped from deep within her body.

Gerhard rubbed and stroked her in the exact way and at the precise speed for her orgasm to flood through her body seconds later. It deepened as it fastened itself to the soles of her feet. It was delicious and went on forever before she shivered with its completion. And yet, satisfaction just eluded her. She yearned for him to enter her, needed the connection and the fullness only he could give her like she needed air. They panted together in a rhythm neither could control. The bathroom's acoustics exaggerated their ragged breathing and moans, and Saira sensed the sounds drove Gerhard wilder.

He kissed her ears, neck, face and devoured her mouth in between fevered words.

"I can't wait, Saira. Please. Oh, God, I can't wait. I'm sorry, my love."

As Gerhard was kissing her and whispering in her ear, she became aware he was unbuttoning his khaki pants, pulled down the zipper. His trousers and underpants fell to his ankles.

Saira felt her eyes widen at the sight of him. He was enormous, rock hard, and pre-come was already leaking from his quivering tip.

He grabbed her hips and moved his hand around the top of her thigh. His thumb came down hard on her sensitive spot again. Rubbing there, he pushed himself into her. They both gasped at the much expected, sudden overwhelming pleasure.

His voice and breath felt feverish on her face and in her neck.

"Are you safe, baby, are you safe?"

Through a haze of altered consciousness, Saira understood he meant birth control.

But she couldn't speak. The only sound she could make was a guttural "huh-huh."

TWENTY-FIVE

A tapping at the edge of Saira's mind broke through the veil of her sleep. Her consciousness rose to wakefulness at the consistency of the sound.

But at once she could tell something was different in her room. A density to the energy around her and pleasant but unfamiliar scents clung to the air. Then, she remembered Gerhard was lying in bed next to her.

She smiled at the feeling of him beside her. The heat from his body was comforting, familiar somehow, and felt as though he'd always belonged here. His arm, over her stomach, was possessive in the best way. She loved how this slight gesture revealed his claiming of her as his.

The tapping continued, and Saira strained her ears to discover where it was coming from. Gerhard moved as he too had woken up from the sound. They sat up, and Saira hesitated for a moment before switching on the bedside lamp.

She turned to Gerhard and couldn't help staring at him. He looked yummy with his bed hair that had fallen over his eyes.

Saira leaned toward him.

"I think someone's at the door."

Although she'd whispered, she couldn't disguise her concern. Whoever was knocking on her door might have heard her.

She noticed Gerhard glancing at the clock and followed his example. It was just after midnight. They turned to look at each other. Smiles hovered around their lips and lit up their eyes as their thoughts turned to the pleasurable way they'd spent the evening together. It had been a long day and no doubt their physical exertions earlier had led to such blissful sleep.

Gerhard indicated with his head toward the bathroom, his voice imitating Saira's whisper.

"Should I wait in there?"

Saira continued to smile as she realized he meant, "should I hide in there?"

But before she could respond, Gerhard was already up. She couldn't help admiring his muscular nakedness as he disappeared into the bathroom. He was a sight to behold, and again she wondered what he did to maintain such a muscular physique.

But she needed to take action, so got up and grabbed her dressing gown from the chair where she'd slung it that morning. She slipped it on as she went to peek through the peephole in the door.

The night outside was inky black. But the lights in the pool, and the fairy lights running along the path to the Lapa, cast just enough light to see the ancient features of Khwai standing in front of her door. It must be about Rundu, she knew at once. But why Khwai would come to her about Rundu, she couldn't imagine. Then it hit her.

Shit.

He was the best tracker in Namibia, by all accounts. If Khwai knew Gerhard was in her room, who else knew it?

When Saira opened the door, the old man's smile stretched

over his ancient face. His eyes almost disappeared among the folds.

He stretched his hand toward her.

"Tjike."

Saira understood it was a greeting and shook his hand.

"Hello again, Khwai. It's lovely to see you, but to be honest, I didn't expect you at my door at this time of the night. Is everything okay?"

Saira noticed though the old man's voice was soft, it told of his strength.

"I have come for Gerhard, please."

"Is it about Rundu? Have you found him?"

By the shift in the energy behind her, Saira knew Gerhard was standing there. He'd come to the same conclusion she did that there was no point hiding in the bathroom any longer.

Gerhard reached over her shoulder and pulled the door open further.

Khwai extended a similar greeting to Gerhard before he turned and melted into the darkness.

Saira noticed Gerhard had dressed. He must have run his hands through his hair, so it looked smooth again, and for a moment, she envied him that gene.

His eyes revealed his reluctance to leave her, but Saira nodded to him.

"It's okay. Find him. I'll see you in the morning."

Gerhard bent down, cupped her head in his hands and kissed her with a fervor that snatched her breath away. Then, he walked backward out the door, throwing her a last air kiss as he closed it.

Saira stayed rooted to the spot and stared at the door. Her thoughts were running in several directions at once.

The passion she'd experienced with Gerhard was unlike anything she'd ever encountered before, nor could she have prepared for it. Who could, without knowing it existed? But it wasn't only the intense physical attraction between them or the mind-blowing sex, was it? It was the emotional connection with Gerhard that had the most impact. There was no going back for her. Even if she could deny it, her soul knew Gerhard was its other half. That he seemed so sure they were meant for each other, only confirmed her conviction.

Saira walked back to the bed, arranged her pillows against the headboard and laid down, clutching Gerhard's pillow to her chest. His scent clung to it, and she pressed her face into it, inhaling as she did so.

Falling this hard for him wasn't what she'd imagined would happen to her and it wasn't a simple thing. There was so much else to consider. Her life and work in London. His life and work here. Her parents. Yes, there were her parents. Would she once again disappoint them? But she couldn't imagine them not falling in love with Gerhard. So, he wasn't a young Indian businessman they'd introduced to her. But he seemed powerful, confident and successful in his own way. His impeccable manners reminded her of her father's old-fashioned ways.

She prayed Gerhard meant every word he'd said about loving her and wanting her because if he didn't, without doubt, he could so destroy her. If falling in love with him happened during their first kiss, joining with him, had melded her soul to his. Her entire body was thrumming with the memory of their lovemaking. If they were to part, she'd never survive it. But with those thoughts came another-would what had happened between them affect their work? She sighed her relief that there were only a few working days left on this project.

She was too angsty to sleep again. As she made her way to the kitchenette to make some coffee, she shook her head and pulled her shoulders back. They were adults and accountable to no one. Then why did she feel so guilty? She'd broken things off with Jonathan. It had to be clear, even to him, that things were over between them.

She took her coffee mug back to the bed and placed it on the bedside table. Squishing some pillows behind her, she leaned back against the headboard.

Sleep probably wouldn't return tonight. Instead, she pulled out her Kindle from the bedside table's little drawer. It opened on the last novel she'd been reading on the flight over to Namibia. But the words meant nothing. Instead, her thoughts remained with Gerhard and his search for Rundu. She knew how important the cheetah was to him and prayed they would find him.

THE SHRILL SOUND of the phone cut through the still morning.

Saira jerked awake and grabbed it.

"Yes?"

"Good morning, daughter of mine, you sound sleepy. Did I wake you?"

Saira turned to look at the clock. Its red neon numbers read six am.

"It's okay. I have to get up, anyway."

"That's good. I wanted to catch you before your busy day starts. How are you, Saira? I know you are nearing the end of your project there. And I wanted to tell you how proud your mother and I are of you."

Saira could feel tears of happiness and gratitude welling up in her eyes.

"Thank you, daddy. That means so much to me."

"You know your mother and I want to support you in your life and your career. If this is what you are serious about, then we accept it, and we will do everything in our power to help you."

Her father, never one to mince his words, was also never liberal with his praise. Saira remembered vividly the few times he'd told her he was proud of her. She couldn't believe he went to the trouble of calling her first thing in the morning to tell her it now. It meant more than anything. She would hold the memory of this conversation in her heart for the rest of her life.

After her father had hung up, Saira sat for moments staring at the phone in her hand. Tears of gratitude flowed down her cheeks. That her parents would visit her in Namibia next week proved their unconditional love for her. It was such an unexpected surprise and made her realize once again how much she was missing them. It meant even more that she finally had their approval about her career choice. All the anxiety about disappointing them on that score, had left her body after the conversation with her father. It might account for the extra teariness as her fears around the subject had been such a deep sense of anxiety for so long.

Now, all she had to do was tell them of her plans to start her own company.

And then there was Gerhard...

TWENTY-SIX

The knowledge that her parents were coming to visit changed everything. Saira had always strived for excellence. Now, she aimed even higher.

Her parents' visit was to support her, yes. But to her, it meant a chance to share with them why she was so passionate about her work, finally. It was the best opportunity to show them that the stories she told through the medium of television affected people's lives, had value and were important in the world.

Following her request for a meeting with Naomi and Kerri, Saira hurried to Kerri's office. The other two women were already there, waiting for her when she arrived. Each held a mug of coffee and was sitting in the lounge area of Kerri's office. Neither of them could contain the curiosity shining in their eyes.

Naomi smiled and winked at Saira as she went to pour some coffee for herself.

"What's so exciting it couldn't wait? Kerri said she could hear it in your voice over the phone."

Saira told them about her parents' surprise visit and was

grateful she didn't have to explain what it meant to her. Naomi and Kerri both seemed to understand the implications and importance of their visit at once.

After the brief silence that followed Saira's announcement, Kerri sat forward in her chair as her thoughts registered in her eyes.

"The moment we have their schedule, we should get Gerhard to collect them from Windhoek. A pity they'd missed the filming, but I'm sure we can treat them to some footage, can't we? And as they're here for one week only, we can schedule in as many activities as you'd like them to experience, Saira. I think they should at least go on a sunrise or sunset safari and visit the waterhole."

Saira couldn't help smiling at Kerri's enthusiasm.

"Yes, I agree. It would be lovely for them to experience at least one safari and the waterhole is something I know my father, in particular, would enjoy. If there is time, I know he'd also love the elephant orphanage, if Johan would have them there?"

Kerri scooted even further forward on her chair, her excitement widening her eyes more.

"Oh, that would be fantastic. Johan would love to have them, I'm sure. Meanwhile, I'll make sure they have the best suite we can let them have."

Kerri turned to Naomi.

She nodded in agreement and added, "And how lucky that Luca would still be here then. I know he'd love to meet them, too."

Saira put her coffee mug down and leaned back in her chair.

Everything was moving so fast. Although she was excited for her parents to visit, she had to calm herself as she still had two more weddings to film. The only thing niggling at the back of her mind was Gerhard meeting her parents first without her presence.

Saira couldn't help being nervous. What would they make of him? Perhaps it was good they'd meet him separately and form an independent opinion of him. Her relationship with Gerhard could come later when, hopefully, they liked him.

Saira got up.

"Right, I'd better skedaddle. Thank you both so much for your kindness regarding my parents. I appreciate it enormously, and I know they will, too."

She turned to Naomi.

"I'll see you later at the wedding site?"

Naomi nodded.

"You will indeed. I'm rather enjoying my role as registrar. And I want to continue doing it when we do more of these."

She smiled at her last statement.

Saira had been concentrating on the pilot, but why not think further into the future?

"Well, that's what we must do, then, Naomi."

As Saira got to the door, she remembered the thing she kept forgetting to ask about.

She turned around.

"By the way, I keep seeing the drone flying over Desert Lodge. I was wondering why it was here. Shouldn't it be out there looking for poachers? Are the guys practicing with this one?"

Naomi and Kerri glanced at each other.

The frown between Kerri's eyes deepened.

"I keep seeing it, too, but thought it was one of yours?"

"No, we only use the drone camera when filming a wedding. We've already filmed enough footage before the ceremonies and need no more. That's why I thought it was one of the poacher patrol drones."

Kerri got up.

"I'll check with Khwai, but I am certain it's not one of ours."

Naomi got up and crossed her arms over her chest, her face serious.

"If it's not one of yours and it's not one of ours, I wonder who the drone belongs to?"

The same thought hit all three women at the same time. They spoke in unison.

"That's how they took Rundu."

Naomi walked over to the window and opened it.

She spoke as she looked for the drone.

"So, Luca was right. Someone has been following Gerhard. But not in the way we thought. Who would have imagined using a drone to follow someone?

"Kerri, could you call Johan, please? He'd know what to do. How to get the drone down."

Kerri didn't respond until after she'd finished sending the text to Johan, even before Naomi's request.

"I'm on it."

Naomi turned to Saira.

"Don't worry, Saira. We'll be discreet in getting the drone down. You guys are prepping for the next wedding and, obviously, we don't want to upset Gerhard. The guards and Khwai are still out looking for Rundu."

Saira felt heat creeping up her neck. How could she tell Naomi and Kerri that Khwai had collected Gerhard from her room last night? She wasn't sure if she was ready for them to know about her and Gerhard yet. But she couldn't help wondering whether the men had already found Rundu.

Saira was still busy with her thoughts when Kerri interrupted.

"Well, if we can get the drone down, we'll know for sure if

it's been following Gerhard and perhaps also, what's happened to Rundu."

Saira glanced at the time and knew she had to leave but couldn't resist the question.

"How will Johan take down the drone?"

Kerri and Naomi shared a knowing look, and Kerri giggled as she responded.

"Haven't you seen Johan's pet fish eagle?"

Saira could feel her eyes widening in surprise.

"He has a pet fish eagle? The sound they make has always personified Africa to me. And the fish eagle will catch the drone?"

Kerri nodded, her eyes filled with laughter and her voice reflecting confidence in her husband's abilities.

"For sure. It's how he's taken down drones from very sophisticated wildlife gangs before. The eagle takes down the drone without destroying it so we can access the information on it."

Naomi stepped away from the window and lowered her voice, imitating Johan's.

"He's a clever man, that bloke, Johan."

Saira laughed. She glanced at the time again. Even though she enjoyed her new friends' company, she had work to do.

"Well, it's something I wouldn't want to miss. Could you let me know when Johan and the eagle arrive, please, Kerri? Does the eagle have a name?"

Kerri nodded, her face mock serious.

"His name is Guardian. Appropriate, don't you think?"

Saira couldn't help the giggle that escaped her.

"I'm guessing he lives near the elephant orphanage?"

Kerri gave her a thumbs up.

"You've got it in one. He's a far better guardian than the guard dogs. Nothing gets past him. Johan rescued him when he was a small chick. Something must have happened to his parents, and he was lucky Johan found him in time. Otherwise, he would have starved and died."

Kerri looked thoughtful for a moment before she continued.

"We still wonder what happened to the parents because fish eagles mate for life. Johan found only the one chick which is normal as they usually lay one to three eggs at a time. The chick imprinted on Johan and accepted him as his parent, instead. It's most likely the reason he answers only to Johan."

Saira's smile told of her wonder.

"I continue to be amazed by this wonderful country and its people and the animals that live here. I can't wait for my parents to experience it. It still feels like some miracle they're able to come here at all. I still can't believe they could arrange it at such short notice."

Naomi turned away from the window.

"Perhaps they'd been planning to surprise you all along?"

Saira nodded.

"That thought had crossed my mind. I can't see how they could swing it so soon, otherwise. And on that note, I must go to work. But I'll see you both later and don't forget to let me know when Johan and Guardian get here? I'm very excited to see how he takes down the drone. Do you think Johan might permit us to film it as part of our pilot? Neville's clever editing skills might allow us to fit it into the story, somehow."

"I'll ask Johan, but I'm not sure what he'd say, Saira. He might want to keep Guardian as his secret weapon."

Saira nodded.

"I understand. Whatever Johan says, we'll abide by his wishes."

Saira shook her head as she walked down the corridor to the beauty room. And she thought London was exciting.

In the beauty room, Mary, Shona, the hairdressers and nail technicians were having coffee and mingling with the crew.

There was no sign of Gerhard, but it didn't worry Saira. It was still early, and everyone was waiting for the bride and her entourage to arrive. They were most likely still having their complimentary breakfast in the Lapa.

Saira checked her phone. Still no messages from Gerhard. She wondered what time to expect him.

Just as she was about to text Gerhard, she received a message from him.

We have Rundu. See you in about an hour. x

Saira stared at Gerhard's text. The day seemed suddenly lighter and brighter.

She texted back.

So happy for you. See you soon. x

She reckoned Gerhard would be exhausted. At least he'd make it back in time for the first wedding of the day. She might suggest he brief the camera crew and get some sleep. That way, he'd be awake and refreshed for the second and final wedding of the pilot, and also awake enough to not only attend but enjoy the party afterward.

Saira walked over to Mary and Shona and brought them up to speed about what had happened with Rundu. Now they'd found the cheetah, she could see no reason not to share the pleasant news. But as Saira spoke with them, she realized that not sharing the information with the rest of the team, who'd all come to know and love Gerhard, was unfair.

"I think I'd better announce it to everyone here. Shona, can you text the news to Naomi and Kerri, meanwhile, just in case Gerhard had sent the text to me only?"

It was a distinct possibility, she thought, judging by the x.

Saira walked over to the sideboard and picked up the bell Mary had provided and which she used to let everyone know their timings. Saira rang the bell until everyone stopped talking and turned to look at her.

"By now you all know Gerhard's cheetah, Rundu, had been kidnapped. Khwai and the anti-poacher patrol guard came to collect Gerhard last night to find Rundu. Gerhard has just texted to say they've found him. They're on their way back. Gerhard should be here within the hour. But I will suggest to him we take up the slack for this wedding, so he can get some sleep to film the last one, and to join us at the party afterward."

Saira suspected the massive cheer and whooping that followed her words had more to do with the reminder about the party than Gerhard or Rundu.

As she poured her second cup of coffee of the day, Saira felt relief and joy flood through her body. Gerhard was on his way back, they'd found Rundu, they were on the last day of shooting weddings, and her parents were coming to visit. It was all wonderful.

The only niggle at the back of her mind said this would soon be over. The crew, who'd lived and worked together as a family unit, would disperse, and go their separate ways. She'd have to bid farewell to her friends here at Desert Lodge, say goodbye to Gerhard for now, and join her parents on their jet to return to London.

Then what?

TWENTY-SEVEN

Today turned out as Saira imagined it would. The busyness kept her distracted from thinking about Gerhard too much.

Everyone went to work in the same way they had for the previous two weddings. They welcomed the next bride and her entourage when they appeared and prepared to pamper them. Gerhard's camera team proceeded as though he was present.

It didn't surprise Saira when Gerhard arrived half an hour later than he'd intended to. His face was ashen from exhaustion but erupted into a radiant smile when he saw her. It wasn't difficult to persuade him to take a break and get some sleep until they needed him for the second wedding of the day.

Vicky and David had been the first bridal party chosen for the pilot, and Saira felt it only fair that their wedding was the final and most fun. She knew she would need all hands on deck for their wedding, and Gerhard was part of that package.

He didn't want coffee but poured himself an enormous glass of fruit juice instead.

Standing beside him, Saira could feel Gerhard's exhaustion even as relief poured off his body.

"So, where's Rundu now?"

He finished the glass of juice and poured another before responding.

"We took him back to the same stable they had abducted him from. Three guards will stay with him at all times."

Saira was in two minds about revealing their plans for the drone. No, Gerhard needed his sleep, and Saira knew if he had any inkling they would catch the drone, he'd want to be there for it. Instead, she hoped he'd be okay watching the footage of its capture later.

That there were no arguments from Gerhard about taking time out, only confirmed Saira's suspicions that looking for Rundu had exhausted him.

An hour later, when Kerri texted to confirm Johan's and Guardian's arrival, Saira hoped Gerhard was in his room and fast asleep.

They'd finished the getting-ready shots they'd needed for the next bride and her entourage, and the camera crew was free for the moment. Saira asked Gerhard's assistant cameraman and a junior to follow her as she joined Kerri and Naomi. Watching Johan work his magic with Guardian was an experience Saira couldn't have imagined. She noticed Luca, Khwai and several of the anti-poaching patrol guards had joined them.

The rogue drone had continued to fly over Desert Lodge all morning. But now, there was no sign of it. Wasn't it always the way?

Saira approached Johan as she contemplated the massive bird at his side.

She couldn't keep her eyes off Guardian as she spoke with Johan.

"Thanks so much for allowing us to shoot this scene, Johan. If nothing else, I know Gerhard will enjoy watching it. But I've already spoken with Neville, who'll edit it so Guardian's mission will remain secret. I can't thank you enough. It'll be awesome."

Johan's smile told of his pride for Guardian and the pleasure he derived from showing off the gorgeous eagle to others.

"I don't work with Guardian in this way often. It's amazing to see his skills, and you would honor us both by featuring us in your pilot in some small way. But it would be good if we could keep his drone catching mission a secret. Neville had mentioned how he intended to make it look as though Guardian captured the wedding camera drone, instead. I suspect it will be hilarious."

"Neville is brilliant. I'm sure he'll do both you and Guardian justice."

Just as Saira was feeling disappointed that the drone seemed to have disappeared, Khwai pointed at the sky.

"There it is. The controller is very clever. He has flown the drone higher. The sun is shining on him. More difficult to see him that way. But Guardian won't miss."

Johan nodded to Khwai.

"Thanks, Khwai. By your reckoning, is it the right time to release Guardian now?"

Khwai nodded and continued to point in the drone's direction even though no one else could see it.

Again, Saira marveled at the old man's hawk-like eyesight. No wonder he could see their tiny smoke signals in the desert on the day their Cessna had broken down. She couldn't believe how long ago that seemed.

But before she could think more about how much had happened since that time, Khwai nodded. Johan, who'd been waiting for the old man's signal, released Guardian into the air.

Everyone watched as Guardian flew over Desert Lodge. He circled a few times before heading toward the drone. His wing-span was majestic. His distinctive call was even more evocative to hear in reality rather than on the many recordings and videos Saira had watched and listened to.

Whoever operated the drone must have seen their group congregating outside the kitchen beside the safari trucks. Perhaps they'd even seen their upturned faces as they looked for the drone. But they hadn't expected Guardian because the drone didn't move away fast enough before the large fish eagle grabbed it in its sharp claws.

Saira imagined even if the drone could fly away, it wouldn't have been able to out-fly Guardian. The eagle was quick, much faster than she'd expected him to be.

When Guardian landed in front of Johan, the drone gripped in his claw, he cocked his head.

Saira could swear he asked, "did I get the right one?"

She couldn't think why, but she hadn't expected such intelligence in a bird of prey.

The drone was trying to take off again, but with Guardian's weight on it, it was going nowhere.

Saira checked with Jim and Mark, the two camera crew members, to see if they got the footage of Guardian capturing the drone. It seemed to happen so fast.

They nodded, and Mark added, "it was quick, but we got brilliant shots."

"Excellent, thanks, guys. Could you please help to get the information we need from the drone?"

Mark curled his lip as if to say, "piece of cake," and nodded.

"Don't see why not? Shouldn't be too difficult."

Saira caught him eyeing Guardian with trepidation.

Johan, aware of the effect, both good and bad, that Guardian had on people, bent down to stroke the eagle's head.

He looked up at Mark as he spoke.

"Just give him a few moments. Guardian likes to appreciate

his capture. He'll soon grow tired of the drone, and then I'll hand it to you."

Luca, who'd had his arm around Naomi, stepped forward.

"That was amazing, Johan. Is it safe to touch Guardian, or are you the only one allowed to do so? I've never been this close to such a magnificent bird before."

Johan squatted down slowly and gestured for Luca to do the same.

"You can touch him. But only if I'm here. Just approach him bit by bit and make sure he can see you. Don't come at him from behind."

Luca imitated Johan's squat. He hesitated before putting out his hand and touching his knuckles to Guardian's head.

"His feathers are softer than I imagined. I'm always amazed how animals keep their white feathers or white fur so clean. He's a charming boy."

Johan nodded, a proud smile hovering around his lips.

"You know, Luca, the fish eagle is the national bird of Namibia."

"No, I didn't realize. It makes complete sense. But don't fish eagles need fish and water? Aren't we too deep into the desert here?"

Johan got up and dusted the sand from his knees.

"Yes, he eats fish and other small animals and birds. You know the big waterhole behind the elephant orphanage?"

Luca nodded and smiled.

"The enormous lake, you mean? It must cost a fortune to keep water in it."

"Right. Well, Guardian has made his nest in an acacia nearby."

Luca nodded as he too got up and wiped the sand from his designer jeans.

"Guardian seems to realize he's caught the drone for you, Johan. Does he often bring you presents?"

Johan's laughter was careful and revealed his awareness that his usual exuberance might frighten Guardian.

"No, not like a cat. I've trained him to retrieve drones out of the sky, and he knows it's not food."

It was apparent Guardian had already lost interest in the drone. He stared off into the sky and flapped his wings but stayed on the drone, locking it to the earth.

Johan was careful as he leaned forward to retrieve the drone. Guardian allowed Johan to take the drone from his claw, and flew off. He stayed in the lodge's vicinity, but it was clear he preferred to be in the air than on the ground.

Saira watched the eagle soar, and out of the corner of her eye, she noticed Mark continuing to film the impressive bird in flight. She wondered if the drone's operators could see them, but then realized Johan and Jim had fiddled with the device and must have turned it off. It sat inert at their feet on the ground.

Saira watched the fish eagle circling above them. He was so free, so unlike her situation at MaxPix and her life in London.

The sudden realization she'd never be able to go back to her old life, hit her full in her solar plexus. She almost gasped aloud at the impact. At some subconscious level, she must have known it, though she hadn't realized it so palpably before. For the first time in her life, Saira felt as though she was standing beside her body, watching herself through eyes that saw a confident, powerful woman. This was not the young, hot-headed girl that had stepped off that plane from London. There were no maybes that tortured her any longer. She knew what she wanted, and she was determined to get it.

In the back of her mind, she heard her father's words as a childhood mantra, "Destiny isn't a point on a map. It's in each step of the journey it takes to get there."

But it wasn't until now, until this moment as she watched the eagle's graceful flight, that it hit her. The full understanding her journey had already begun, that her experiences here had instigated profound changes in her. There was no going back for her. She would forever be her evolved self, continuing to grow as the years and fresh experiences presented themselves.

She could see it as clearly now as she imagined the fish eagle saw his world, his path.

It felt good.

TWENTY-EIGHT

Naomi and Kerri were standing on either side of Saira. The three of them leaned over Mark's shoulder to watch the footage he'd rescued from the drone.

Naomi touched Saira's arm as she asked the question.

"Where did they find Rundu?"

"I haven't spoken to Gerhard about it yet. But I overheard Khwai talking to Johan. It sounded like an abandoned farm three hours' drive away from here. No wonder it took them the entire night to get there, rescue Rundu, and drive back. Khwai's powers of tracking still seem miraculous to me."

Saira had continued to watch the footage from the drone as she responded to Naomi. But it wasn't what she saw, rather than what she'd heard, that made her take note.

"Wait, Mark. Go back…"

Mark ran the footage back for a few seconds, then stopped.

Saira put her hand on his shoulder.

"Go back a little more."

Mark did as she asked and ran the footage back in small increments, stopping each time, checking with Saira.

When he found the right spot, her hand tightened on his shoulder.

"There... Did you hear that? Go back again please, Mark."

Naomi and Kerri asked in unison.

"What are we looking for?"

But Saira was trying to get control over her breathing. She felt as though she was choking.

Her voice sounded strangled when she got the words out.

"I could swear that's Jonathan's voice. How can it be?"

The three women looked at each other. The same question showed in their eyes.

Kerri was first to break the silence.

"It can't be Jonathan. He isn't in Namibia anymore."

Naomi leaned forward.

"Play it again please, Mark."

Again, Mark ran the footage.

Now they knew what to focus on, Jonathan's voice was unmistakable.

His words were clear.

"If that bitch thinks she'll ditch me for some fucking German prince, she's got another think coming. He's obviously a disgrace to his family, which is why he's hiding here in the middle of the desert where no one can find him. God knows what else he's guilty of. The least we can do is rescue the cheetah. He's probably holding it illegally, anyway."

A woman's voice giggled. Her accent was local and sounded familiar, but Saira couldn't place it.

"And I bet even a German prince can be done for illegal wildlife trading. Think of the money he'll pay. And how desperate is she? She doesn't even care that his family has done terrible things. If you ask me, you're better off without her."

Jonathan's and the woman's laughter faded as the drone took to the air.

Naomi's voice was tight with anger.

"Mark, can you tell how long the drone had been filming Gerhard?"

But Saira heard the voices around her as though she was underwater. She'd known Jonathan was a vindictive person, but this was on a whole other level. Perhaps she should have known he'd do something like this, been prepared.

Mark's voice responded to Naomi's question.

Saira felt drawn to his words when she heard him say, "Difficult to tell. He may have more footage downloaded at his end. But I have no way of knowing how long he's been filming. The footage on this SD card appears to be for one week only."

Naomi and Kerri spoke in unison.

"Does it show them taking the cheetah?"

Mark scrolled back through the footage.

No images appeared of them abducting Rundu. But there were many comments from Jonathan and his female cohort that showed they'd been behind Rundu's kidnapping.

Kerri spoke the words they were all thinking.

"I wonder if this will be permissible as evidence in court?"

Mark's voice sounded thoughtful.

"That I don't know. But I'm sure Jonathan wasn't supposed to film the wedding ceremonies."

He turned to look at Saira.

"Right, Saira?"

"What? He filmed the weddings?"

"Yes, look."

Mark ran the footage backward.

A silence thick with disbelief descended on the room.

Everyone watched the drone filming the weddings from several angles, but mostly from above. Its microphone, of the highest quality, captured every single word spoken.

Saira heard Kerri's fingers fly over her phone and knew she was contacting Johan.

"Johan can get in touch with his cousin, Nick. Times like this, it's a blessing to have the ex-Police Chief in the family. He'll know how to deal with this, but can we make a copy of the footage, meanwhile, Mark?"

Mark glanced at Saira for permission. When she nodded, he started the download.

"Doing it now."

Kerri had stopped typing.

"Excellent. I'm sure Nick would want a copy, anyway."

Naomi was staring at the screen, listening to her voice as she performed her role as registrar, crossed her hands over her chest.

She spoke the words Saira had been thinking.

"Well, apart from the kidnapping charges for stealing the cheetah from Gerhard, not to mention stalking him, hasn't Jonathan just broken the contract you have with MaxPix, Saira?"

The area around Saira's heart felt warm with recognition at the truth of Naomi's words.

She turned to look at Naomi and saw smiles curling around hers and Kerri's mouths as they contemplated her.

"You make an excellent point, Naomi. I was just thinking the same thing."

Kerri's eyes glittered with excitement.

"This is exactly what we've all been wishing for. Now, you can get out of that dreadful contract, Saira, and the pilot will be yours for your new company. Congratulations."

Before Saira could respond, Kerri embraced her in a tight hug. When she stepped away, Naomi took her place. She gave Saira a less-tight hug, but one that conveyed excitement for Saira.

Mark twisted around in his chair and extended a hand to pump Saira's.

"Congratulations, Saira. It's been great working with you. When you start your new company and have space for me, I'd be delighted to continue working for you."

Saira's laugh wasn't as exuberant as she would have liked. The bitterness Jonathan's words and actions caused, still sat in her mouth.

"Thanks, guys. But steady on. I still have to talk to Max, and I can't imagine he'll let the pilot go without a fight. He's invested money in it, after all-"

Naomi interrupted her.

"Like I said before, Saira, Luca has one of the best lawyers in the world working at Armati. We must get the info to Roberto. He'll sort it out for you. You won't have to talk with Max if you don't want to."

Saira nodded her thanks to Naomi, but before she could speak, Kerri continued where Naomi had left off.

"Max doesn't deserve your attention or energy, so don't even think about being fair to him, Saira. You're a decent human being. But you don't owe Max or Jonathan anything. Those two men made your life hell. And I'll bet Max only sent you here because you're probably the only young female producer at MaxPix and this series is about weddings, right?"

Again, Saira nodded.

She couldn't help being amazed by Kerri's perceptive observations. Once again, as hesitant excitement swirled in her body for her dream's manifestation coming closer, she felt grateful for such wonderful friends.

When Kerri stopped talking, Naomi resumed.

"Jonathan may not be aware, but he has messed with the wrong guy. Gerhard can be a formidable enemy. I don't envy Jonathan. He and his girlfriend were right describing Gerhard as a prince. He may have abdicated his official role, but what neither Jonathan nor his partner knows is that Gerhard is still a prince. He still has access to people, institutions and funds Jonathan can't even dream of."

Saira felt light-headed as the meaning behind Naomi's words penetrated her brain.

Wait, what? Gerhard a German prince? Why had he never mentioned it? Why had no one told her?

She wondered what his surname was. She'd never thought to ask. Perhaps it would have rung a bell. But now, his home that looked like a colonial castle made sense.

Naomi must have sensed Saira's bewilderment.

She turned to Saira.

"Sorry, Saira. I can see you didn't know. Gerhard doesn't make a big deal of it. It's not a secret exactly, but he doesn't like us to talk about it. I think there's some grim family history he'd rather forget."

Kerri's support for her friends filled her voice.

"But just because Gerhard doesn't like us to mention it, doesn't make it any less true. The fact remains, Gerhard is an abdicated German prince."

She turned to Naomi.

"You're right, hun. I don't envy Jonathan when the full wrath of Gerhard descends on him."

Mark had swung his chair around, jumped up and stood facing the three women.

His hands on his cheeks, his mouth had formed a perfect silent "O." His wide eyes traveled from one to the other.

"Does it mean I didn't hear this conversation?"

Three pairs of eyes turned on Mark. They spoke in unison.

"Yes."

Naomi held up her hands, taking responsibility for her mistake.

"I shouldn't have said anything. So, this conversation cannot leave this room."

A blush had crept into her cheeks.

"I'm sorry if I spoke out of turn. But I feel so incensed about what Jonathan has done to all of us. Gerhard doesn't deserve this. Over the years, he's proved to be a wonderful friend, kind, supportive and helpful to those in need. We're lucky to have him here. The least we can do is to keep his secret. I'm sorry I let it slip out."

She turned to Saira.

"I'm sure he'll tell you when he's ready to do so, Saira. We all know you have a special place in his heart."

Naomi's smile showed she was trying to make light of the situation.

"Lucky girl."

Saira turned her head to hide the heat in her cheeks from the others.

Shit.

Their secret was out, too. She should have known. But theirs paled by comparison to Gerhard's bomb of a secret.

Peter and Manda were going to flip when they heard it.

Saira sensed yet another brief shock going through Mark, but he pretended not to hear the secret about her relationship with Gerhard.

His eyes remained thoughtful.

"You have my word. I'll keep my mouth shut."

He pressed his lips together, mimed zipping and locking his mouth and throwing the key over his shoulder.

His eyes darted to Saira as he spoke.

"That includes all the secrets."

TWENTY-NINE

Saira focussed on what Jonathan had done and what it now meant for her and the future. She didn't want to think about the secret Gerhard hadn't shared with her and why.

To combat her restlessness and growing excitement, she'd spent much of her lunch break researching a name for her new company.

Flame Productions sounded perfect. The flame presented her desire to produce excellent shows, and the image gave a sense of drama, life. As the opportunity had presented itself here, in Namibia, it was also her tribute to the Flame memorial in Windhoek. She'd talk to Vince soon about designs for a logo.

Her head was spinning. Things were happening so fast. Luca had contacted his lawyer, Roberto, at once, to get Saira out of the contract with MaxPix. Johan did the same with his ex-Chief of Police cousin, Nick, who had alerted his successor. The police were already on the hunt for Jonathan and his female companion.

Saira would tell her parents soon about the change in her career path, though she could guess what their reactions would be. She'd have to wait until her contract with MaxPix had been severed, and she kept possession of the pilot before approaching her team. But she hoped they'd want to stay and continue to work with her.

Exhaustion must have overtaken her at some point. When the alarm sounded, she felt groggy but ready for the last wedding of the pilot.

As she left her room, everything felt different. She had a weird sense of having woken up from the deep sleep that was her previous life. Perhaps it happened if you didn't live your heart's desire, she thought. Maybe no one is truly awake until they do so.

Even the sky was bluer, the air fresher and infused with the scent of flowers as she made her way back to the beauty room.

When Gerhard arrived, Mark caught Saira's eye. His nod was imperceptible, and she prayed things wouldn't be awkward around Gerhard for the two of them. But true to his word, Mark behaved in his usual way toward Gerhard. If only it would be that easy for her.

But everyone was in such high spirits for the last wedding, no one would notice any weirdness or awkwardness.

Saira breathed out as she contemplated those around her. It could be difficult dealing with Gerhard's secret later. She wasn't looking forward to it. First, she had to get through the wedding.

The sounds of excited female voices carried toward the room as the next bride and her posse arrived. Vicky's voice sang out over those of her entourage. Only her mother's voice vied for supremacy with her daughter's. The volume went up several decibels when the women walked through the door. Saira wondered if there was a way to dial down the level of their excitement. It seemed too big for the room.

The women oohed and aahed at the sight of the cameras and beauty paraphernalia. They accosted the hairdressers and nail technicians with their requests. But their eagerness helped get them to their different stations, so things could progress at a pace.

A waitress offered champagne and tiny canopés.

The noise increased until it sounded like the reception party was already well underway, even though the wedding was still to come. The women's exuberance rubbed off on the crew, and the light-hearted session got underway with much banter and jokes.

Saira could see great shots to add to the excitement she'd wanted for the pilot.

Perhaps a few mishaps were unavoidable as the effects of the champagne took effect on empty, jittery stomachs. Several pots of nail varnish met their end when over-dramatic hand gestures swept them off the tables. But no color splashes reached the bridal dresses or the camera equipment. Saira reckoned the room would need a new carpet, though. Shona had found plastic sheets from somewhere and had covered the mess so the many feet in the room wouldn't trample nail varnish everywhere.

The group smashed some champagne glasses, and crew members rushed to collect every tiny sliver of glass before someone in bare feet stepped on it.

Vicky's mother threw a hissy-fit when her hairdresser pulled her hair tighter than she liked, and a bridesmaid had the sense to vomit in the corner. Staff cleaned the mess, sprayed the room and opened more windows.

Vicky and her mum kept crying and spoiling their make-up, which gave their make-up artists a trying time.

But somehow, despite everything, when six o'clock arrived, Vicky and her bridal party were ready and looked magnificent.

Mary and Shona led the women out of the room, and through the French doors. A short distance from there, outside the kitchen porch, their decorated safari trucks waited to drive them to the wedding site.

Gerhard and his assistant, Mike, got into the truck with Vicky and the mothers, and Mark and Jim went with the bridesmaids.

When the trucks had left, Saira and Kerri grabbed what they needed and headed for their vehicle where Mary and Shona were already waiting for them.

Shona scooted up to make space for Saira.

"We're the last ones. Everyone else is already there."

Kerri glanced at Shona as she tapped the guard who was driving them on the shoulder.

"Can you overtake them, please, Piet? We must get there before the bride arrives."

Piet's mischievous smile gave consent as he winked and stepped on the gas.

When they found the other trucks, Piet gave them a wide berth as he drove past them. The women in the other trucks waved and hooted, their exuberance continuing. It amused Saira when the response from those around her was less than enthusiastic, including her own. She sensed everyone wanted this wedding over. Vicky and her mother had caused too many problems. Then there was Michelle, Vicky's weird best friend and erstwhile bridesmaid, and the drama she'd created.

As Saira watched the faces surrounding her, she realized she wasn't the only one eager to see this group on their way.

Piet ensured Saira's group arrived before the others.

They had just enough time to find their places before the bridal vehicles arrived. But it didn't surprise Saira when Vicky and her entourage made an entire production of disembarking from their trucks. Having got to know this group, no one would have expected anything different from them. When their squealing and over-the-top acting died down, Vicky's father took her arm. The San singers began their beautiful song, and the ceremony got underway.

Saira wanted to savor this last wedding of the pilot. Who knew if any others would follow? She looked around at the blended families. Their genuine smiles were happy for David and Vicky.

Around them, the tall poles created a safe circle. Fires crackled, flickered and danced in their upturned iron buckets. Apart from the setting and the San singers' voices, the fires lent an air of African-ness for Saira. As she inhaled a contended breath, she realized they'd scented the flames.

How had she not noticed it before?

The fires reminded her of her new company name, and images of a cool logo danced in her mind.

When the singers stopped their song, Naomi's voice reading the wedding proclamation, brought Saira back to the present.

She felt satisfied with their achievements so far. They did the best they could and had learned an enormous amount. What a shame if the TV series didn't take off?

Once she was sure it was hers, she'd do everything in her power to ensure it didn't fail. It would be such a waste of the time and effort she and her team had put into the production of the pilot, not to mention the abundance of talent they'd provided.

The guests surrounding her interrupted her thoughts with their gasps, oohing and aahing. Saira realized Johan was walking up the aisle ahead of a tiny ellie ring bearer. Johan must have briefed everyone beforehand because no one tried to touch the ellie. But several people dabbed tissues to tears, most likely at the thought the ellie was an orphan.

The ceremony was unexpectedly sedate.

But the moment Naomi announced David and Vicky were husband and wife, pandemonium broke out. People were whooping and squealing with delight and crowding around the happy couple, trying to get the first congratulatory hugs and kisses in. Though rowdy, the group's antics made for great shots. Saira watched Gerhard, and his team took advantage of the boisterous, colorful scenes. Out of the corner of her eye, Saira saw Johan leading the small ellie further away from the noise through the trees, where he'd parked his special adapted elephant truck. She prayed the sudden noise of the people yelling and screaming hadn't further traumatized the ellie. But she knew Johan would care for the sweet little elephant as he would for a child.

As she turned to glance at Shona and Mary behind her, she noticed Khwai and Luca standing on the sand behind the wedding site. Between them sat Rundu. The cheetah sat still, awaiting his turn to pose with David and Vicky. His ears flicked as his amber eyes followed Gerhard's every move.

Saira only noticed the unfamiliar vehicle after it had stopped behind the two men and the cheetah. But Johan's truck soon obscured it. He'd loaded the ellie and was on his way back to the lodge. Saira guessed Johan knew the occupants of the unfamiliar vehicle as he'd stopped to chat before driving off. The other truck turned around and followed Johan.

Saira had to hide her curiosity behind her professional smile.

But she couldn't help noticing Kerri's eyes shining as though she had great trouble containing some juicy news.

Saira smiled as she reminded herself never to tell Kerri a secret. But then, Kerri had kept Gerhard's secret so well, hadn't she?

THIRTY

Saira and her team stayed until all the guests had left. She wanted to savor her last memory of this magical place before the staff dismantled it. Staff from Desert Lodge had joined her team, and already the site looked emptier as they'd carried items to the waiting trucks. The rest of the film crew had gone with the wedding party to film their return to Desert Lodge.

Gerhard hadn't left with the others. Instead, he came to stand close beside Saira, his arm touching hers.

"Penny for your thoughts? You seem miles away."

His nearness felt comforting, but she didn't trust her voice.

When she didn't respond, he continued.

"Luca and Naomi had chosen the right spot for a wedding site, don't you think?"

Saira's voice sounded strange to her ears when she responded.

"Yes, it's uber-romantic. I'm glad we could gate-crash it to shoot the weddings for the pilot here."

But Saira wasn't interested in small talk. She couldn't stop thinking about the secret he'd kept from her. How to broach it with him?

As though he could sense her thoughts, he stepped away so he could look into her eyes.

"Now we're done filming, we need to talk."

He took her elbow in his firm, warm hand and led her away from the surrounding racket.

They walked in silence. When they reached the nearest dune, he helped her to sit down on the still-warm sand.

From here, the wedding site was even more picturesque. Saira wondered if they'd had the foresight to film from these angles and then remembered the drone footage. If they won their case against MaxPix, it might even allow her new company to use the excellent footage from Jonathan's drone.

Gerhard snapped her back to the present when he took her hands in his.

"Saira, there is something important I have to tell you. I didn't do so before because I wanted you to get to know me first. Once you know what it is, I'm sure you'll understand my reasons for doing it this way."

Saira nodded.

Her heart was beating in her throat. Here it comes.

Gerhard locked his eyes to hers. His voice sounded serious.

"First, let me say, I've never felt this way about anyone. I know we haven't known each other for long. But I know one hundred percent you're the woman I've waited for all my life. Do you feel the same for me?"

How could she deny what was in her heart? But she couldn't help being terrified about what his revelations would mean for her.

Again, Saira nodded, not trusting her voice to come out right.

Gerhard contemplated her for a moment before threading her fingers through his and leaning back against the dune.

Saira shifted to a more comfortable position to get ready for his story.

"Before I was born, my parents came to Namibia on vacation from Germany. Our family is old, and it's sometimes difficult for members to go anywhere without being recognized. But in Namibia, they were anonymous. It gave them freedom. They loved their time here, and my mother told me I was conceived here during that time. To cut a long story short, my father died in a tragic accident soon after their return to Germany. Mother, distraught at losing the love of her life, and desperate to cling to her last memories of him, returned here. Nine months later, I was born."

Saira shifted deeper into the soft sand.

Gerhard kept looking straight ahead as though he, too, was terrified of the effect his next words would have on their fledgling relationship.

"My family is wealthy and influential, and the last of the royal members still left from the House of Hohenzollern."

Gerhard glanced at Saira.

Though her heart was beating faster, she remained still, waiting for him to continue.

"Mother made an agreement with the family that when I reached fifteen, I could decide whether to take up my official duties or remain here. If I stayed, I would have to abdicate my title."

Again, Gerhard glanced at Saira.

His uncertainty showed in his eyes, but she nodded for him to continue.

"Of course, I received the best education. They flew tutors here from Germany, and they groomed me for princedom."

Gerhard looked away as if the memories hurt him.

"It was a lonely existence. But I never blamed Mother."

Things were starting to make sense to Saira. His regal

bearing and the way he seemed separate from everyone else, were give-aways she'd noticed before but not known the meaning behind them.

When she remained silent, Gerhard continued.

"During my schooling, I learned of my ancestor's role in almost annihilating two native tribes in Namibia. It was a terrible moment in history when he ordered people to be committed to a barbaric concentration camp. The place was called Shark Island. Perhaps you've heard of it?"

It cost him, she could see, speaking of these things. But her heart broke at his determination she should know him fully. It was difficult to hide her shock from Gerhard, who must have read it in her eyes.

She couldn't speak, nodded instead.

"That anyone could do something so cruel and unnecessary, was beyond my understanding. That it was a member of my family was incomprehensible and unacceptable. I had to help, even after all these years. Though I could never fix what they'd done.

"I decided to stay here and help heal the wounds my family had caused so many people. It meant abdicating my title, but it also meant Mother and I could establish crucial funding for the Herero and Nama tribes to better their lives. I'm proud of the work we're doing here, and my family in Germany approve."

Gerhard brought their hands to his lips, kissed the back of hers.

"There, now you know my tragic secret."

He turned to face her, his eyes unreadable. When he spoke, his voice was a gravelly whisper.

"Are you still mine, Saira?"

Saira loosened her fingers from his, cupped his face and kissed him with all the reverence she felt.

Her heart was beating so fast, she hoped it stayed in her

chest. She would always be his, share his life. What else would she do with the overwhelming feelings of love for this beautiful, amazing man?

"You will always be the love of my life, Gerhard. Thank you for sharing your story with me. It all makes sense now."

"What do you mean?"

Oops, she'd let that slip out.

She bit her lip before speaking.

"Naomi and Kerri might have let it slip that you're an abdicated German prince. But they only did so after we heard Jonathan mention it on the drone footage."

Gerhard turned his body toward Saira.

"You knew this entire time? Why didn't you say something?"

"Well, they said you didn't like to talk about it. And I thought you'd tell me in your own time. I was right, wasn't I?"

Gerhard pulled her hard against his body. His passionate kiss stole her breath.

When he let her go, he stroked her cheek and tucked her hair behind her ear as though he couldn't stop touching her.

"You're perfect for me, Saira. I can't wait to spend another night with you, a lifetime with you."

Saira nodded and kissed him again.

They were panting when they broke apart. Somehow, he was lying on top of her, their bodies molded together, already expressing their need for each other.

He looked up, then jumped up and pulled her to her feet.

"Come, we have to go, or we might miss a lift back to the lodge."

It was almost entirely dark now, and Saira had to strain her eyes, but she could make out only one truck near the empty site. Everything had gone. No one could tell there was ever a wedding site here.

Gerhard grabbed her hand and ran toward the truck.

Khwai had been waiting for them and beamed when they reached the vehicle, their breaths racing.

Saira felt her cheeks flush, and she knew it was from more than just the sudden exertion of running to the truck. She remembered Khwai's hawk-like eyesight. But the ancient Khoisan tracker said nothing as he drove them back to Desert Lodge.

Above them, the sky had pulled over its black blanket. Stars sparkled like trillions of diamonds strewn on it.

As Desert Lodge came in sight, Saira felt her smile broadening.

Gerhard shoulder-pumped her.

"Why the smile? What goes on in that smart, beautiful head of yours?"

"I think the penny just dropped."

She glanced at Khwai as she mouthed to Gerhard.

"You're a prince. I've slept with a prince."

Gerhard threw his head back and roared.

"You should see your face."

"But you don't understand. My parents will flip! No one else could ever exceed their expectations for me."

Gerhard's voice still carried the trace of laughter as he spoke.

"And that's a good thing?"

"Better than you can imagine. For once, I won't disappoint them."

"I can't imagine they ever thought you'd disappointed them."

Saira's sigh told of her lifelong inner battle.

"I'm not what you'd call conventional. I can't live the life they want for me. That must disappoint them."

Gerhard contemplated her for moments.

"I'm sure you've never disappointed them."

"How do you know?"

Gerhard took her hand in his again, intertwining their fingers.

"There's something else..."

She scooted a little away from him so she could look into his eyes.

"What? More secrets?"

Gerhard looked sheepish.

"I'm afraid so."

But before Gerhard could continue, Khwai stopped the truck under the porch outside the kitchen. As though the old man knew they had something to discuss, he bid them goodnight and left.

For moments Saira and Gerhard sat in silence, regarding each other.

Gerhard spoke first.

"Don't be mad, okay? We meant it to be a surprise. Your parents are here."

"What do you mean, they're here? They can't be. They're only arriving tomorrow."

"No. They arrived on Friday."

Saira smirked.

"You're just trying to minimize the shock factor you dumped on me earlier. I spoke to my dad on Friday, and he was in London. Stop playing. Let's go. I can hear the party is in full swing, plus I'm so hungry, I could eat a giraffe."

Saira touched the door handle to open it, but Gerhard pulled her back.

"No, please, listen, Saira."

He seemed so serious, she let go of the door handle, prepared to give him a chance to explain.

"Your parents and I have been in touch for a while now, and-"

"What? Why?"

Gerhard continued as though she didn't interrupt him.

"It's best we get to know each other as soon as possible. I'm serious about you, Saira. I'm not letting you go."

He rushed on before she could interrupt him again.

"They agreed to visit with Mother and me over the weekend. The reason they didn't tell you they were here was because they wanted to stay out of your way while you were working on the weddings. To be honest, they spent more time with Mother than with me, but they seemed to enjoy one another's company. We wanted to surprise you with them at the party."

Saira sat still. Her head was spinning.

To all the gods of the universe, her parents knew about her and Gerhard? They'd been staying with him and his mother all weekend, and no one had told her? She might never forgive any of them.

She crossed her arms over her chest.

Her voice was a growl.

"I don't know whether to smack you or kiss you."

Gerhard's smile lit up his face.

"I'd prefer the latter. Your lips are so soft, and they do all kinds of sexy things to me."

Saira couldn't contain her disobedient smile.

"Stop trying to be charming. I'm cross with you."

"I can see that. The fire in your eyes is driving me wild, woman."

He grabbed her and pulled her into his body. His kiss cleared her mind of all thoughts.

When they broke apart, she kept her hand against his chest. His heart thumped beneath her fingers.

"So, where are they now?"

Gerhard clasped her hand in his.

"They're waiting for us in Kerri's office."

Saira's heart thudded with excitement and trepidation in equal measure.

How would her parents react to her and Gerhard being together? How would she tell them about her imminent career, and possibly also lifestyle change? If she'd understood Gerhard correctly, they were heading toward serious coupledom. Though it thrilled her, she wasn't sure they would be.

Gerhard got out. She knew he'd walk around the truck to open her door, so she waited. Now, even his quaint manners made sense. As she waited, she saw the unfamiliar truck again. Someone had parked it under a nearby camel-thorn tree, just outside the circle of light from the porch.

When Gerhard opened her door, his smile almost blinded her.

She took his proffered hand and looked into his eyes as she allowed him to help her from the truck.

"Please, tell me there are no more secrets?"

Was it her imagination, or did his smile just broaden?

THIRTY-ONE

The scene that met Saira and Gerhard when they entered Kerri's office would live in Saira's mind forever.

As expected, Luca and Naomi, and Kerri and Johan were sitting on the sofas in the lounge area of Kerri's office. Two unfamiliar men sat opposite them. Drinks and bowls with snacks littered the coffee table in the middle of the area.

But Saira's eyes went to her parents at once. She felt her smile broaden at the sight of them. They were sitting beside a regal-looking woman Saira assumed was Gerhard's mother.

It was better than good to see her parents. Saira forgave everyone at once for keeping their presence in Namibia a secret from her for the entire weekend. When they saw her, they put their drinks down, got up as she bounded over to them and embraced her when she reached them.

From the radiant faces surrounding her, Saira knew everyone had kept the secret of her surprise. How could she feel anything but loved? How could she ever repay their kindness?

Gerhard introduced her to his mother, who insisted Saira called her Annette.

Her voice was friendly, and her smile warmer than her

austere appearance suggested. But Saira felt awkward calling Gerhard's mother by her first name. She resorted to Countess H. when that's how the others addressed her.

Saira felt their group was complete when Luca introduced Roberto and Nick, the two strangers. She knew it would be good to chat to them both later.

But before Saira and Gerhard sat down, Kerri got up to address the group.

"I've arranged for dinner for us in the dining room. No one will disturb us there as everyone is at the party in the Lapa. Shall we go?"

Everyone took their drinks and followed Kerri.

Lovely, low lighting in the dining room, produced a gentle intimacy. The long table in the middle of the room spoke of elegance. The cutlery, crystal glasses and silverware on it were gorgeous. Tea lights and flowers made a stunning centerpiece. Name tags on each place seated the dinner guests, alternating males and females.

Gerhard sat at one end and his mother opposite him.

Everyone had just taken their seats when waiters with hostess trolleys bearing wine, water and food arrived.

Wine poured, plates filled, the feasting could begin. Chef had outdone himself, and Saira suspected the delicious vegetarian dishes were in honor of her parents. Conversation flowed with ease, and before Saira got her head around everything that had happened tonight, the waiters served coffees and dessert.

When the port and cheeseboards with dried fruit and walnuts arrived, Luca pinged a knife against a glass as he stood up and pushed his chair back.

He winked at Saira before he spoke.

"I know we kept the secret of Saira's parents being here from her. But we wanted her to concentrate on finishing the pilot. I hope you can forgive us, Saira? Mr. and Mrs. Shah? We promise to make up for it, starting tonight."

He looked between them, then introduced Roberto, who stood up as Luca sat down.

Roberto's deep musical voice resonated around the room as he spoke about his conversation with Max and the agreement he'd made on Saira's behalf with MaxPix. Roberto made it appear as though it was nothing. But Saira wasn't so sure it was that easy. She knew Max. She knew how stubborn he could be, how tenacious and how devious.

Roberto's voice was mesmerizing.

Saira almost missed the important information about the annulment of her contract with MaxPix and that she was now the proud owner of the pilot they'd shot. Roberto had ensured nothing would stand in Saira's way. He offered to help her set up her new company.

The offer came as a favor to Luca, Saira thought. Luca must have asked Roberto to do so.

Roberto suggested meeting with her and Luca in the morning. Saira glanced at her mother to gauge her lawyer opinion. But she appeared satisfied with Roberto's work and suggestions and joined in the applause when Roberto sat down. Saira felt it was better to keep her business dealings separate from family affairs and determined to appoint Roberto as her lawyer for Flame Productions. They'd have to work fast. But she had full confidence in her team to deliver the final cut next week. She was already looking forward to her meeting with the two men in the morning.

But the surprises weren't over yet.

Next Nick took his turn to bring everyone up to date on the Jonathan situation.

Despite his former grand position in the police force, Nick's down-to-earth manner delighted Saira and her parents. It turned out Michelle, the wayward bridesmaid, was Jonathan's partner-in-crime.

The news shouldn't have surprised Saira, as she had thought them well-suited. Still, it hurt that after all they'd been through, Jonathan would choose someone like Michelle to take revenge on her.

Nick confirmed the couple had been apprehended and were languishing in a Windhoek jail, awaiting their fate. He explained Michelle might get away with pleading innocence as a victim in Jonathan's evil plans. But Jonathan's future didn't look too bright.

Cheetahs were an endangered species, and the authorities more than frowned on kidnapping them. It was also illegal to stalk someone using a drone or film private ceremonies, like weddings, without prior consent.

Everyone laughed at Nick's statement that "Jonathan's goose was cooked."

The irony escaped no one as a goose on the menu tonight was a dinner option.

Though Saira enjoyed all the wonderful surprises, she worried that she should appear at the party. But as she thought of excusing herself from the dinner, Gerhard got up.

He winked at her as he pinged his knife to a glass to get everyone's attention.

"I have one more surprise for Saira."

She cocked an eyebrow at him. Hadn't she asked him earlier if there were more surprises? Her instincts had been right. Now, it seemed her body knew something before she did. Her heart galloped at the thought of what Gerhard might say, and she wiped her clammy hands on her thighs under the table.

Gerhard continued, oblivious of Saira's trepidation.

"It won't surprise our friends here that Saira and I have become more than colleagues."

He turned to look at her as he spoke.

"In Saira, I've found my other half, the woman I've waited for my entire life. That she appeared in such a pleasing package is a bonus."

Everyone laughed at Gerhard's small joke.

"That she feels the same, is more than a bonus."

He turned to the faces surrounding them.

"We just know when we meet the one. I knew she was it for me the moment I laid eyes on her. Despite her telling you otherwise, I feel it took her longer to admit I was the one for her. She called me many names in the beginning. I recall words like Neanderthal and oaf coming from her beautiful mouth."

Saira couldn't help blushing and giggling at the same time. She thumped him on the arm.

He roared and exaggerated his injury before continuing.

"I'm telling you all this because, despite the rocky start from her side, she has acknowledged she can't live without me either."

He turned to her again.

His eyes locked onto hers as his voice became serious.

"It's one reason I invited your parents to stay with us, Saira. Your father was gracious enough to hear me out when I asked for his permission to marry you."

Gerhard got down on one knee in front of her and extended his hand in which he held a black velvet ring box.

"Will you make me the happiest man in the cosmos by becoming my wife, please, Saira?"

Saira thought she'd lost her hearing, or the sea-like sound was that of people clapping. But she experienced again that weird sensation she'd felt so often with Gerhard. Despite others surrounding them, she had the sense they were the only two people in the universe.

For moments, she sat frozen while Gerhard opened the box

and took out a stunning ring. When Gerhard and the ring became too blurry to see, Saira realized she was crying, and that he was waiting for her to respond. She wiped the tears from her eyes, felt her cheeks ache from the broad smile on her face, and threw her arms around his neck.

Her voice was a whisper. It was all she could trust it to do.

"Yes. Oh yes. I'd love to."

Gerhard held her tight against his body. She felt his heart thudding in his chest, and his breathing increased at her answer. Then, he eased her away and slipped the platinum ring bearing a single giant pink diamond on her finger.

She stared at the ring for moments before she cupped his face in her hands and kissed him gently.

The applause grew louder. Everyone was standing, clapping and cheering the couple. Johan's voice rose above the others'.

Gerhard stood, pulled Saira up and with his arm around her shoulders, beamed at the others around the table. But Saira's ears continued to give her weird information about her current reality.

Meanwhile, Kerri had arranged for champagne, so everyone had a glass when they'd finished congratulating the couple.

No one appeared in a hurry to leave the joyful celebration and retook their seats, apart from Gerhard. He remained standing, his body turned toward Saira.

Reverence for her pervaded his voice when he spoke.

"I am the happiest I could ever have imagined, Saira. Thank you for accepting my proposal and my ring."

He pulled his phone from his trouser pocket.

"Your life will now change not only in the usual way when two people throw their lives together. But you will also join the German royal family. Yes, I have abdicated my title. But the world is a strange place. People, it seems, remain obsessed with royalty everywhere.

"As a courtesy, I had to inform the current head of the Royal Household. This was his reply."

Gerhard read the email from his phone.

"Congratulations to you both. We wish you lifelong happiness and joy."

Gerhard hesitated for a moment.

His voice reflected his irritation when he continued.

"If our British cousins could allow a woman of color into the Royal family, I don't see why we couldn't do the same. GF."

Silence descended on the room.

Gerhard returned his gaze to Saira.

"I've been struggling with whether to read you his last sentence. But I feel it's only fair you know exactly what you're getting into."

Saira glanced at her parents.

Racism existed everywhere. She remembered their stories of how difficult it had been for her immigrant grandparents. But by the time she went to school, she'd experienced far less racism than they had. Though now the Prince's message had reminded her of it, there were instances. But Saira didn't want to spoil her happiness with the awful memories.

Before she could respond, the Countess spoke.

"I hope you can forgive our family members who live in Germany, Saira. GF lives ensconced in his castle, hardly ever comes out and has forgotten how to be civil."

She glanced at Gerhard.

"Mind you, he has always had terrible manners."

She looked back at Saira.

"You won't find the rest of us behaving in such an appalling manner."

Saira's smile at the Countess wasn't only to placate the woman. Saira surprised herself when she noted the Prince's reaction didn't bother her at all.

Again, before she could respond, her mother got there first.

"We've brought Saira up to respect all cultures. Our friends come from diverse backgrounds, yet they are all welcome in our home. Their friendship enriches our lives."

Saira saw her father nodding in agreement, but he remained silent. His eyes flicked from her to Gerhard.

The atmosphere in the room had changed. The conviviality of earlier had evaporated.

The Countess got up.

"Let's not allow GF's insensitivity to spoil our lovely evening together. He doesn't deserve our energy. His clumsy attempt at what I suspect is supposed to be a joke, was his only contribution here tonight.

"Raj? Parul? Shall we leave the youngsters to their party?"

She turned to Gerhard.

"Gerhard, bring Saira to the house for breakfast tomorrow. Eight will be good."

Then, she thanked Naomi and Kerri and swept from the room.

Saira's parents hugged her again, pride for her shining in their eyes before they followed Gerhard's mother.

Gerhard and Saira accompanied them to the strange truck Saira now realized was one of Gerhard's.

The Countess was already behind the wheel and waved as the three of them drove back to the home Gerhard shared with his mother.

Gerhard held Saira's hand in his and tucked a stray curl behind her ear. He seemed so vulnerable, as though he stood naked in front of her.

His eyes were dark with apprehension, his voice a hoarse whisper.

"Are you still mine?"

Saira cupped his face in her hands before responding.

"Yes, my prince. That was a brave thing to do, and I'm grateful you did it. I want our relationship to have no more secrets."

Gerhard's grin turned wicked and sexy. He narrowed his eyes.

"Well..."

Saira play-slapped his arm and laughed. She knew he was only joking. All the secrets were out.

Hand-in-hand they walked toward the Lapa where the party was in full swing.

The ring on Saira's finger nestled in between their intertwined fingers as though it had always been there.

FROM ANGELINA

Building a relationship with my readers is the very best thing about writing. So, please feel free to subscribe to my Newsletter - https://angelinakalahari.com/contact/. If you prefer, you can email me at angelina@agelinakalahari.com.

You'll receive occasional email notifications about freebies, new stories and novels, YouTube videos, podcasts, short stories and much more.

The first thing you'll receive upon subscribing, is an exclusive novella called Diary of Naomi, a Desert Elephant – it's the story of what happens to ellie Naomi.

Elephants in Namibia are the toughest in Africa. But orphaned elephants are the toughest still. And they need to be.
All elephants must travel great distances to find food to live on and they're renowned for their magnificent memories and deep emotions.
In this novella, discover what happens when they find the people responsible for making them orphans?

On my website - https://angelinakalahari.com/ - you'll find

lots about books - mine and other authors' books I enjoyed reading. There are videos with readings from my books, short stories and much more just waiting for you to enjoy.

Here are more places for you to connect with me:

Amazon Author Page: https://tinyurl.com/yyxdohld

https://www.facebook.com/authorangelinakalahari/

https://twitter.com/angelinakalhari/

https://www.instagram.com/angelinakalahari/

www.pinterest.com/angelinakalhari

http://www.youtube.com/c/AngelinaKalahari - I'd love you to subscribe to my YouTube channel, too – it's where I post free audio chapters of my books, interviews with other authors and talks about love.

THANK YOU

Thank you for reading *Heat in The Desert*.

If you enjoyed it, you might also like the previous, and the next books in the series.

As all authors, I appreciate enormously your short review on Amazon or Goodreads stating why you liked the novel. I cannot stress how important reviews are. They enable novels like *Heat in The Desert* to live in the world.

ALSO BY ANGELINA KALAHARI

In the first novel in the Desert Love series, *Under A Namibian Sky*, we meet Luca and Naomi.

A beautiful love story that will capture your heart.

No one remains lost. Love is the deepest healer of all.

"The story was so compelling, I simply couldn't put this book down." - Amazon reviewer.

Naomi leads the exhilarating, carefree life of a desert guide.

Then tall, dark and handsome billionaire, Luca arrives to shatter her peace. Luca, heir apparent to the Armati supercar dynasty, visits Desert Lodge to photograph and paint African elephants. His charm and wit endear him to everyone, and he surprises Naomi when he doesn't behave like the other spoiled industry princes they receive there. Shy Naomi doesn't know what to do when Luca teases and flirts with her, but she can't help falling for him. And it seems he feels the same about her.

What intrigues Naomi most is the pain she reads in Luca's dark eyes. But when he's comfortable enough to reveal its cause to her, his vulnerability allows Naomi to share her secret heartache with him.

As both have suffered terrible betrayal and hurt in the past, will they have the courage to admit their intense soul-connection?

Explore *Under A Namibian Sky,* an emotionally riveting love story, the first novel in the captivating *Desert Love* contemporary romance series today.

Disclaimer: This novel contains some heat and a happy ending. Don't forget, it's also available in Kindle Unlimited.

UNDER A NAMIBIAN SKY

ONE

"Naomi!"

Naomi knew that tone of voice.

She hurried barefoot across the cool, dark slate tiles. She sat down opposite her Auntie Elsa, the nickname almost everyone used.

Naomi crossed her long, bare legs. She eyed the menus and various email print-outs scattered on the coffee table that separated their two sofas.

Naomi sighed.

It looked like work... lots of work.

Elsa Smith's melodic voice had carried through the main house of the lodge.

Naomi's guardian, adoptive mother and boss, comfortable in her mid-fifties, was sitting in the guest lounge. Her reading glasses were balanced on the tip of her nose. The heat had frizzed her short steel-gray hair. She was checking through the new menus Chef had prepared in time for their next guests' arrival and doling out tasks to her adoptive daughter and other staff.

The airy, shaded room, where the grand old house's thick walls thwarted the afternoon's heat, was just about the best place to be. It also helped that the blazing Namibian sun threw its rays on the other side of the house at this time of the day.

Auntie Elsa was still busy sorting through the menus and, although aware of Naomi's presence, didn't look up as she spoke.

"Look at the email on top of that pile. Kerri printed it on pink paper, so I guess she must have thought it was important. Remind me to congratulate her. She was right."

Naomi knew what the pink paper meant.

"Is it another American wanting to 'observe' African elephants?"

Naomi made air quotes around the word, observe.

She picked up the sheet of paper, but before she could read it, Auntie Elsa snorted.

"No, this time it's an Italian 'prince'."

Auntie Elsa mimicked Naomi's air quotes around the word, prince.

Naomi sighed again.

She removed the sunglasses she had placed on top of her head and ran a hand through her long, straight, blonde hair.

Oh, no, not another spoiled, egotistical top brass from some fast-paced industry coming to 'relax.'

She'd be willing to bet he'd be the bane of everyone's life for the duration of his stay here, as they all were. But turning them away, Naomi knew, wasn't a choice as they paid well.

It had become a source of amusement among the staff who had made a game of trying to guess how much over the odds these guests would pay when they checked out.

Auntie Elsa had her photograph taken with each of them,

and then the framed photos were hung on the walls in the well-appointed dining room for all to see. It worked. Every time. These rich guys clearly moved in similar circles, and even when they didn't know each other, they recognized the faces when they saw the photos. They seemed to want to outdo each other, even here.

Naomi ran her finger down the page as she read.

"Hmm... this is different. It says here he wants to photograph and paint elephants. I'm not sure he knows what he's talking about."

Naomi re-read the email just to be sure she'd got it right the first time. That's when she noticed the familiar logo.

"Oh, and he's not just any prince this time... he's the Armati prince, no less. From the supercar dynasty, if I'm not mistaken?"

Auntie Elsa looked up and smiled.

"Yes, he is. And I thought you would make the perfect guide for him, Naomi. You're very good with these types, and God knows we could use his money. We need to update the sanitation system for the entire lodge. The repairs and upkeep of this place seem never-ending, and the costs of doing so just go up year after year. This booking has come at just the right time. I don't know what I'd do without you, Naomi. What would we all do without you, my girl?"

Naomi returned Auntie Elsa's smile.

No pressure then.

Auntie Elsa checked her watch.

"Well, I'm almost done with these new menus, and I suppose you'd better get going. The new prince will be here within the hour."

Naomi's head snapped up.

"Really?"

She turned the email over and saw attached to it his arrival schedule sent by the private airplane company from Windhoek.

Auntie Elsa gathered the menus and the other emails and got up.

"I've allocated suite twenty-two for him as it's the biggest and most secluded, and suite eleven opposite, for his secretary, who is accompanying him. I believe Kerri has already arranged for the rooms to be thoroughly cleaned again, even though it was done just this morning. But perhaps it would be a good thing if you checked it, don't you think? We don't want to give him a reason to complain about any of the simple things, do we? And make sure Khwai brings all their luggage directly to their suites. He's getting forgetful in his old age."

***

Promptly, on the hour, the sound of the small plane alerted everyone to their guests' imminent arrival.

Khwai was already waiting under the big camelthorn tree when Naomi got to the landing strip. It was on the other side of the grand main house with its gabled rafters. The old Khoisan man's face beamed when he saw Naomi.

He walked toward her, hand outstretched in greeting.

"Tjike."

Naomi returned his smile and greeting and stood by his side as they watched the Cessna plane flying closer. Naomi and Khwai glanced wide-eyed at each other when the aircraft was near enough to identify. It wasn't the usual bush plane they'd been expecting. Instead, a small jet was flying toward them. Only a few guests could afford such luxurious transport to the lodge, and they were always the biggest pains in the butt.

Naomi's heart sank further at the thought of how much more challenging than she'd imagined her life could be over the next few days.

The Cessna jet came down on the hardened part of the long, sandy driveway created as a landing strip for the small planes. It stopped amid the tiny sandstorm it had generated.

Khwai walked toward it, and Naomi followed with trepidation. The jet's door swung open, and a man's head appeared. Naomi and Khwai stopped nearby to wait for him to disembark.

The man who came down the short ladder looked to be in his late twenties or early thirties, a good few years older than Naomi, at any rate. His muscular body was evident at once and further enhanced by his immaculate dark blue jeans and a tailored white shirt. Naomi glimpsed a scattering of dark hair on his chest, peeking out from beneath the unbuttoned shirt. A somewhat thicker coat on his forearms peeped out from where he'd rolled up the shirt's sleeves.

Naomi didn't know what she'd expected, but this was not how she imagined Mr. Armati to look.

Mr. Armati saw them, raised a hand in greeting before reaching back to take the hand of an older lady and leading her carefully down the ladder. Her short dark hair was in sharp contrast to her stylish white pants suit and flat white shoes. When she stood next to Mr. Armati, she ran her hand down her clothes, the other hand clutching a brown leather handbag. Then she looked up, and a beautiful smile lit up her face. She stood tall and straight, but he was a whole head taller than her.

Naomi wondered if it was his mother. They looked so much alike. But then she remembered the woman had to be his secretary.

Mr. Armati turned towards the plane and pushed the ladder back inside the body of the jet before he closed the door. He heaved a large black bag over his shoulder with such ease it appeared to be lighter than it undoubtedly was. Long strides toward them further showed his athleticism and easy, aristocratic bearing. The lady kept pace with him. Her confidence and fluid movements belied the fact that she was so much older than him.

"Buongiorno. I'm Luca. This is Santina. I'm okay to leave my jet here? You're not expecting any others to arrive soon?"

His voice was deeper than Naomi had imagined. Although his English was perfect, she delighted in the slight Italian accent that appeared so exotic to her ears. Experiencing all the different accents was one perk of working with so many foreigners.

"Yes. No. I mean, yes, it's okay to leave your jet here."

Naomi felt silly for having stumbled over her words.

"You don't have a pilot?"

Her question was such a superfluous one, even to her ears, that she felt herself blush at her clumsiness.

"No. I fly myself. Much more exciting and fulfilling, si?"

Luca didn't appear to need her response and instead offered his hand in greeting to Khwai. The old Khoisan man smiled and nodded and tried to take Luca's bag. But he held on to it and handed Khwai a much smaller, lighter bag to carry, leaving a reassuring hand for a moment on the old man's shoulder.

There was no way he'd be this kind to Khwai when no doubt he'd be demanding, rude and unreasonable, soon. Why would he be trying to impress them? How long would it take before his true colors emerged?

Naomi had seen this kind of behavior from other princes before. It never lasted. It didn't impress her.

Santina smiled and shook Naomi's hand.

"Buongiorno. How lovely it is here."

Her voice, though authoritative, was clear and carried the musical tones found so often in Italian voices. Her smile was even more engaging up close, and her eyes reflected her powerful spirit. Santina's warm personality and elegance made an immediate positive impression on Naomi.

Luca moved toward Naomi, his hand resting for a moment on Santina's back, and they smiled at each other - warm smiles.

Their affection for each other seemed genuine. Then Luca's hand enveloped Naomi's.

He was gorgeous at a distance. Close-up, he was the most handsome man she'd ever seen, looking more like a model than a spoiled, rich, Italian prince. His smile displayed straight, white teeth from a full, sensual mouth. Tall, much taller now he was in front of her, his physical presence crackled with energy. His hair was so black it shone blue in the sun, and intense eyes, like pools of the darkest water, rooted her to the spot and robbed her of her ability to think, much less speak.

Feeling foolish and like a peasant in front of this dazzling man, she almost tripped as she stepped back when he leaned forward to kiss her on both cheeks. It was the European way. She'd forgotten.

He grabbed her elbow with his free hand and pulled her upright.

"The sand is so soft here."

He smiled again.

For moments, Naomi stood dazzled by his beauty. The soft, erotic, expensive fragrance of his cologne, and his gorgeous dark eyes, with lashes so long they touched his cheeks when he looked down, was overwhelming. It felt as though she was continuing to fall. But his hand, hot on her elbow, kept her steady.

He may look like a God, but she knew at some point he'd behave like one, and not the good kind either.

Naomi felt the minor victory of taking back her power, as she extricated herself from Luca's grip on her arm.

She could feel her hair flick as she turned to lead them to their suites.

"This way."

Ahead of them, Khwai, carrying Luca's smaller bag, was

already rounding the corner of the house on his way to the guest suites.

Naomi glanced at Luca from beneath her eyelashes.

He was chatting and laughing with Santina as they walked side by side.

He wasn't what she'd expected. But she was prepared for the inevitable change in character. Perhaps Santina's influence will keep him from becoming too demanding. He seemed very respectful of Santina.

All the same, thank goodness he'd be here for only a few days.

THE INSPIRATION BEHIND UNDER A NAMIBIAN SKY

Around two o'clock one morning, unable to sleep, I switched on the television.

As I flicked through the channels, I came upon a BBC Four documentary in which literary novelist, Stella Duffy, took on the challenge of writing for Mills and Boon (Harlequin in the US). I believe it was part of a celebration of their one-hundredth birthday and a re-run of an earlier program.

What fascinated me particularly is how impactful romance has been on society and on women. Perhaps it's not surprising, but I hadn't realized romantic fiction is largely written by women for women. By contrast, most other art forms have been fashioned and/or developed by men. But romantic fiction looks at the world through the eyes of women.

Of course, romance novels have changed drastically over the years. These days, romance novels feature smart, strong, savvy characters in real-life situations that appeal to smart readers. Not all readers of romantic fiction are women, of course, but the vast majority are. I suspect there are as many reasons that people read romantic fiction as there is romantic fiction in the world.

It soon became clear from the documentary that writing romantic fiction, however, was rather more difficult than I'd imagined it to be.

Mills and Boon know a thing or two about romance novels as they'd been in the business so long. Perhaps that's why they're so difficult to please. They know instantly whether a romance novel will appeal to their readership. Many have tried to write romances and have failed. But there is good news.

There are courses on offer and reading as many good romance novels as you can, also helps. The program showed Stella Duffy joining specialist romance writers' courses and her progress as she wrote her first romance novel.

As it was two o'clock in the morning, I thought writing a romance novel sounded like a great idea because that's the time when all great ideas are born, aren't they?

Visiting Mills and Boon's website, I learned they required three chapters and a synopsis to gauge my suitability as their next superstar romance novel writer. When I read they were particularly keen to find writers who were either born in Southern Africa or wrote novels set there, I thought I'd scored the jackpot. Being from Namibia and having lived in South Africa, I had at least one of those two requirements in the bag.

I read their guidelines and sat down to write a story I'd like to read. I agonized over it, re-wrote it multiple times, dreamt about it, talked about it to anyone who'd listen, and sent it to all my closest friends for their brutally honest opinion. Satisfied I could do no more, I hit the submit button and started to write something else.

To my utter surprise, I received a long email back from them, expressing interest in my story but asking for changes. I duly implemented the changes, again driving my poor friends loopy with my requests to check even the smallest changes until I felt I had something Mills and Boon might like enough to commission. But a few weeks later, when I received a short rejection email, the characters in Under A Namibian Sky started to scream at me. They were alive and wanted to live in the world. They wouldn't be denied.

It brought me immense pleasure to revisit the world I'd known in my youth. Writing Under A Namibian Sky felt as though I was on holiday in Namibia. I could feel the sun on my skin, breathe in the dry, hot air and see the vastness of the desert in my mind's eye as I wrote. I know the people, the characters. Some are my family members. Others are dear friends.

Of course, I took a few creative liberties here and there, and those who know Namibia well will recognize where I've endeavored to make the story more exciting, more dynamic.

True, this novel is not a Mills and Boon novel, but it's the first in the Desert Love series.

I'm delighted that readers of this novel wanted to know more and it's a real pleasure to return to Namibia to write the rest of the novels in the series.

MORE IN THE DESERT LOVE SERIES

If you've loved Luca and Naomi's story in *Under A Namibian Sky*, then you'll be thrilled by *Love In Modena*, the follow-up novella to that much-loved contemporary romance novel.

"Often I am left with a feeling of 'what happened after' in romance books, and it was really refreshing to read a follow-up story." – Amazon reviewer.

Naomi has found her prince, her Luca, her soul mate. In Modena, she also found her place in the world with him. But she can't let go of Namibia so easily, not now she's become the new owner of Desert Lodge.

Luca, the heir apparent to the Armati supercar dynasty, understands Naomi's dilemma. Their decision to split their time and responsibilities between the two countries seems like the perfect solution.

Theirs is a lifestyle others can only dream of.

But neither expects that an unforeseen foe in their midst would test their relationship to the limits.

Get your copy of *Love in Modena* today to find out what happens to Luca and Naomi once they leave the desert.

Disclaimer: This novella contains some heat and a happy ending. Don't forget, it's also available in Kindle Unlimited.

***

In the next novel, *Starlight Over the Dunes*, we meet an artist and a Hollywood A-lister. Each sought out the desert to contemplate and struggle with their own demons. But the desert is the last place they imagined meeting someone who could be their soul mate. Could they help each other? And will it lead to love?

***

There are more books to come in the series as I adore writing love stories set in my beloved Namibia. I hope you'll enjoy them as much as I love creating them.

Won't you join me?

LOVE IN MODENA

ONE

Their home. Hers and Luca's.

Naomi sighed her contentment.

The villa felt like a cozy nest despite its size.

Love makes a house a home, Auntie Elsa had always said, and Naomi couldn't agree more. Her adoptive mother had been a warm, wise woman, and Naomi still missed her as though she'd died only yesterday. That four months had already passed, seemed like a dream.

But Naomi suspected the level of her heartache about Auntie Elsa's death, had much to do with her new home and life here in Modena, and the love she shared with Luca. It was like nothing she could have imagined, so much better on every level.

None of the romances she'd read as a teenager had prepared her for the joy that overflowed in smiles which refused to leave her face, even at the most inappropriate moments. She knew the light that enveloped her soul now, was one she'd never want to lose.

Naomi stretched out her long legs in front of her and reclined on the sunbed.

How amazing to think the same sun shining here on her in Italy was the one that had shone on her in her beloved Namibia, that shone now on the people she loved and had left there. But the sun felt different here, somehow. Softer, friendlier, with none of the harshness of the desert, but none of its underlying excitement, either.

Naomi took a sip from the iced drink that stood on the small table next to her sunbed.

At least, this part of life reminded her of life in Namibia when, on days off, most people liked to relax next to a swimming pool with a drink in hand. She'd have to hold Luca to the swimming pool he'd promised to build her.

When Naomi had first laid eyes on the sun trap the balcony outside her new bedroom had created, she'd ordered two sun loungers and an umbrella for the balcony. She'd envisaged the two of them spending time here together, relaxing and prolonging the vacation mood of their honeymoon for as long as possible.

Once she'd got used to being in Italy and work took over, she knew the initial feeling of being on vacation would evaporate. Such a shame Luca seldom joined her here. Instead, he seemed hell-bent on having her vacation mood last as long as was humanly possible by showing off as much of the surrounding area as he could, when he could.

On his days off, they'd drive around in one of his Armati sports cars. He'd hold her hand on his thigh, his enthusiasm shining through as he introduced her to the breath-taking Italian landscapes that whizzed past as they drove. He'd drive to some little family-run restaurant where everyone knew him, where they accepted her into their bosom with typical Italian gusto and served the best food Naomi had ever eaten.

She'd have to watch her waistline with all these delicious meals. It was one reason she looked forward to her daily meeting with Santina when the two women could enjoy the almost private pool facilities at Armati HQ.

Naomi realized she must have fallen asleep when her alarm alerted her to the imminent arrival of her Italian language coach.

She grabbed her floral caftan and walked through the sumptuous bedroom. How could the bed not draw her eyes to it-their bed? Luca had ordered a brand-new super king size bed for them to share now they were married.

Like her old one at Desert Lodge, this was a safe place. At Desert Lodge, her room and her bed were her sanctuary from the ever-present guests.

Here, it was her escape from a culture she didn't understand yet, and a safe place to reconnect with who she was in this exotic world she'd hope to inhabit a hundred percent one day.

But now, too, it had become a place of wanton abandon in the arms of her lover and husband. It was where their trust expressed itself in the way they loved each other, where Luca taught her what he liked and where they experimented to find out what she liked.

Yes, it was again her oasis in life, but oh, what an oasis.

She hurried down the corridor toward the double marble staircase that ran through the center of the impressive foyer.

At first, the house had taken some getting used to. It differed a great deal from Desert Lodge. The grand old German house at the edge of the Namib Desert was all she'd known as home. She'd spent most of her life there after Auntie Elsa and Uncle Wouter had adopted her following the tragic death of her parents.

Luca had told her his house in Italy-theirs after their wedding in the desert-was big and filled with marble. He didn't exaggerate. She had to give him that, but if anything, he'd down-played it somewhat. The villa was much larger than she'd imagined.

Her first impression was that the entire interior consisted of marble. The massive double marble staircase connecting the upper rooms with the foyer was only the beginning. Counter-tops and tiles in the bathrooms and kitchen also sported the finest marble, as did the floors in the foyer and throughout much of the villa. The sumptuous carpets in the dining room, living rooms, the bedrooms and hers and Luca's studies, masked the marble underneath.

Luca had been worried it was too much, or it would feel too cold, but Naomi had loved it at once. She couldn't imagine Luca living anywhere else, even though it didn't display much of his personality. But as he was now hers, she wanted to be where he was, and with touches from her here and there, she'd trans-formed the villa into a home for them. Despite its size, everyone who visited remarked it now felt cozy and welcoming.

Luca had teased she might consider a career as an interior designer because she'd done such a good job with their home. He'd only been joking, but she'd enjoyed every second of putting their stamp on the villa.

As Naomi came down the staircase, she could see Francis-ca's silhouette through the frosted glass of the front door.

Luca had beamed when she'd told him she'd wanted to learn his language. He'd wasted no time finding the best language coach in the area.

The short time it took for Francisca to help Naomi get to grips with Italian had surprised her. At first, Naomi couldn't even make out where one word stopped, and a new one began. But now, four months later, it was making sense. When she felt brave, she ordered items and meals in Italian, and it always amazed her when people actually understood her.

An hour later, just as her lesson with Francisca ended, Naomi heard Santina's melodic voice as her mother-in-law opened the front door. Santina had always had a key to Luca's home, and there was no reason to change that arrangement now Naomi and Luca were married.

"Naomi! Are you home?"

Santina knew Naomi was there, but it was her habit every day to call out the same phrase upon entering. It had fast become a token of comfort to Naomi in her new life.

Naomi hugged Francisca thank you, and together they walked from the library to meet Santina.

Santina was admiring the enormous bouquet of lilies in a Murano glass vase on top of the round marble table.

She looked up when Naomi and Francisca came into the foyer.

"Ah, there you are. Hello, Francisca. These are gorgeous, Naomi. And they smell so lovely."

Naomi smiled and went to hug Santina.

"Aren't they just? A gift from Luca."

With arms around each other, they waved Francisca off through the open front door.

Naomi felt blessed Santina was part of their lives in this way. But Santina's arm around Naomi's waist somehow transported her back to that moment Luca had discovered Santina was his birth mother.

Naomi knew it could have gone terribly wrong. Luca had been furious, feeling they'd lied to him all his life. Naomi knew he'd been blaming himself for years for Cecilia's disappearance, convinced his mother had left because of him. His young mind couldn't imagine anything else for her departure. What made it all much more painful, was that his father, who'd loved Cecilia with the passion of youth, was never the same afterward. The pain Cecilia's leaving inflicted on Enzo had absorbed him entirely. He was incapable of sustaining any relationship with his young son.

Instead, Luca had been packed off to boarding school. There, rumors first reached him Cecilia had run away with a wealthy shipping magnate who could afford her the lifestyle she'd supposedly always craved. In time, the rumors turned to 'truths,' even in Luca's mind.

How could it not affect his view of women? If Cecilia could leave Enzo, whom she'd professed to be her forever soulmate, and Luca, whom she'd called her 'little prince,' what woman would stay? How could he trust anyone to stay with him when there would always be someone else willing to offer more?

But he'd confided in Naomi it relieved him she was so different, sincere and loyal. Despite Luca's fears, he'd admitted he'd dared to hope for something better when he'd realized Naomi was his forever soulmate.

She'd felt comforted knowing his heart had broken for her when it became clear her beloved Auntie Elsa was at death's door. It was the moment Naomi knew for sure she belonged with Luca.

But who could blame him when it became too much to be told the truth about his birth at Auntie Elsa's deathbed? Auntie Elsa's imminent death had finally spurred on Santina to tell Luca the truth. At first, he couldn't believe Santina would love Cecilia so much she'd give her the child Cecilia had craved and could never have. That he'd turned out to be that child had shamed him, almost undone him. For hours he'd raged and doubted Santina and Enzo's noble words and thought it just a facade behind which to hide their sordid affair.

Yes, Naomi could see how easily it could have gone wrong.

While Luca had been ranting, it became clear to Naomi that he'd continued to think of Cecilia as his mother. Who could blame him? In his mind, Cecilia had always been his mother. He hadn't known another.

Naomi had pointed out to him Cecilia had never been his mother, Santina hadn't only given birth to him but she'd always been there for him. Only then did realization enter his over-wrought mind. Only then could he forgive them all.

But the best news was that through telling their story, Enzo and Santina freed themselves to marry. They became Luca's parents, united. No one could have hoped for a better outcome.

Naomi's smile reflected how much she'd grown to love Santina.

"Do we have time for our swim today?"

Santina checked her watch.

"Let's go check if everything's ready for the party, first. Enzo's birthday feels different this year."

Santina's smile betrayed her pride.

"I've celebrated it with him every year since I first met him, but this is the first time I'll be attending it as his wife."

Naomi nodded. She knew only too well how marriage could change one's feelings.

"I can relate to how things can change. But I'm so glad you're married now, and Luca knows you're his mum. Thank God you've always been there for him. Now he can honor you as his mother who gave him life. There's been such a change in him since you told him Cecilia wasn't his birth mother, but you are."

Santina squeezed Naomi's shoulders.

"You're far too modest, Naomi. Luca told me how you'd helped him to see the truth. Much of his acceptance of what had happened is down to you. And I would never have had the courage to tell Luca the truth if it wasn't for my dear friend, and your adoptive mother, Elsa. I'll never forget what she's done for all of us."

While they'd been talking, Naomi had picked up her handbag and keys.

"I could never repay Auntie Elsa for all she's done for me, either. She'll always live in my heart. And the first thing I'll do when Luca and I return to Desert Lodge is to visit her grave. I can't believe we have only two months left here before we'll leave for Namibia."

Santina touched Naomi's arm.

"Will you put some flowers on her grave for me, too?"

"Of course. I'm sure Auntie Elsa would love flowers from you, Santina. I can't tell you how thankful I am the two of you became such close friends, and you were there for her when she needed a friend such as you. I know you miss her, too."

Naomi held open the double doors for Santina to exit first before she locked them and walked to the Armati supercar Luca had gifted her. But she wasn't confident to drive as fast as Luca did and took the corners rather more sedately than the car could go.

Santina had chosen the large restaurant near the Armati headquarters to host Enzo's birthday party again this year.

Ristorante La Luna was the Armati team's usual venue for meals and meetings away from the office. Since it was within walking distance from the office, people could pop back to the office when they needed to. The party was sure to continue into the early morning hours, and it interfered with the workaholics' schedules at Armati.

Ristorante La Luna was the perfect solution.

Naomi followed Santina into the restaurant but stopped dead in the doorway. Luigi and his staff had transformed the restaurant into a tropical garden. The lush plants with exquisite flowers filled the space most artfully. Their fragrance permeated the air, almost obscuring the delicious aromas wafting from the kitchen.

From her first day in Modena, Naomi had met Luigi once a week when she went for lunch there with Luca.

Luigi was flamboyant and gregarious, the total opposite of his childhood friend, Enzo, and Naomi delighted in his company that felt like the sun. But through their good-natured banter, it was obvious the two men had remained close throughout their lives. Fierce gardening rivals, Luigi agreed wholeheartedly that Enzo's gorgeous castle boasted the most beautiful garden Naomi had ever seen. It was the reason Santina had sold her modest home and moved into Enzo's castle after she and Enzo got married. He couldn't bear to part from the garden he'd spent years and a fortune creating. Since Santina had always loved the garden, it was a pain-free decision for them. Now, Luca and Naomi joined them there almost every Sunday for lunch. But Naomi still struggled to believe the castle she first saw when Luca drove her home to Modena, belonged to Enzo. It was what she'd always imagined a castle to look like.

Naomi left Santina and Luigi and made her way to the toilet at the back of the restaurant. Here, Luigi had placed large potted palm trees and lined the area between the mirrors and the wash basins with mosses and tiny pink flowers. It transformed the stylish bathroom into an oasis of serenity.

Just as Naomi closed the door to the cubicle, she heard the bathroom door opening. She could make out the voices of two women, chatting and laughing, friends. But as she listened, not only was she astonished to realize she could understand what they were saying, but their words weren't what she'd expected to hear.

"Well, I still don't get what he sees in that little desert mouse," Voice One said. "She's so plain. So unlike who I thought he'd end up with, you know?"

"I know exactly what you mean," Voice Two said. "She

doesn't even speak the language."

The women laughed, and Naomi got the impression they weren't referring to a language comprised of words.

"Do you remember the last party at his house?" Voice Two asked.

The delay and muffled sound of Voice One's response indicated she was applying lipstick.

"Hmm, how can I forget? I'm sure that party was the reason I got to be his secretary when Santina left."

She almost purred as the words left her mouth.

"If only all interviews were so interesting and exciting. I'm still waiting for the de-brief if you know what I mean?"

The women laughed again.

"Don't give up," Voice Two said. "He'll soon tire of her and then there you'll be, ready for your de-brief and whatever else might follow."

"I know, and I agree," Voice One said. "It can't come soon enough. Just imagine... living in that villa, having all that money, having him... And it's not for lack of trying. It wasn't easy to find the drugs and when you get them from the internet, you never know if they're real, do you? But whatever they were, they worked better than I could've imagined."

The women's callous laughter clamped a tight band around Naomi's chest, making breathing difficult.

Voice One snorted as she came to the end of her laughing fit and simultaneously tried to speak.

"By the way, do you like this new top? I got it specially..."

Their voices faded as they left the bathroom and the door shut behind them.

Naomi stood rooted to the spot. She felt as though someone had poured a bucket of ice water over her after punching her in the solar plexus. An immediate headache threatened behind the tears that stung her eyes.

LOVE BEYOND REASON SERIES - WOMEN'S FICTION

The Healing Touch

How do you live in a world without your voice, without passion, and without James…?

Isabelle spent her career as an opera singer and her life married to an emotionally unavailable man. With the onset of the menopause, Isabelle loses her most precious gift - her voice. As time marches unforgivably on, Isabelle yearns to experience the love and passion she'd always dreamt of in her operatic roles.

Throwing herself into her work, Isabelle finds her soulmate in the least likely of moments. When James auditions for the lead in one of her shows, Isabelle discovers the one thing she has spent her life searching for - him.

But when James unexpectedly dies, Isabelle must forge a new life for herself in a world that is suddenly unfamiliar and forever cold.

Is it too late for her to find the love she craves, or could Angelo be the healing touch to save her fragmented soul?

Inspired by true events, *The Healing Touch* is a mesmerising story of loss, heartbreak, passion and love in many guises.

If you liked The Notebook, then you'll love The Healing Touch.

Explore *The Healing Touch*, the first novel in the captivating *Love Beyond Reason* series today.

"Profoundly moving, delightfully evocative and totally absorbing... reminds me of novels by Nicholas Sparks."

- Mary Anne Yarde, author of the award-winning series The Du Lac Chronicles.

Disclaimer: This novel is written in British English, contains some heat and a happy ending. Don't forget, it's also available in Kindle Unlimited.

***

Next in the *Love Beyond Reason Series*
FOREVER AND EVER LOVE

The reincarnated love Angelo Antoniou and Isabelle Cooper share will never give up their yearning for happiness.

In Ancient Egypt, their undying love as a princess and a high priest, is born. But their love is forbidden, and as she dies tragically, they swear an oath to find one another again.

Eighteenth-century Venice sees them finding each other again, but once more, their love is thwarted.

Now, in present-day London, they find one another once again. But as she's married to someone else, does it mean they still have to fight to be together or can they taste true happiness and fulfillment in this lifetime?

A HUGE THANK YOU

To the best editorial team in the world – Hester, Irma, Linda, Julia, Elizabeth, Kate, Colette and Mia – thank you so much for reading, commenting, suggestions and helping me to create a world in which to escape and bask for a while.

Without you, this novel would not have become the story it has. I'm grateful you asked all the right questions and helped me to create a wonderful story we can all be proud of.

To Jane Dixon- Smith for the most romantic cover.

ABOUT THE AUTHOR

Author photograph ©www.Bobieh.com

Angelina Kalahari has worked for over thirty-five years as an operatic soprano, stage director and voice teacher around the world.

She received recognition for her contribution to the music, culture and economy of the UK from Queen Elizabeth II at Buckingham Palace.

Angelina has always regarded herself as a storyteller, either through music or through acting and directing. She honed her storytelling skills from a young age, writing and telling stories to her siblings at bedtime. It became a habit over the years. She has many finished novels, children's stories and plays. Her publishing journey as an indie author began with *The Healing Touch*, a Women's Fiction story, based on true events.

Born in Namibia, and having lived all over the world, she currently lives in London, UK, with her husband, her fur cat daughter, a rapidly diminishing population of house spiders and a smallish herd of dust bunnies.

She has recently come to the conclusion that drinking vast amounts of tea holds the key to life.

.

Printed in Poland
by Amazon Fulfillment
Poland Sp. z o.o., Wrocław